ENDANGERED

ENDAN

GERED

Eliot Schrefer

SCHOLASTIC INC.

FOR KINSUKE

This book was originally published in hardcover by Scholastic Press in 2012.

ISBN 978-0-545-16577-8

Copyright © 2012 by Eliot Schrefer. All rights reserved. Published by Scholastic Inc. SCHOLASTIC and associated logos are trademarks and/or registered trademarks of Scholastic Inc.

12 11 10 9 8 7 6 5 4   14 15 16 17 18 19/0

Printed in the U.S.A. 40
This edition first printing, January 2014

The text type was set in Centaur MT.
Book design by Whitney Lyle

NOTE: THROUGHOUT THIS BOOK, CONGO
REFERS TO THE DEMOCRATIC REPUBLIC
OF CONGO (THE COUNTRY FORMERLY
KNOWN AS ZAIRE), NOT NEIGHBORING
CONGO-BRAZZAVILLE.

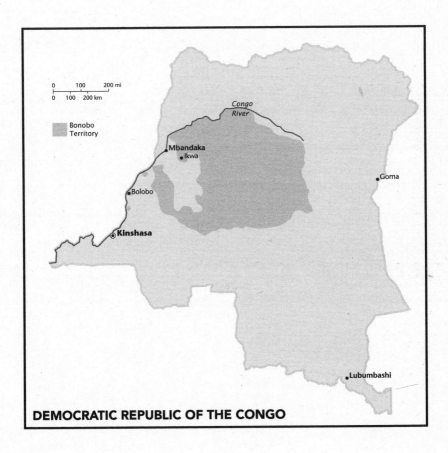

DEMOCRATIC REPUBLIC OF THE CONGO

ENDANGERED

Part One:
Otto

ONE

KINSHASA, THE CAPITAL OF CONGO

Concrete can rot. It turns green and black before crumbling away. Maybe only people from Congo know that.

There was a time when I didn't notice that sort of thing. When I was a little girl living here, it was a country of year-round greenery, of birds streaming color across clear skies. Then, when I was eight, I left to live with my dad in America; ever since then, coming back to spend summers with my mom meant descending into the muggy and dangerous back of nowhere. The fountain in downtown Kinshasa, which I'd once thought of as the height of glamour, now looked like a bowl of broth. Bullet holes had appeared up and down it, and no one I asked could remember who had put them there. When I looked closely, the pockmarks overlapped. The Democratic Republic of Congo: Where Even the Bullet Holes Have Bullet Holes.

Kinshasa has ten million people but only two paved roads and no traffic lights, so the routes are too crowded to get anywhere fast. Almost as soon as the driver left the house to take me to my mom's workplace, we were stuck in traffic, inching by a barricade. A police roadblock wasn't common, but not all that unusual, either. Some of the Kinshasa police were for real and some were random guys in stolen uniforms, looking for bribes. There was no way to tell the difference, and it didn't much change the way you dealt with them: Show your ID through the windshield. Do not stop the car. Do not roll down the window. Do not follow if they try to lead you anywhere.

A man was approaching each car as it slowed. At first I thought he was a simple beggar, but then I saw he was dragging a small creature by its arms. I crawled over the gearshift and into the front seat to see better.

It was a baby ape. As the man neared each car, he yanked upward so that it opened its mouth into a wide grin, feet pinwheeling as it tried to find the ground. The man had a lame foot but got around agilely, his scabby stump pivoting and tilting as he maneuvered. Behind him was a rusty bike with a wooden crate lashed to the back, which he must have been using to transport the ape.

Already that morning, I'd seen plenty of animals suffering. Grey parrots crammed so tightly into roadside cages that the dead stood as tall as the living; a maimed dog howling in a crowded market, flies swarming the exposed bone of her leg; a peddler with half-dead kittens tied to his waist. I'd learned to shut all of it out, because you couldn't travel more than a few miles in Kinshasa without seeing a *person* dying on the side of the road, and I figured dying humans were more important than dying animals. But it had always been my mom's philosophy that the way we treat animals goes hand in hand with the way we treat people, and so she'd dedicated her life to stopping men like this one, bushmeat traders hoping for a sale. Dedicated her life so fully, in fact, that when my dad's work in Congo ended and he had to go back to the States, she'd stayed on and they'd divorced. Our shared life as a family had ended.

It appeared that the ape was having the time of his life, grinning ear to ear. But when I looked closer, I saw bald patches and sores. He'd been restrained by a rope at some point; it was still tied around his waist and trailed in the dirt.

"Clément, that's a bonobo," I said stupidly.

"Yes it is," he said, his gaze flicking nervously between me and the man.

"So stop the car!" I said. Irritation — at being stuck in this car, at being stuck in this country — fired away.

"*Te*, Sophie, I cannot," he said.

"This is precisely what my mom fights against. She would insist that you stop, and you work for her, so you have to," I said, waving my hand at him.

"No, Sophie," Clément said. "She would want me to contact her and have the Ministry of Environment deal with it. Not her daughter."

"Well, *I* insist, then."

In response, Clément locked the doors.

It was a pretty weak move, though, since there weren't any child locks in the front seat. The car was barely rolling because of the roadblock traffic, so I simply opened the door, jumped out, and sped back to the trader. He swung the baby bonobo up into his arms and greeted me in Lingala, not the French that Congo's educated classes use.

"*Mbote!* You would like to meet my friend here, *mundele*?" he asked me.

"He's so cute. Where did you get him?" I asked in Lingala. I spoke French and English with my parents, but was still fluent in the language of my childhood friends.

The man released the bonobo. The little ape sat down tiredly in the dirt and lowered his arms, wincing as his sore muscles relaxed. I kneeled and reached out to him. The bonobo glanced at his master before working up the energy to stand and toddle over to me. He leaned against my shin for a moment, then extended his arms to be picked up. I lifted him easily and he hugged himself to me, his fragile arms as light as a necklace. I could make out his individual ribs under my fingers, could feel his heart flutter against my throat. He pressed his lips against my cheek, I guess to get as close as possible to my skin, and only then did I hear his faint cries; he'd been making them for so long that his voice was gone.

"Do you like him?" the man asked. "You want a playmate?"

"My mom runs the bonobo sanctuary up the road," I said. "I'm sure she'd love to care for him."

Worry passed over the man's face. He smiled nervously. "He is my friend. I have not harmed him. Look. He likes you. He wants to live with you. He wants to braid your hair!"

He knew the way to a Congolese girl's heart.

The man began to plead. "Please, *la blanche*, I have traveled six weeks down the river to bring this monkey here. There was a storm and I lost all of my other goods. If you do not buy the bonobo, my family will starve."

Looking at the man, with his crippled foot and greasy ragged tunic tied closed with woven palm fronds, it wasn't hard to believe he was close to starvation.

By now Clément had parked and huffed up the street to join us. Undoubtedly he had already called my mom. "Sophie," he said. "We need to leave. This is not the way."

He didn't get it. "Stop worrying! If we wind up in trouble, I'll tell Mom it was all my idea." The baby ape reached his fingers under my collar to touch my skin directly. "How much do you want for him?" I asked the man.

"The sanctuary doesn't buy bonobos," Clément said, stepping between us.

"He is my property," the man replied. "You cannot take him from me."

"It's not going to come to that," I said. I wished Clément would go away; he was on his way to ruining everything. I turned to dismiss him, but paused. Clément was staring back at the roadblock. From his worried face I could tell he'd clearly decided these weren't true police but the other kind: drunk men with guns and a hunger for bribes. Already they were watching us curiously. It was risky to be out of our car at all in this part of the capital. People were robbed — or, for girls, much worse — all the time. But I was going to get this bonobo to give to my mother.

"One hundred American dollars," the man said. "One hundred dollars and you can have him."

"Te!" Clément said. "We will not pay you for what you can't legally sell."

The thing was, I *did* have that kind of cash on me, right in my front pocket. Shouldn't have, but I did. The notebook money.

When I'd first arrived in the States years ago, I'd been the only African girl in the whole school. I'd gotten plenty of looks, with my plastic slippers and hair whose kinkiness I hadn't decided whether to embrace or fight. When Dad had picked me up from school after the first day, I'd tearfully told him he had to tell me what a mall was and then go straight there.

There was only one nice thing anyone said to me in my early America days, but I heard it over and over: My notebooks were really cool. It turned out that the year before there had been some sort of stationery arms race among the kids, with each trying to have the most unique pens and paper. I pulled out these shiny Congolese foolscap notebooks, roughly bound, with big green elephants stenciled on the front. I gave them all away, making do with plain old spirals, and the five girls I offered notebooks to became my closest friends.

Each time I left to be with my mom for summer break, the American kids would ask me, "So, Sophie, you're going back to Congo; what's it like?" and I'd say, "Poor," and we'd move on to the important business of notebook requests. A ton of them. Even now that we were fourteen, not eight.

I still had my friends' money. My free hand went to my pocket.

"No, Sophie," Clément said, watching me. "Your mother would forbid it."

"This is *for* my mother," I said. "Saving bonobos is the most important thing for her."

The bonobo's skin was feverish, baking against mine. He was still making his almost-mute cries.

Any moment, those men with guns might get involved.

"No," Clément said to the man. "Take the bonobo back."

Reluctantly, the trader reached out. I could feel the weak legs wrapped around my belly tense and tremble. I'd seen it at my mom's sanctuary — young bonobos spend years hanging on to their mothers. Without that constant affection, they die. The baby had spent weeks with this man, but he already preferred to be with me. What did that say about how he'd been treated? He had probably been in that cage the whole time, with nothing warm to touch. If I let him be pulled off me, the cage was right back where he'd go.

Supporting the scrawny bonobo bum with one hand, I pulled the cash out of my pocket and handed it to the man. It was less than he'd asked for, but the trafficker took the thick wad without counting and backed toward his bike.

"*Te, papa,*" Clément called after him. "We will not buy this bonobo! Come back."

I buried my face into the baby's neck, felt his pulse beat its hot and fragile rhythm.

The transaction finished, the trader got on his bike and cycled away.

Clément hurried me back to the car and refused to say a word to me all the way to the sanctuary. I sat in the back, the bonobo in my lap. He wrapped his legs around me and kept his arms at his side; they must have gotten hurt when the man dangled him all morning.

I was no bonobo expert, but he was the ugliest I'd ever seen. He was practically bald and covered with scabs, his belly wrinkly and stuck out. It, too, was nearly hairless, covered in only a soft gray down. On each hip bone, where the rope had been rubbing, was a pus-filled blister. The pinkie was totally gone from one hand, and the next finger was only an angry red nub.

"He's missing fingers," I said to Clément.

He didn't break his silence.

"Why would he be missing fingers?" I asked.

I gently lifted the bonobo's hand, but he tugged it away, turning his head to stare quietly out the window, his fingers making knitting motions over his rope. *Leave me alone.*

Staring at him was the only thing in the world I wanted to do. He didn't meet my eyes. There was no seeing in his looking.

I pressed my forehead against the window and watched what he watched as it passed by outside: the lifeless streets of the wealthy district with its guards dozing against front gates; day laborers crowding job boards; swamps of trash picked over by street kids; chickens with wrung necks thrown flailing into ditches; boys pushing a truck until the engine kicked over. It was a big change from the tidy American scene I'd left two days before.

The bonobo either hadn't been given anything to eat or had refused it — he was so thin. Nothing was coming out now, but he had had major diarrhea sometime recently; the hair on his legs was matted and stinky. The breath that came from between his chapped lips was hot and dry. He had nothing left in the world except me, and we had known each other for just minutes. For all I knew, he could have only hours left to live. No wonder he was trying to shut everything out.

So what? I thought against the quaking in my heart. *He's an animal.* But I couldn't feel it. Despite myself, I cared about him.

I stroked the bonobo's belly, and for a few moments he half closed his eyes. His breathing slowed as if he might fall asleep, but then Clément hit a bump and the bonobo startled. Suddenly panicked, he sat up and stared about.

"Shh," I whispered. "You can relax. No one's going to hurt you now."

Even then I knew it was a dangerous promise.

TWO

We turned off the paved road and switched to crumbly dirt. Village women, marching with giant plastic basins balanced on their heads, parted as we rolled past. From its spot on its mother's back, a baby wrapped in a bright shawl peered into the window, waving a thin arm when it saw the bonobo. Clément eased by a pickup truck, long broken and rusting in the middle of the road, and then we made a sharp turn into the jungle. Trees closed in on the car as we rattled down a muddy trail. A small painted sign announced we were nearly there.

The sanctuary was located on the former campus of a state school that had closed after it got shot up during one of Congo's wars. After years of lobbying, Mom had finally convinced the government to give the plot to her. There have always been laws against killing or selling bonobos in Congo, but the government had trouble enforcing them before because there was nowhere to place confiscated infants. The sanctuary was a collaboration between the government and the international donors my mother had chatted up.

As we pulled in, crowds of butterflies burst into the air, swirling and settling in flecks of color against a backdrop of vivid green. As I stepped out with the bonobo, he stared at the butterflies passionlessly, but his eyes did dart around as he watched them. I decided this was a good sign and rocked him cheeringly in my arms as I held him close.

"Do you see Mom anywhere?" I called to Clément, nervously scanning the sanctuary grounds. I knew she wanted it to be the

Ministry of Environment that confiscated bonobos, in order to make it clear that it was the government of Congo taking people's property, not her. But I hadn't had that option. That man would have disappeared with this bonobo if I hadn't paid him. The failing heart I cradled in my arms would have stopped. If her life's work was really to take care of these apes, wasn't saving one the most important thing?

"No. She must be in back," Clément said, sounding as relieved as I was that we wouldn't yet have to face my mother.

I passed along the grounds, black-and-white magpies and long-tailed red birds scattering as I went. I could hear, from afar, the high-pitched cries of the bonobos in their enclosures. When we reached the veterinarian's office, Patrice greeted me warmly. "Miss Sophie, you are back from America?"

"Yes, sir," I said in English.

Patrice chuckled, then stopped when he saw the bonobo. "*Oh, là là.* On the table," he said.

He placed a cushion on the operating table, which was really just a desk repurposed from the former school, and I laid the bonobo down on it. Patrice immediately had his grimy old stethoscope out and laid it on the little ape's chest. The bonobo looked alarmed, so I held his hand and stroked his scabby forehead.

"He's cramping, I think —" I started to say, before Patrice raised his hand to shush me as he listened for the heartbeat.

Patrice lowered the earpieces around his neck and sighed. "He's not in good shape at all. A lot of fluid around his heart. Where did you find him?"

The bonobo started whimpering again, so I took him back up into my arms. He resumed his now-usual position, his forehead against the base of my neck. "A man was selling him on the N-I. Do you think he'll be okay?"

"There was another roadblock today," Clément interjected. "It's an odd sign, no? Have you heard about anything unusual happening in the capital?"

"Go tell the boss," Patrice said, dismissing Clément with a hand gesture before turning back to the bonobo. "He's extremely dehydrated, and we'll need to get fluids into him as soon as possible if he's to have a hope of surviving. Our IVs haven't been working, but I'm going to put one in anyway and hope for a miracle. Sophie, could you put him back down and hold his hand and make sure he doesn't resist?"

The ape sighed as I pulled him off me. A healthy adult bonobo is much stronger than a human, but this little guy couldn't have resisted me no matter how hard he tried. I stroked his arm to keep him calm as Patrice worked the needle in. He didn't fight at all; I wondered if he was simply exhausted, or if his previous owner had been brutal enough that he didn't dare protest.

"He keeps wincing every once in a while — I think he has cramps," I repeated. His little face was so like a human's, and no one grew up in Congo without knowing what stomach cramps looked like.

"Fluids first," Patrice said. He hung the bag on the side of a cabinet and flicked the tubing going to the needle, trying to make the saline flow. His face crinkled as he peered.

"Do you need me to take his temperature or anything?" I asked.

"Maybe you could find your mother and let her know about him," Patrice said.

"I'd rather stay here."

"I was afraid of this. The IV won't work," Patrice said, scowling at the rubber tubing. "We need to buy new ones, but, you know, they aren't easy to find." It was one of those things about living in Congo, that I'd once been used to but now found hard to bear: You find something you like or need and then it gets taken away and no one can promise it's ever going to come back.

Patrice removed the line. "I'm going to do some preliminary tests for diseases. Want to give him a bath in the meantime?"

I lifted the bonobo from the table, gently cut his mangy rope away, and brought him to the sink. He tried to screech, but since his voice was almost gone, it sounded more like a rustle. I made sure the water was nice and warm, and he calmed down once it started running along his body. He balanced on my arm using both hands and one foot, watching curiously as the runoff swirled down the drain. All sorts of things were in it: clumps of poo, crawly mites, more of his hair. He liked getting soaped up, I thought, enjoyed the feeling of my hands on his body; he stared into my eyes the whole time and rasped less frequently. I dried him with a fluffy towel and wrapped him tightly. Only his face showed through. Since he was nearly hairless, he looked almost like a real human baby. Three delicate little fingers protruded from the towel.

He needed to get fluids into him, I knew, and without an IV, we'd have to do it the traditional way. There was milk in a mini fridge in my mom's office, so that's where I headed. I had the bottle in hand and was trying to coax the bonobo to drink when my mom came in from the outside, wiping her hands on a rag. Clément was a few steps behind.

"What happened?" my mom asked, immediately across the room and crouching next to me, her strong hands on my hair, on the bonobo, warmth everywhere.

"He was on the side of the road and he's not drinking, Mom," I said, my voice teary. "He's going to die if we don't get something into him. I knew I had to do whatever it took to get him to you."

"This bonobo has lost the taste for milk," my mom said, her arms still around me. "He must have been traveling for a long time."

He reached a hand to her face, as if to touch it, then got shy and let it drop. He was immediately in love with my mother. It happened with every bonobo. I'd spent my childhood wishing I was like Snow White, that little birds and other woodland creatures would flock to me if I raised my arms — but whenever I tried they always ran away, and I felt totally rejected. My mother, though — everything she came across adored her.

She was true Congolese, tough and warm, with an amazing broad face from which her soft brown eyes shone. Mom was skilled at charming her way around corruption, which had helped her cut through the endless red tape it took to get the sanctuary off the ground.

I'd started to wonder, though, about what went on underneath. Because I saw her only on vacations, we didn't have the day-in, day-out knowledge of each other that most mothers and daughters have. It's not like she was a stranger; we had too much history for that. But at the same time, I couldn't say I knew her well. Or at least well enough to see her thoughts.

I gave her a big kiss on the cheek. "What are you going to do with him?" I asked.

"Let's keep trying to get him to drink," she said.

Patrice appeared in the doorway and kneeled beside me and the bonobo, another needle in his hand. "I'm going to send a blood sample to Kinshasa, see what diseases he might have. We'll have to keep him separate from the other nursery bonobos for a few days, until I get it back." The bonobo barely noticed as Patrice took his blood, he was so fixated on my mom.

"Come, *mon p'tit*," Mom cooed. "You can drink. Aren't you thirsty, even a little?"

When I put the bottle to his lips, though, he only chewed on the nipple and squeaked.

She sighed.

"What do you think happened to his hand?" I asked, putting my arms around my mom and resting my head on her fleshy shoulder, all three of us a pile of comfort.

There was a flash of annoyance in my mother's eyes — even though she instantly tried to hide it, her instinct was to tell me I was asking a stupid question. Stupid, I guess, because the answer was so obvious. It took her that moment to remember that I didn't live here, that in Congo her daughter was essentially an outsider.

"Superstition," she said. "Soup with a bonobo finger in it is supposed to make a pregnant woman give birth to a strong baby. Putting another finger in the bathwater keeps the baby strong."

"I hope the stupid baby gets polio," I said, and surprised myself by even sort of meaning it. I kissed the top of the bonobo's head. I imagined him in his crate, crying against the bars, someone lifting him out only to chop off a finger. Plunging him back into the crate, then pulling him out a few days later to take another. "He looks so sad, Mom. I don't know what happened. He was grinning ear to ear when I found him."

"They grin when they're happy, but also when they're terrified," she said. "He was probably scared out of his mind. And now he's not sure whether he wants to bother fighting."

Patrice corked the blood vial and went for his jacket. "I'll drop this at the clinic when Clément heads back to Kinshasa," he said. "Can I take the sanctuary van? Are you ready to leave for the night?"

"In a minute," my mom said. "Will you wait for me?"

Patrice left, and Mom sat there quietly for a moment, stroking both me and the bonobo.

"He'll be okay here when we go back to the house?" I asked.

Her home was a roomy two-story building in a guarded complex in Kinshasa. I was envisioning one particular spot on the floor, a pile of imported Tunisian pillows, perfect to curl up in and e-mail friends. "Who's going to take care of him overnight? One of the guards?"

"Darling," my mom said slowly, "I need to talk to you about something. What you did today was wrong."

This was the thing with my mother — she could never admit there was a space between right and wrong. Remaining at the sanctuary had been right, just as coming to America with me and my father would have been wrong. She couldn't be honest with me; she had to present her heart as not so much a compass as a two-way switch.

"I know what you mean, Mom, about getting the ministry involved, but if I'd wasted any time that guy would have —"

"Do you remember when someone threw a rock through our window, back when I first started the sanctuary? You were too young for me to tell you at the time, but that was a wildlife trafficker whose bonobo I'd confiscated. It is very important that we are not the ones to take what people see as their property. We can only provide the place where the bonobos come to live. Do you understand the difference?"

I rolled my eyes. I was nearly fifteen, not ten. "I paid the man, so he can't get mad. And we helped a bonobo." I held up my hand to stop her from countering. "Mom. I get what you're saying. But this bonobo would be dead or missing another finger by now if I hadn't bought him. He needed to be in your sanctuary. And now he is."

"I've got calls in to the ministry right now, trying to get them to track that man down."

"He wasn't that bad," I said. I remembered his ratty clothing, his calling the bonobo a friend.

My mom's eyes flashed. "He's very bad, Sophie. You made a big mistake by giving him money. I can see you're starting to understand the gravity of what I'm saying, so I won't bring it up again. But you have to be wise about these things. You have to learn when to ignore suffering so that you're strong enough to fight it when the time is right."

I didn't agree, not exactly, but I didn't fight back because I was ready for lecture time to be over. I wanted to hand the bonobo to a nursery worker who would know how to get him to drink, and then get into that van and head home to dinner, a phone call to Dad as he woke up in the States, and satellite French TV.

"Are you done with your office stuff for the day?" I asked. "I'm ready to go pass out."

"Yes," she said, kissing the top of my head and getting up. "It's been a long day, hasn't it?"

"Yes," I said, standing. I hadn't yet adjusted to the time zone. Or the time. Or the zone. The bonobo whimpered at my movement. Another cramp must have come over him; his face scrunched up all over again. "Make sure you tell whoever's looking after him tonight to rub his belly. It seems to help. And to change the dressing on his blisters. One of them is oozy."

"You can do it yourself," she said.

"What do you mean?" I said. "We're taking him into Kinshasa?"

"No. We're staying here. You two can sleep on my office couch tonight, and we'll introduce him to the nursery mamas tomorrow. Then we'll get one of the upstairs rooms set up for us to stay in for the next few weeks. I'll run home tonight, have dinner with your aunt as planned, and bring your clothes and books when I come to work tomorrow. You need to offer him milk at least every two hours. Use my alarm clock."

"Mom! You're not serious."

She gave me one of her enveloping hugs, all vivid heat and batik fabric. "He can't roam free in the nursery until he's out of quarantine, and we have so many young bonobos right now that I can't spare one of the mamas to take care of him. I'll stay here, too — there's always plenty for me to do. You will see this through, Sophie."

"There's no way I'm staying in this creepy place after dark."

She looked pained — she'd spent her life setting up this "creepy place," after all. "There's electricity and satellite Internet access, and plenty of food in the office fridge. The usual security guards will be on duty. They'll keep us safe. And that bonobo is your responsibility. So yes, you are staying here."

"What do I do if he gets worse during the night?"

She shrugged sadly, as if to say that if he were meant to die, it might be tonight or it might be tomorrow, and there was no difference. Soon after, she was gone, and the bonobo and I were closed into her office as the rest of the sanctuary went dark.

I trusted that the guards were solid if my mom was okay leaving me with them, but I still figured to stay extra safe I'd barricade myself in her office with the bonobo until morning. I raided the kitchen, got plenty of warm milk, made myself an omelet with chopped mango on the side, and settled in with my mom's laptop. First thing to do was go online and track down my dad. He was awake, and we were video chatting within a minute.

Now that I was almost in high school, now that I was talking online to my father in his business suit while he ate his breakfast, I felt like an adult — and, more important, a member of the world and not only of Congo. As he told me about his upcoming work day, I fished under the neck of my shirt and brought out the silver chain that he'd given me for my fourteenth birthday.

He was being typical Dad, excited and scattered. Once he'd finished his monologue about his construction projects, he closed with an exuberant "I miss you so much! How are *you*?"

In response, I tilted the laptop screen so the little bonobo came into the picture.

"Whoa. Sophie, is that a ferret?"

Of course my dad knew exactly what a bonobo looked like; he had spent plenty of time around the sanctuary back when my parents were together. "It's the baby Jesus," I said, bowing my head piously and lifting one of the bonobo's arms so he made the sign of the cross.

"Sophie!" my dad said, scandalized. His side of the family is Italian-American and pretty religious.

"What?" I said. "I thought that would score me points with a Catholic."

"What's his actual name?"

"He doesn't have one yet," I said. "You know Congo. Here you don't name babies until you know they're going to survive."

My dad got his teasing face on. He's an elegant, skillful teaser — you feel loved the whole time he does it. "Until then you'll, what, assign him a number? What if he *does* die? Unless he's named and baptized, he won't go to ape heaven."

"I don't know, Dad. What do *you* think I should name him?"

"Tilt the screen more so I can get a better view." I did. "Wow! He's so *ugly*." Dad said the word reverentially, like ugly was the most marvelous thing in the world.

The tired bonobo's head bobbed as my dad and I talked. But some terror kept wresting him awake. The moment he'd be about to nod off, he would startle and cry out.

"Don't talk about him dying," I said. "Bonobo Number Eight is going to live."

"Eight's sort of an appropriate name. Considering the state of his fingers."

My dad had picked up a very African sense of humor during his years in Congo. Everyone here constantly laughed at tragedy, as if insulting misfortune would keep it at bay.

"I'm not calling him Jesus. And I'm not calling him Number Eight."

"*Otto*, then. Everything's prettier in Italian."

And so he became Otto, baptized with rejected milk.

He didn't sleep that whole night, which meant I didn't, either. I stayed awake in the semidarkness, watching Otto try to fend off his exhaustion. At first I assumed he was keeping himself awake because he was afraid of nightmares, but then I started thinking that maybe he'd been asleep when they'd come to take his fingers. It was warm in the office, so I unwrapped his towel and put him under my shirt so he could grip me directly, skin on skin. He seemed to like that, and started panting softly. He clutched and clutched, sometimes shivering and sometimes sweating, his panicky heartbeat beating its wings against my chest.

I dozed for spurts in between attempts to get him to drink. I'd noticed how calm he got while I was talking to Dad and figured he enjoyed the vibrations of my voice. So I sang, starting with the couple of Congolese lullabies I could remember and soon transitioning to hip-hop. Whenever Otto's bottle went cold, I carried it to the water boiler my mom used to make tea, bathing it in hot water until it was body temperature. He never drank, though. How long had he already gone without sustenance? It wasn't as though he was running on some nuclear reactor; unless he took something in soon, he'd wind down and stop.

Sometimes his belly would clench like he was trying to poo, but nothing ever came out. I knew he'd had diarrhea before, from the stains he'd had when I found him, but his not having any now was more worrying than reassuring. He was probably all dried up inside. Maybe that explained the cramps. I pressed the bottle against his mouth, poured some milk on my fingers and tried to dribble it in. Nothing doing.

My mom called a couple of times during the night. I suspected she felt bad about departing: If she hadn't had a dinner date with my aunt, she would have stayed. Unlike my dad, though, she wasn't the type to come out and say she regretted leaving me alone. Instead, she talked about how dangerous it was to be on the road after sunset, I guess to imply why she hadn't returned. There is no word in Lingala for *evening*, because this close to the equator the sun goes down very quickly, and day becomes night almost without warning. Even before I learned how to cross a street, my parents taught me to keep track of time in the afternoons to make sure I didn't get caught outside. Especially if you were a girl, the moment night fell you stayed where you were and locked the door.

"How are you doing over there, sweetheart?" my mom asked.

"I still can't get him to drink anything," I said, voice cracking.

"Keep trying," she said. "The nursery mamas will be there at dawn and they'll help you. But in the meantime, just keep trying."

During my childhood, I'd only half listened when my mom talked about the sanctuary, that half more from affection for her than from actual concern about the glorified kennel she'd spent hundreds of thousands of dollars getting together. But now I asked her everything she knew about bonobos. I looked online, too, not that there was a ton of info about them. They were way less famous than the other great apes, the chimpanzees, gorillas, and orangutans, even though a recent study showed they were our closest relatives, sharing over 98.7 percent of our DNA.

Otto still hadn't taken in any milk by morning. One time he dozed for ten minutes before startling, and that was the night's one minor victory. Otto and I shuffled out of the office, and what a sight we must have been. Neither of us was smelling too good: I'd gone twenty-four hours without access to deodorant, and Otto was giving off odors of spilled milk and passed gas. His little remaining head fuzz and my crazy 'do were both sticking up at odd angles. Looking like a case study for evolution's rejects, we headed into the nursery.

THREE

Mom's sanctuary was divided into three parts. There was a main structure, then a thirty-acre electrified enclosure where the adult bonobos lived, and the nursery, where the orphans spent their early years. The nursery was a one-room building with a fenced yard, the site (appropriately enough) of the former school's kindergarten. A mural on the wall showed painted children smiling in front of a rainbow. It had probably been beautiful once, but now it was covered in smashed bananas, and there were always rambunctious bonobos running around in front of it, occasionally humping the painted-on kids.

Otto and I crossed the sanctuary lawn slowly so he wouldn't get alarmed by new people or new apes. I'd be keeping him in my arms, anyway, since he couldn't come in direct contact with the other bonobos until his health was cleared. As the high-pitched calls of the young bonobos grew louder, Otto tried to pivot to see what the fuss was. I turned him around so he was facing forward, unlatched the gate, and went inside.

Motion exploded above me, and I was simultaneously bitten in the leg and kicked in the head.

Two black flurries scurried away, giggling maniacally. Mama Evangeline ran after one, a stick raised in her hand. "Songololo! Eh!" Then she saw me and stopped. "Eh, eh, mamas, *la princesse* is here!"

It sounds sweet, but *princesse* was no compliment. "Hello, mamas," I said cautiously. Three women approached me, each draped in baby bonobos. Baby bonobos clutching ankles. Baby bonobos slapping bosoms. Baby bonobos sitting on heads and swaying, trying to jump from one mama to another.

In the wild, bonobo infants spend the first five years of their lives virtually attached to their mothers. When they're really young they cling to her belly, and when they get older they ride on her back, like a jockey. The guidelines on how to keep a young bonobo healthy are pretty short: When they're with their mothers, they're happy and healthy; when they're not with their mothers, they begin to die. Remove a chimpanzee from its mother, and it will still play with its friends and chow down on whatever you put in front of it. Remove a bonobo from its mother, and it immediately despairs. For a long time, zoos couldn't keep any bonobos, because they kept dying. It sounds crazy now, but for a long time veterinarians didn't think an animal's emotional state could affect its health. It took years for scientists to figure out that unhappy animals get sick easier.

After everything each orphan had been through to get to the sanctuary, when a new one arrived it was an uphill struggle to lift its despair enough to stay alive. The bonobo had to feel like it had a mother again, and as soon as possible. Back when she had only a few bonobos to take care of, my mom bonded with each one. I remember her trudging through our house with a bonobo on each leg and each arm as she got me ready for school. Once there got to be too many bonobos, she hired local women to be full-time ape mothers. I wondered if they listed that as their occupation on official forms.

Except for Brunelle, the mamas loved to tease me. Maybe they knew I never really understood why all this money should go to a home for apes when people all over Congo were dying in poverty. Or maybe they noticed I didn't visit much. Possibly they liked to hassle me because I was half-white, and they assumed I needed to be taken down a notch. Or four.

Profiting from my hesitation, the bonobo named Songololo scampered over to kick me in the shins and run off again, laughing her head off the whole time. Clearly she was on the mamas' side.

"Hi, Sophie," Brunelle said. She was younger than the other two mamas, and in past summers we would spend hours in the nursery, doing each other's hair. Brunelle came from poverty in a nearby village, and was so good at her job that my mom hoped she would one day head the sanctuary. I was about to respond to Mama Brunelle when Songololo took a flying leap off Mama Evangeline's head. She missed me and sprawled in the soil, then picked up a big handful of the dirt, sprinkled it over her body, and proceeded to lick it up.

Mama Marie-France grunted and nodded. She was three hundred years old and not about to make small talk with anyone.

"That's the ugliest bonobo I have ever seen," Mama Evangeline said.

Mama Brunelle looked like she was going to say something nice, but then another bonobo infant sucked in a mouthful of water from a bucket and spat it at her. The bonobo ran away, and Mama Evangeline chased after it.

"Oui, princesse," she called over her shoulder. "We have been hoping you would finally get a nice Congo boy, but couldn't you have found one that was better-looking?"

Even Mama Brunelle thought that was hilarious.

I'd hoped Otto would perk up around other bonobos, but he didn't seem to have attention for anything but my torso. His eyes were doing their almost-closing thing. Maybe he would finally fall asleep.

Mama Marie-France came over, peered at Otto, and snorted.

"All done yet, ladies?" I asked. I switched Otto to my other hip, anxious to get past the hazing. I'd put bandages over Otto's blisters, and they squished as I moved him, like he was wearing a diaper. The babies didn't wear actual diapers — they delicately moved away and pooed elsewhere if they needed to go. "Because I need your advice."

"Maybe she's worried that they can't afford a place of their own," Mama Brunelle hooted, unable to resist. "Maybe Sophie is worried she'll have to move into the jungle and live with her bonobo mother-in-law."

"Really, Mama Brunelle?" I said. "You too? Listen. I can't get him to drink, and he hasn't —"

"Peed or pooped?" Mama Brunelle finished, suddenly serious.

"They're still in the honeymoon period," Mama Evangeline said. "He'll start pooping around you soon, believe me."

"Quiet, mama. Not peeing?" Mama Brunelle said. "Sophie, you may be a fourteen-year-old widow." Her tone had gotten severe. She scrutinized Otto, gently stroked his ear. He inclined his head toward her, though he kept his eyes closed.

Mama Marie-France finally spoke up. Her French wasn't very good, so she spoke in Lingala. "Not a widow," she said. "They can't get married. No ring finger!" Proud of herself, she put her hand into a pouch at her waist and stuck a handful of guava leaves into her mouth, a local cure for diarrhea.

Mama Evangeline loved that jab. Mama Brunelle, though, put her arm around me and steered us away. Following her lead, Mama Marie-France dropped her teasing and huddled around me and Otto, chewing away. While Mama Evangeline used her stick to bat away any nursery bonobos who came over to investigate, the other two mamas helped me wet Otto's bandages to remove them without yanking out his hair, and to soothe ointment over his hip wounds. We put a dollop on his ring-finger stump, too, since it was still a little scabby. He closed his eyes and scrunched up his face, looking baffled by all the attention.

The other nursery bonobos swarmed Mama Evangeline as

she heated up bottles for the morning feeding, until one of them discovered a dung beetle and they surrounded it instead, shrieking from the far side of the yard as they goaded one another to touch it.

Leaning against a wall was a muscular adult female bonobo; she was sitting there so quietly that I hadn't noticed her before. She watched me masterfully, her eyes sparking.

"Anastasia," Mama Brunelle explained. "The queen of the enclosure. Songololo's her child and usually lives with her in there. But we noticed Anastasia was rejecting her, so she's in the nursery for today. Which means mom's here for a couple of days, too. She's not a great mother. Maybe because she was raised among humans and was never taught how to take care of an infant."

Anastasia stared at me, frank and unfriendly: *Do not mess with me, hairless one.*

No wonder Songololo felt she had the right to dropkick me the moment I walked in. As the alpha female's daughter, she would be the crown princess out there in the enclosure. I lay in the grass so I wouldn't have to feel Anastasia's eyes on me, and stared at the clouds while Otto yawned and dozed. Whenever he jerked awake, I tried to tempt him with a few choice berries from the nursery's supply. Nothing doing. Every time he startled, I'd blow on his mouth until he pursed his lips for a kiss.

Eventually Mama Evangeline looked tired of batting bonobos away, so I said good-bye to the mamas and wandered with Otto back to my mom's office.

I found her doing her morning e-mail. "Mom," I said before she could speak, "I'm really sorry about yesterday."

She hugged me and stroked Otto. "Darling! How is our little bonobo?"

"Not good," I said. "I can't get him to drink, and he hasn't peed or anything."

We discussed Otto for a while. Usually Mom named the bonobos after towns in Congo, but she liked his name, especially since it was easy for Lingala speakers to pronounce. Though she tried, she couldn't disguise how worried she was that he'd die.

"Maybe we could try flat soda?" she finally proposed. "Who doesn't like soda when they're sick?"

I transferred Otto to my mother and went to the kitchen to get some orange soda. When I returned to the office and saw her holding Otto, I had a crazy thought: *It's a good thing my mom's here to help me take care of my baby.*

Of course I didn't say that, but poured the soda into a glass and put it in the sun to warm up a bit, then dipped in a soft wooden spoon and held it to his lips. When he smelled the soda, Otto's eyes opened. For the first time, his face showed an expression other than pain or despair: curiosity. Slowly he brought his lips forward and sipped, then took in the whole spoonful. Hands shaking, I poured another and held it to his lips. He drank it too quickly, and most of it dribbled down his chin. It beaded on the down of his face, the droplets glowing bright orange in the morning sun, like jewels.

FOUR

Sometime during my six years in the States, I began to hate the Democratic Republic of Congo.

For starters, it majorly failed to live up to its name. It was, in fact, the least democratic place on Earth. For fifty years the country had been headed by dictators and warlords, guys who led the country into civil wars and then barricaded themselves into their estates while they waited for dinner to be flown in from Europe.

In Lingala, *yesterday* and *tomorrow* are the same word: *lobi*. That had begun to capture so much of Congo to me, that there was only a now and a not-now, that moving forward was much the same as moving backward, that what we were heading into could easily look the same as our past. Back in the 1940s, there were over a hundred thousand kilometers of road in the country. Under the dictators they had all gone to ruin, and now there were fewer than a thousand. (An old joke: What did Congolese use before candles were invented? Lightbulbs.)

Things had gotten a little better in recent years, but anything that happened to the rest of the world between the 1950s and the 1990s never really made it here. Cell phones, yes. But landlines, not really. MP3s, yes. But videos or cassettes, eh. You'd come across movie posters glued to abandoned buildings, but they would be for black-and-white films. There weren't any movie theaters anymore.

Kinshasa residents with money lived like colonists in a hostile land, shuttered into manor houses with guards stationed in front.

Everywhere they went, drivers accompanied them. Once, when I was six or seven, my friend's driver hit someone and couldn't stop, because a mob could have formed and pulled them out of their car. I had to cancel my eighth birthday party because of *le pillage*, and spent it on the floor of my bedroom with Mom and Dad, our lights out so as not to attract attention, singing "Happy Birthday" in hushed voices, the birthday candles the only illumination in the room.

Not that I'm complaining about a ruined birthday party — I was lucky to be fed and alive. The ruling forces of Congo had been fighting wars for years. When it wasn't the Rwandans, it was the Ugandans. When it wasn't the Ugandans, it was the Zambians. When it wasn't the Zambians, it was other Congolese. On average, twelve hundred Congolese had been killed every day since 1998.

Five point four million. And it wasn't nearly over yet.

I knew there was great stuff about Congo. The second-largest rain forest in the world, wildlife everyone else gets to see only in the alphabet animals that hang over children's cribs. Brilliant greens, blues, and reds only your imagination could match. A lively, loving people. It was just that those same people occasionally took up their machetes and chopped one another up by the millions, and those vibrant red shades weren't only from blossoms pouring off sun-soaked tree branches. During my childhood, Congo was the best place in the world because it was the only place in the world. Now I really got why someone would want to live somewhere else if she had the option.

On a morning like this, though, when Otto and I walked through the nearby woods to pick him some gourds so sweet that they dripped sugar over our fingers, when a blanket and the hot sun were all we needed to feel the earth turning deliriously under our bodies, I found it easy to forget the bad parts. Maybe I was thrilled that after two months, Otto was finally getting better, and my happiness lapped over to Congo itself. Otto had grown a layer of soft black down, and his swollen malnourished belly had shrunk. He pooped and peed like you wouldn't believe, and it put me in a good mood every time he did.

The lab in Kinshasa ruined his first blood sample and asked us to send another, so the results on what diseases Otto might have weren't in yet. He seemed all good to me, though. With daily scrubbing, his skin had cleared up, and he didn't scrunch up his face from cramps anymore. But we had to keep him out of direct contact with the other nursery bonobos until we knew for sure, so for the time being he and I were each other's only company.

The first week of that summer, my mother and I had been inseparable. Then sanctuary business consumed her, and I saw her only occasionally throughout the day. We tried to have dinner every night, but it was often rushed, and when we did talk, it was usually about work. If she was guilty of not noticing me, I was guilty of letting her get away with it. She was so passionate about her bonobos that it seemed selfish to speak up about myself.

Otto and I spent one morning lounging on the bank of a pond outside the sanctuary's administration building. We were reading a bonobo coffee-table book. Well, I was reading, and he was trying to hump the pictures. I wasn't sure what to do with him, since if I walked around with him for too long my back began to hurt — as he got healthier, he also got heavier.

He got bored of the photographs and started snoring away. The moment I budged, though, he would be awake and staring around in panic. His voice was back, and he sounded like any other baby bonobo as he cried until I held him. I wondered what went through his mind that wrenched him awake.

By late afternoon he'd filled up on sleep, and we played airplane. I'd seen the adults in the enclosure play that way with their infants, lifting them into the air with their feet and holding on to their arms as the babies whizzed around. My legs weren't nearly as agile as a bonobo's, but Otto didn't know what he was missing and was blissed out, closing his eyes in giddy pleasure and wheezing noisily. He even smiled once. A smile!

Everything still wasn't in tip-top shape in his stomach, apparently, because he grimaced if my toes pressed too hard on his abdomen. So I thought it was better if we quit after a few minutes. We lay there together, sweating in the sun, listening to the birds make their rapid calls over the drone of the insects, to the singing coming from the farmers from the nearby village. I decided our lives needed a little excitement, so I stood up to go to the office to see what I could find for us to do. I thought I'd leave Otto in the grass for the few seconds it would take, but he immediately murped and pulled himself up me, settling around my torso.

In my mother's office was a cupboard full of old games. I was hoping to find a ball inside, but they'd been lost long ago. I'm a total fiend for Scrabble, so I pulled it off the shelf. Otto shifted to my back to get a better view of what I was doing as I set up the board on my mother's worktable. I placed Otto in one chair and me in another and gave each of us a letter rack. Otto immediately picked his up, nibbled on one end, tossed it across the room, and scampered over to retrieve it.

I poured out the letters. Otto loved the noise, smiling and making the raspy noise I was coming to recognize as laughter. So I took up the tiles and poured them out again. He loved it even more this time, jumping onto the table and clapping. I did it again, and he beamed at me and plunged his fingers into the letters, sifting through them like sand.

Apparently Otto was a Scrabble fan, too.

I placed a word, which he promptly demolished. Eventually he stopped wrecking my words, instead watching me with a very serious expression as I placed them. Within half an hour we'd worked out a system. On my turn I'd get whatever score my word was worth, and on his turn he'd get twenty points if he hadn't chewed any letters.

Eventually my mom came in and called us to dinner. She and the workers ate on the patio outside of the administration building. The sanctuary chef was pretty amazing, so in my two months here I'd made sure not to miss a single meal. Normally bonobos weren't allowed near the offices, since they tended to make a mess anywhere they went, but since Otto was attached to me for the time being, we got special permission. Besides, I liked to think he had good table manners.

I knew my mom had something unusual planned, since she made sure Otto and I sat beside her, and grinned mischievously as the food came out.

Emile, the chef, was already laughing as he brought out steaming plates. Patrice and the mamas clapped wildly. Because I had to lean back in my chair to keep Otto from pressing into the table, I couldn't see what the joke was until the food was in front of me.

It smelled delicious and looked weird. Mounds of meats and vegetables in rich and fragrant sauces. Something was unusual about them, but what . . .

"Now," my mom said, "this is actually Mama Brunelle's idea. It wasn't hard for us to see how much you're missing the States, so we brought some of the States to Congo."

Emile was beside himself with pride as he pointed to various dishes. "We have barbecue manioc, tilapia-in-a-blanket, and goat cheesesteak."

"Thank you, everyone," I said, my voice hiccupping.

I'm sure the food was great, but I couldn't taste it. I was too moved. I'd been condescending to them; I thought it was in secret, but they'd been aware of it the whole time — and instead of holding it against me, they'd indulged it.

To top it all off, Otto even ate a tilapia-in-a-blanket.

Later that afternoon, Otto and I were video chatting with Dad when I heard bicycle tires grind the gravel out front. A man's voice I didn't immediately recognize called out. Through the barred glass I could see my mother's bright dress, and Patrice next to her, shaking his open hand at someone. I hastily said good-bye to Dad and brought Otto outside.

The minute I saw the man, I froze.

It was him — the trafficker who'd sold me Otto. He was wearing the same torn and oily smock, had the same rusty bike leaning against a tree. On the back was a crate, covered with a cloth.

No one was speaking when I came outside, but I recognized a look of outrage on my mom's face, and the familiar stance of Patrice trying to calm her down.

When Otto saw the man, his body went rigid. Then he was pushing against me and was down from my arms and on the ground. He started making his high-pitched cries. His lips parted and he gave that same awful terrified smile I'd last seen the day I'd found him on the side of the road. Otto made a few steps toward the man and then stopped, looking at him, then looking back at me. Crying piteously the whole time, he held his arms out for me to lift him, even as he was walking away from me and toward the man.

"Sophie!" my mother said. "Take Otto inside, right now."

I quickly stepped to Otto and lifted him from the ground. He wrapped his arms around me without complaint, even as he kept his eyes trained on the man, crying in a strangled tone I hadn't heard from him before.

The trafficker seemed genuinely glad to see Otto. His face brightened. "You are looking so healthy, my little friend! Do you like your new home?"

"Sophie," Mom repeated sternly. "Inside, now."

"*Te*, don't go!" the man said. "I want to say hello!"

I hesitated, not because I wanted to hear anything the trafficker said, but because, as much as it made my stomach drop to see him, I would have felt even worse if I gave up a chance to give him a piece of my mind. "You," I said, "have to promise you won't sell any more bonobos."

Sensing the tension in my voice, Otto went rigid and cried louder.

"It is not that way, mademoiselle," the trafficker said. "He is my friend! We like each other, don't we, *mon p'tit*?"

"His name," I said icily, "is Otto."

Patrice beckoned me to go inside.

"*Malamu*. His name is Otto. Please do not go away yet, mademoiselle!" the trafficker said to me. "I have more friends for you."

For a moment I didn't realize what he meant; then the world narrowed and wobbled. "What do you mean?" I asked.

The man yanked the cloth from the back of the bike. There, clutching each other and shivering in a cage, were two baby bonobos. They'd been caught much more recently than Otto: They looked healthy and still had their hair and voices. Their limbs stuck out at awkward angles through the wooden bars of the cage, and at the sudden sunlight they cried loudly, scrambling over each other to try to get out. One of them made an arms-swaying motion I recognized from Otto when he wanted to be picked up.

My mom had her arms around my shoulders, trying to force me away.

"Do you like them?" the trafficker asked. "They are adorable, no? There are two, so it is more expensive, but maybe one hundred twenty-five dollars for them both? They need a home, they need someone to take care of them like my lucky little friend there. Of course I'm willing to bargain," he added, seeing my stunned expression.

The cries of the infants made Otto shriek louder.

"Sophie, go back inside," my mom said one last time.

Despite myself, I thought about my bank account in the States. It had over two hundred dollars in it. If I convinced the man to give me enough time to get into town, and if by chance one of the Kinshasa ATMs was actually working today, I could get the money out and then come back here . . . but no. It was my buying Otto that encouraged the man to come here with these two more bonobos. I sat down, right where I was. My legs refused to hold me up.

I hadn't fainted, but nonetheless I couldn't get my body to move. I'd pinned Otto's arm under me as I fell, and I sensed from somewhere remote as he pulled his arm away and crawled onto my chest, staring worriedly into my eyes. Screeching softly, he stroked my face, pulled my lips with his fingers to get them to talk. Somehow I marshaled the concentration to lift an arm and pull him close. I turned my head to the side and watched my mom.

She stopped being a person and became something like weather, lifting her body to all its formidable height and, with one blow, knocking the man to the ground. She stood over him.

"These creatures are nearly human, and to kill them is murder! Do you want to spend your life in prison? I have friends very high up, and they will take you away and you will simply disappear from the world. I called them the moment I saw you coming up the walk. Maybe you will not be lucky enough to make it to prison. Maybe I will have them slit your throat and feed you to the zoo crocodiles."

Believe it or not, those weren't the big guns. She didn't believe in witchcraft, but she knew her audience.

"I am a sorceress, do you know that as well? I have touched you now, and my curse is already running through your blood. If you ever harm a bonobo again, my spirit will come at night and cut off your toes. Then it will feed them to you, one by one."

The man scrambled to his feet and jumped for his bike.

"Take them, Mom!" I gasped. "Get those bonobos before he's gone."

But the man heard me and freed a knife he'd lashed to the side of the bike.

Undeterred, my mom stepped closer. "Do you think I'm scared of you because you have that little knife? I —"

But she stopped, because the man swung the knife, not toward her, but toward the two screeching babies in the cage. Mom held up her hands.

"If you don't take your curse off me, witch, I will kill them both right now," the man said.

"Okay," Mom said quietly. She mumbled some nonsense words. "I take it off you."

The man waved the knife at her threateningly. "They are my property, and you cannot take them away. Do you want me to starve, madame? You will call your powerful friends and tell them to turn back. If you try to follow me, I will kill one. If you continue, I will kill the other."

He got on the bike, the knife pinned precariously between his palm and the handlebars.

Patrice tried to pull me up from the ground as he went inside to get help. But I resisted, and he disappeared through the front door without me.

I sat up on the ground and pointed wildly at the man. "Mom! You have to stop him!"

But she was frozen still. "We cannot be the ones to take them. That is what caused this in the first place. And I believe him that he would kill them if we tried."

"But, Mom —"

"I already told you to take Otto away. Go inside!" she said, whirling on me furiously. I got to my feet.

The bike was almost all the way down the driveway. The trafficker hadn't had time to put the cover back on the cage, and I would forever remember the image of the two little bonobos in back. They clutched each other as the bike bounced over the dirt road, then finally turned a corner and vanished.

The only one of us to run after the bike was Otto, who dashed forward on all fours. He got only a few yards, when he fumbled and fell in the dirt. He looked back at me in confusion. I expected to see him angry or upset, but his expression was wistful. It said: *Why has my father gone away again?*

My mom locked herself in her office for an hour. I sat on the floor outside her door, listening as she called the Ministry of Environment, then various other government contacts. With everyone she talked to, she started calmly and then got angry when they couldn't help her; the space from one emotion to the other kept narrowing until eventually she was like, "Hello, is this Monsieur Ngambe? *Mbote*, monsieur, thank you for taking my call. A TRAFFICKER HAS TWO BONOBOS AND YOU IDIOTS WON'T HELP ME!"

She slammed down the phone one last time. There was only an ominous silence from inside her office.

When the door whizzed open, Otto got scared and climbed to the top of my head, gripping me by covering my eyes. I pushed his hands up to my forehead so I could see.

"Sophie," my mom said quietly, "no one will be able to save those bonobos. Patrice and Clément are off looking for them, but it doesn't look good."

"I'm sorry, Mom."

She put her face in her hands. "How could you, Sophie?"

"I'm sorry! I've told you a million times."

"I've spent years trying to put an end to the market in baby bonobos. Slowly, they stopped appearing in Kinshasa. In one moment, you reestablished it."

I lifted Otto's hand so it looked like he was waving at my mother. "But she saved me!" I said in a fake bonobo voice.

Instantly I knew it was a mistake. Her face darkened with fury, but she didn't say anything, buried her anger, and held me. Held me like she knew I really needed to be held. She whispered against my ear, because she couldn't hold it in: "Sophie. You know the only way they can get a young bonobo is by killing its family, yes?"

I'd known it but not really known it. I started imagining what horrors Otto had endured: the murder of his mother as he clung to her, having her shriek and bleed all over him as he saw the rest of his family butchered and smoked. And not just that terrible moment: It had been followed by weeks fighting the cord tied around his waist, surviving hundreds of miles of canoe travel down the Congo River to Kinshasa, all the while remembering his mother chopped down.

Otto squirmed out from between us, gasping from my crushing hug, and sat on my mom's head.

I needed her to say it wasn't my fault, even though I knew it was. I took her hand. "I know we're a very lucky family, Mom, that I'm so blessed I get to go to high school abroad and that when I'm here we don't have to worry about having food to eat. That I'm one of the only people in Congo who can decide to give a man sixty dollars that I was going to spend on notebooks."

But she wasn't going to let me off that easily. "If you were that man, Sophie, with no belongings in the world and no job, what would you have done? His only way to feed his family was to go back into the jungle and kill more bonobos so he could steal two infants so some rich girl would give him five months of income on a whim. So he did it."

She had to say that. The bonobos meant too much to her not to make that point to me. I told myself that even as my heart broke.

"So would I," she continued. "If you were starving, I would kill as many bonobos as it took to keep you fed."

I knew she was upset about the two infants, but she wasn't making me feel any better. I *did* see what I had done wrong. "Don't you realize how guilty I feel already, Mom? It's not like I meant for all of this to happen."

"Darling, I'm really upset right now. Please, go upstairs with Otto and let me deal with this problem."

I unwrapped Otto from her head and pressed him to my chest. My fingers played over his ribs and he panted happily. *He felt his first tickle with me*, I thought, somehow pleased within my frustration and sadness. At least something in this horrible world was working right; Otto was getting tickled.

But my mom . . . I worried that, as much as she tried, she would now always have this feeling of disappointment every time she looked at me.

FIVE

I slept terribly that night, especially since Otto woke up every hour or so to eat. By morning, evidence of his hunger was piled at the side of the bed: the remains of eight mangoes, two cartons of milk, a knee-high pile of sugarcane husks — the ones that I was able to rescue from Otto's mouth before he wolfed them down whole — and a mound of peanut shells. Though sugarcane gave them a run for their money, peanuts were quickly becoming his favorite food. I'd shell them and then he'd delicately peel them further with his front teeth — he didn't like the papery red coverings.

When the sun came up I went to brush my teeth and returned to find Otto spread-eagled on the bed, asleep. Near daybreak he'd moved on to oranges, and their juice matted the hair around his face as he snored away. I sat beside him and tried to wake him, but all he did was sleepily crawl into my lap, producing occasional citrus burps.

Finally I had him awake, out of bed, and bathed. We lumbered to the front yard, where Patrice was directing the staff as they unloaded metal cages from a truck. Bonobo-sized cages. "What's going on here?" I asked, jostling Otto on one hip. He playfully slapped my cheek and murped.

"The trip to the release site. Four more bonobos are going."

My mom's most recent success had been to get a forested island set aside as a bonobo preserve. A local tribe served as wardens to keep the bonobos safe from hunters, in return receiving funding for a local school and clinic. The project had been a success, and she was adding four more bonobos to the original six. Ideally, all the orphans would end up there someday, settling in with their new families. But this latest transfer hadn't been scheduled to happen until after I went back to the States.

"The plane schedule," Patrice explained when I asked. "We have to fly them in on a charter since there aren't any roads going north. We'd reserved a plane for next month, but for some reason the government's grounding non-commercial flights starting tomorrow, probably to get bribe money. So it has to be today or never."

"Where's my mom?" I asked.

"She's off with the handlers in the enclosure, getting the bonobos ready for sedation. Want to go say hello to her?"

I wasn't sure how to answer. We hadn't had a fight last night, not really, but I could tell she didn't know where to put her misery over my mistake, and I was scared to find out where things stood today. So I changed the subject. "I assume no one found those two bonobos?" I asked.

He shook his head sadly.

"Is there any way I can help you guys here?"

"You should keep Otto away. We have to tranquilize the adult bonobos to travel, and seeing the dart guns can be upsetting to the infants. Reminds them of the last time they saw their mothers, and they think the same thing is happening all over again."

So Otto and I played more modified Scrabble while I sneaked glances at the driveway through the window. My mom held and comforted the adult bonobos while they slowly fell asleep. She looked like she did in the photos of her holding me as a child — except, bizarrely, with giant hairy apes in her arms. Once the bonobos were out cold, the men lifted them into the cages and then heaved those into the back of a truck to be transported to the airport. My mom presided watchfully over the whole process, barking out reprimands whenever the men banged the cages. Once the bonobos were secured in the truck, it hit me: They had to fly north, then take the cages by dugout canoe up the Congo River until they reached the release site. And once they got there, they had to introduce the bonobos, make sure they were adjusting, and make their way back. Last time they'd been gone for weeks.

I was scheduled to fly back to Miami in ten days.

It wasn't like I thought my mom would leave without saying good-bye, but just in case, I had to get out there to tell her I was sorry one more time before she left. There was no e-mail or phone access out in the jungle; if for some reason I didn't catch her, I'd have to sit with my guilt until she got back.

I hesitated. She was out front with the sedated bonobos, where Patrice had told me Otto couldn't go. I hadn't been apart from Otto since the day I'd found him. Sitting him down in his favorite chair, I motioned for him to stay still while I backed toward the door. He stared curiously at me for a few seconds, wondering at this new game, then scampered over and wrapped himself around my leg. Humming softly, I set him back on the chair and held out my hand for him to stay. He was soon off the chair and running to me, but before he reached me I ducked through the doorway and, heart breaking, slammed it in his face.

He hit the door audibly and began to cry.

"It's okay, I'll be right back!" I called out, which only made him cry harder.

I stood there, torn by his loud shrieking. He wasn't ready to be apart from me, not even for a minute. The decision was instant: I wouldn't be going outside to talk to my mother. I'd give up on that so Otto wouldn't give up on me.

I reopened the door. Otto was stunned for a minute and then, screeching happily, leaped into my arms. It's like I hadn't existed while the door was closed, and now I'd magically come back to life. He shivered against me, his murps only gradually quieting into contented gurgles as he calmed down.

"Sophie."

I turned around and saw my mom at the end of the hallway, framed by the front door to the sanctuary. I rocked Otto and stared at her. "Hi, Mom."

"I have to leave early for the release," she said.

"I know. Patrice told me."

She rubbed her head. "Honey, I'm so sorry. But I know you'll understand this is our only chance for months to do the relocation. I've been preparing a year for this moment, and those four bonobos are at the perfect state to transition. If I let this chance go, I don't know when everything will come together again." There was so much in her expression: a profound sadness to be leaving me at all during the short summer I would be home, and a principled stance that she shouldn't be too warm to me so that I learned my lesson.

Also, the weight of history. Years ago, my dad patiently begging her to move to Florida with him; he had to go to America for work and to enroll me in a good high school, he'd argued, but she could come with us. Her raging back that she'd founded the only sanctuary in the world devoted to bonobos and couldn't abandon it. She knew it would mean splitting us all up for a few years, but she couldn't give up her life's project.

That was how she put it.

Her life's project.

Their marriage could have survived the years apart, but I guess it couldn't survive what my dad realized in those fights: Family would always come second for her.

And she was choosing bonobos over family again. It made me angry, but I couldn't find the words to tell her.

As if reading my thoughts, she said, "We've had a great two

months. You're flying back next week, anyway. Patrice and Brunelle will make sure you get off to the airport okay."

I've learned my lesson, I wanted to tell her. *You don't need to punish me.* "I get it," I said. "You're doing what you have to do. I'll be fine."

"How would you feel about flying back to Miami early?"

My mom's proposal caught me off guard. What I felt was: *Absolutely not.* Now it was a matter of making sure she didn't make me go. "You can't be serious, Mom. You'd have to pay for a whole other plane ticket."

"That's fine, Sophie. I don't mind."

"It's really that I can't leave Otto, Mom. I know the surrogate mothers are great, but he's bonded to me and it would kill him if I abandoned him."

She sighed and nodded. "I imagined you'd say that. Remember, you're going to have to leave him soon anyway, so you have to pick one of the surrogate mothers and transition him over. I think he'll be a good fit for Evangeline, and you'll see, he'll be more adaptable than you think. Patrice and the mamas are experienced with the process. If you need it for any reason, your aunt and uncle's number is in the phone book at my desk. And you know your father will be calling to check in all the time, online or through Patrice's cell phone."

"I know. I'll be fine, don't worry."

"The plane's waiting. I have to leave now, Sophie."

"Yes."

After a long moment she took my hand, gave Otto a warm rub on the head. I held myself to her, felt her warmth. "I'm so sorry, Mom," I whispered. I was sorry for the two little bonobos and, I guess, obscurely apologizing on my mom's behalf, for her choosing to stay six years ago and breaking us all up.

"I know you are, darling," she said, stroking me. "Don't worry about that anymore, okay? Shh."

"Thanks, Mom," I said. "I love you." Of course there were a lot of darker feelings I had toward her then, too, but in all my guilt I wanted to be consoled more than be right. We held each other for a while, but not long enough; then she turned around and was gone.

That night I was able to fall asleep but woke before dawn, mind looping from Mom to Otto to those two little bonobos in the crate. Once it was light out, I took Otto for our morning walk. He enjoyed being outside so early, because there were more birds on the grass to try to catch. When we headed back, I found Patrice near the enclosure's electrified fence, high on a ladder to wash the solar panels. I left Otto ineptly hunting finches and joined him.

"Hello, Sophie. Hello, Otto!" he called down. Otto murped once in acknowledgment and then returned his concentration to what was important.

"Patrice," I said, "did my mom sound okay to you when she left?" I'd never opened up to Patrice before, but he and Mama Brunelle were the closest I had to friends here, and I needed to talk to someone.

"Yes, Sophie," he said, smiling. "Why do you ask?"

"Nothing. She was mad at me about those two bonobos."

"She has a big heart, that's all. She's going to be fine," he said.

There was a heaviness to his words that I couldn't quite figure out. "What do you mean, she's going to be fine?" I asked.

He looked surprised. "I . . . I'm sorry, I thought someone told you, and that's why you were asking."

"No. What's going on?"

Patrice let out a long breath. "It's nothing to get worried about, it really isn't."

"Patrice. Tell me."

"On the way back from dropping your mother and the bonobos at the airport, we were stopped downtown. No one was on the street. There were more fake police. And more UN trucks, even though they didn't seem to be doing anything. It's like we were suddenly back to the early 2000s."

"You think the fighting is going to come back to Kinshasa?" We had plenty of street crime, but all the actual warring in recent years had been way in the east of the country, a thousand miles away.

"I don't know. Maybe we're all getting worked up."

But Patrice wasn't the type for paranoia, which made me all the more concerned. "So what do we do?" I asked.

He shrugged his skinny shoulders. "Nothing. Just keep your eyes out."

"Will my mom be okay?" I asked.

"Yes," Patrice said, though his voice was distant. "It is safest to be far away from the capital if war comes here."

"Oh," I said, relieved . . . until I realized, of course, that we were the ones in danger.

Part Two:
A Country
No More

SIX

I spent that weekend in a slushy mix of anxiety about the country's instability and delight at watching Otto fill out into a handsome young bonobo. He'd been improving for a while, but he looked fully healthy for the first time. The mamas still made fun of me for having an ape husband, but at least they couldn't make fun of me anymore for having an *ugly* ape husband. Though his hair had become thick, it was still uneven, so for the time being he had a punkish look. Fittingly enough, too, since he had a big mischievous streak that was coming out in full force. He knew when to stop, though: He'd steal a magazine and hide it, and then once he'd laughed for long enough he'd gallantly take my hand and show me where he'd put it. With his sweet smile and big eyes, it was all very charming.

Almost the moment my mom left, Otto and I came down with amoebas. I won't go into exactly how we knew, but it involved poo and the color yellow. But the infection was minor and, since Otto was eating well by that point, we got through it by Monday. That same day his results came back from the lab in Kinshasa, and I was officially the guardian of a healthy baby boy. For my last few days in Congo, at least.

Well, maybe not such a baby. Patrice had first thought Otto was two years old, but it turned out he was that small only because he'd lost so much weight during his travels. He was filling out so quickly that Patrice now thought he was closer to three and a half or four years old. Still young, but a kid more than an infant.

He'd become really good on his feet. Or off his feet, I guess I should say. Otto was still an unsteady walker, staggering a stretch and then holding my hand for a second before getting up the courage to toddle farther. But when he was near a tree — or a drainpipe, or a car, or (as I learned the hard way) a wobbly filing cabinet — he would suddenly be up in the air. My idea of space was limited to left, right, front, and behind, but he had a wonderful sense of *up*. He'd disappear from my hands, and I'd look around for him, getting panicked, until I'd hear a telltale raspy laugh and find him dangling from a ceiling fan, revolving on one of the blades.

He still wasn't ready to meet other bonobos, though. I'd walk into the nursery with him, and the others would come over curiously, but Otto would clutch me hard and whimper until we left. Like a kid too young for kindergarten, he simply wasn't ready.

I loved video chatting with Dad, but otherwise my social life was pretty narrow. That's why Otto and I were on our own when we met the strangers. We were taking a walk along the sanctuary's overgrown driveway . . . well, I was walking, and Otto followed me along the treetops, calling down to me, amused that I would be so silly as to choose the ground when there were thrilling branches to swing from. He would go for minutes through the jungle canopy, then come across something that scared him — a snake under his fingers, a snapping branch, a songbird flying in his face — and he'd be in my arms. Then he was back into the trees again.

The sanctuary was far from any major road, so I was shocked when I turned a corner and saw four guys trudging up the driveway toward us. Two of them had mangy-looking dreadlocks. All wore mismatched army uniforms.

I backed up, my body tensed. My skin felt like rubber.

One of them held up his hand. "*Zila, mundele.* Don't run. We're lost, and we need you to guide us."

I didn't want to help them find their way. I wanted to get out of there. But if I ran, they might follow, and I definitely didn't want that. "What are you trying to find?" I called out in French, crossing my arms over my chest.

"What's up the road?" the man asked. "Where are you coming from?" He was speaking Lingala, but his accent sounded like a Swahili speaker's. Eastern Congo?

"I have to go," I said, backing farther down the path. I heard branches bending in the canopy over my head. Otto was up there, watching. I prayed that, like most bonobos, he'd be shy of strangers. If he didn't try to join me, the men might not notice him.

"Wait, *mundele*," the man said. "*Olobaka Français?* What's your name?"

I hated getting called *mundele*. Back before 1960, when Congo was still a colony, the Belgians would say "*suivez le modèle*" when they wanted the black Congolese to behave. *Follow the model*. The French had morphed over time, so now any white person was called a *mundele*. It was a sarcastic way to paint anyone who was white as stuck-up. While my dad is white, my mom is black. But no one treated me like I was halfway. I was either bled-through black Congolese or the *mundele*. I'd inherited these face spots from my dad, not the pinpoint kind common to the Congolese, but broad leafy freckles. Sometimes I thought that's what tipped things over, whether someone could see my freckles. I was black only to those with bad vision.

"I'm leaving. Good luck finding your way," I said.

The man in front advanced, holding out his hands. "Is there a school nearby?"

"A school?" I asked, confused. Subtly but naggingly, the situation was spinning out of control. I quickly decided I wouldn't answer, no matter what he said back.

The men said something in Swahili, then suddenly they were all moving toward me. I was nervous, but not really scared — I was only a hundred yards away from the sanctuary entrance, and if I sprinted, they wouldn't be able to catch me before I got to safety. But then I saw one man reach down beside a tree and pick something up — a rifle.

All of a sudden the trail was full of movement. I heard a loud crack from above, and then Otto was on the ground before me. He held out his arms to make himself look bigger and stormed the men, barking loudly. They jumped and fled a ways down the path before it must have come to them that the charging monster was only two feet tall. When the men stopped, Otto lost his nerve and ran headlong back to me, nearly bowling me over when he leaped into my arms. He barked at the men, buried his head in my chest in fear, barked again, then hid his face away.

Three of the men started laughing, but the smallest one was rattled; he lifted the rifle and aimed it at us. Otto started caterwauling when he saw the gun, jumping back to the ground and charging. This time the men didn't scatter, but watched him unsmilingly. Otto stopped short a few feet in front of them, peered at the man with the gun, then ran back to my arms.

Finally seeing that Otto was no threat, the man lowered the rifle. "Is that monkey yours?" he asked.

"Please get out of here," I said, heart slamming. As steadily as I could, I turned my back on them and walked up the path. I kept my ears pricked, listening for any sound of pursuit. Nothing. Otto stared over my shoulder and barked, full of endless bravery now that he was in my arms.

Once I reached the sanctuary door, I allowed myself to turn around, head faint and legs trembling. But the men were gone.

When I told Patrice, he took Clément out to scout for the men, but couldn't find any sign of them. From my description, he thought they were *kata-kata* — "cut-cut" in Lingala — a catch-all local term that could refer to renegade guards or deserters from the Congolese or Rwandan or Zambian armies. Congolese politics were such a confusing mess that *kata-kata* came to refer to anyone you didn't want to meet. Many of the roaming soldiers didn't themselves know who was paying for their weapons. Seeing my anxious expression when the *kata-kata* were mentioned, Patrice assured me there was nothing to worry about. But I noticed he double-checked the locks on all the doors and windows of the sanctuary that night.

Otto had been simple before, representing only himself. Now whenever I looked at him I'd see the image of those two little bonobos in the cage. His life stood for those other two lives. And it stood for my own guilt.

Our history had become complicated. Maybe that's why we were both drawn to Pweto.

The adult bonobos kept to themselves, hiding away in the center of their large enclosure. I would hear them calling to one another, especially at the end of the day when they were bedding down, but I didn't see them very often, only when one happened to be near the fence while foraging.

But Pweto was different. He had to be kept by himself, and his one-ape enclosure was a lot smaller than the main one. Because his arm was crippled, he didn't spend much time in the trees, just sat all day by the piece of stream that snaked through his space, in full view of any who walked by as he stared into the water.

Something terrible had happened to him. He was missing an ear, and there was a hole in his cheek. One arm had a hunk missing and dangled uselessly. While the other bonobos loved to frolic, he barely moved all day.

Otto was fascinated.

We parked ourselves at the edge of the fence, where I did my summer reading while he watched Pweto. This quiet, motionless adult was apparently more Otto's speed than the rowdy nursery bonobos. One hand resting on my leg for assurance, Otto sat and called for Pweto to come play. Occasionally Otto got frustrated and approached the fence, calling louder. He never tried to touch it, though, not since the first time he'd grabbed the metal and gotten hurled backward, left with frizzed hair and a shocked expression. Now he was very wary of the magic in the wires.

That afternoon Mama Brunelle joined us when she went on break. "Pweto used to be our most energetic bonobo," she said, looking wistfully at him.

"He didn't arrive this way?" I asked, surprised.

"Oh, no," Brunelle said. "He was the most popular and handsome bonobo in the nursery. Really could do nothing wrong, especially with the young ladies. Then, early last year, one of the females in the enclosure gave birth to a little girl bonobo. Pweto was fascinated by the baby, and would carry her on his back, whizzing around the trees to make her smile. It earned him a lot of points, but then one time he went too fast. The baby slipped off his back and fell to the ground and died. The Pink Ladies turned on him."

"The Pink Ladies?"

"That's what we call them. Bonobos are matriarchal — that means that the females are in charge. Because bonobo females spend all day together and help care for one another's children, it makes them very close, so they're able to band together and have power over the males. Even though the males are bigger and stronger, if any of them steps out of line, the Pink Ladies gang up on him and teach him a lesson."

"Other *bonobos* did that to Pweto?" I asked. Bonobos always seemed so sweet and friendly. I didn't know they could be savage like that.

"The baby girl bonobo was the infant of Banalia, one of the Pink Ladies. When she saw it was dead, she got furious and attacked Pweto — and her allies joined in. Before Patrice and his staff could get in there with tranquilizer guns, he was almost dead."

"Poor Pweto," I said. "All he did was make a mistake."

"They kept him apart for a while, and once he'd healed they tried to slowly introduce him back. As soon as he was back near the females, they went after him as if no time had passed. So he has to stay by himself."

Otto and I watched Pweto until the sun set. Even when Otto would occasionally call a greeting, Pweto wouldn't react. Only once did he look back at us, and when he did, his eyes were empty, empty, empty.

Otto and I went to my room to video chat with Dad before dinner, but I'd just established the connection when the satellite link went down. I went into the hall to find someone who might know anything, and found the building quiet. Finally I discovered where everyone was: huddled around a shortwave radio in my mother's office. "What's going on?" I asked, and was immediately shushed a dozen times over.

The radio crackled and popped as a weak signal struggled to get through.

"Why aren't we watching the television?" I asked, only to get shushed again. Intrigued, Otto made a bonobo version of a shushing sound back.

Finally words came through: "... confirm that the gunfire this afternoon was indeed ... seen emerging from the capitol building with the defaced body of ... thought to be the actions of the TLA, or Trans Liberation Army, a militant group from the east, with links to Hutu groups in Rwanda and Burundi ... fleeing the capital, where the army has been seen infighting and ... those who are home, stay home ..."

The signal cut out for many seconds.

"What's happened?" I whispered to Mama Marie-France, seated next to me.

Her face was severe. It had always been that way, but now it seemed like she'd been holding it tight in preparation for this moment, for the inevitability that everything would again fall to bits. "The president has been shot," she said.

"Is he dead?"

She nodded gravely.

The president is dead? Though I was in shock, I finally got out: "Does that mean the vice president's in charge?"

"No," she said. "It means no one is in charge."

I hugged Otto to me so tightly that he whimpered in protest.

"I'm trying the UN station," Patrice said, fiddling with the radio dial. The United Nations had been in Congo since war broke out in the 1990s, and had reserved a frequency for emergency communications.

"We have to get in touch with my mom," I said as the radio whizzed through varieties of static.

No one answered at first. Everyone was in a private, horrified zone.

"We can't get in touch with your mother," Clément said quietly. "The networks are down, and she is somewhere on the river with the bonobos."

"Then I have to call my dad in Miami," I said.

"Shh!" one of the staff said. Of course — they were all worried about their families, too.

Patrice found the UN station. It broadcast in Belgian French: "... imperative that no one be on the roads. Until a stable transition government is in place, avoid interaction with any military or police or anyone who identifies as such. To reiterate, as many as a thousand people in the capital are already dead in street rioting, with reports of many more. Counterattacks from loyalists have resulted in confusion and a spike in opportunistic violence, so being in the open is inadvisable, as most victims have died in the streets. Stay calm, but treat this situation with utmost caution. Many armed groups are on the main roads, with no affiliation or central organization. The governments of the United States of America and Belgium have already announced their intent to evacuate all citizens and France is expected to follow; specific directions will follow on this station. Again, this has been a broadcast of the United Nations command center in Kinshasa. This message will repeat until further information becomes available."

Patrice turned the volume down.

"What do we do?" asked one of the gardeners.

"We stay put," Patrice said. "You heard them. This will go like it has gone before. We will hope no one tries to enter our homes. And the roads are where you die."

"What are you talking about? Everywhere is where you die," Mama Evangeline said.

"We'll stay here for now. No one is going to attack the sanctuary," Patrice said.

"Maybe not for a few days. But once there is no government and ten million starving people in Kinshasa? The first thing that happened in '94 was they tried to eat the zoo animals. We might as well be sitting on a herd of cattle here. Not to mention the US currency they'll figure we have in our safes from our foreign donors."

"It's not going to come to that," Patrice said. "Not this time."

But he didn't give a reason why, and despair, already heavy in the room, grew crushing. It was something about the way Patrice said "this time"; assassinations and coups were baggage the Democratic Republic of Congo had been lugging on its own for a long time. Why should anyone expect magic intervention now?

Since we couldn't risk the road, everyone stayed overnight in the sanctuary. The mamas curled up in the nursery with the young bonobos, the gardeners pulled blankets and pillows into the shed, I shared my little room with Emile the chef, and Patrice and Clément encamped in my mom's office. The rebels must have taken down the Internet and cell networks, as we could establish no communication with the outside beyond what we heard on the shortwave radio. Throughout the night, I groggily trudged into the office, nodded to Patrice and Clément, and made herbal tea. No one talked, but we'd sit together and listen to the repeat of that same broadcast. Then I'd wander around some more, hoping to get tired. Otto seemed to love the sleepless chaos and chirped happily at the restless people we passed in the hall.

The first light of dawn found Otto and me sitting on the front step, staring into the jungle. I couldn't see anything, but I listened for footsteps. I listened for those four men I'd seen the day before. I listened for the sound of a vehicle approaching. I listened for gunfire from the nearby village. I listened for the first sign that death was on its way.

•   •   •

Around noon, Patrice yelled out that the UN broadcast had changed. We all piled into my mom's office.

It started with reports of increased fighting in the north and east, on the borders of Sudan, Rwanda, and Burundi. And in Kinshasa. The president was dead, and people said it was Hutus, formerly from Rwanda, who had killed him, but it was feared that his intended replacement had also died in the fighting. No one from the TLA had stepped forward to take control, and the capital was falling apart. Banks and stores were looted. Corpses clogged the streets, mainly those of loyalists to the dead president and anyone who looked like a Tutsi, the ethnic group historically opposed to the Hutus. Most of the staff came from Tutsi families, so the atmosphere in the sanctuary was pretty grim. The mamas worried about their children holed up with their husbands back in the capital. The consensus in our group was that people who stayed inside weren't being killed, but the radio had said nothing about that, and we'd agreed on it only because it made us feel better.

The UN warned us that many of the slayings were being conducted with "white weapons": machetes, clubs, and knives, so-called because they killed without noise. At the close of the broadcast, the announcer said, "Any citizens of the USA, or EU countries with Belgian reciprocity agreements, will be airlifted out of Kinshasa's N'Djili Airport at 20:00 tonight on marked UN planes. The respective embassies request that any applicable citizens be at the airport no later than 17:00. Any citizens whose addresses are registered with the embassies of the USA, Belgium, or France and living outside the confines of Kinshasa proper will be picked up by an armored UN vehicle between now and 16:00."

"Your dad is American. You're a US citizen," Patrice said.

Everyone stared at me. It felt terrible to be singled out for rescue, when the rest of the staff would have to stay here. "I'm sure they'll come back for you guys," I said.

Mama Marie-France snorted. "They're going to fly out sixty million of us?"

Perhaps to save me from embarrassing myself, Patrice led me into the hallway. Otto gripped my torso and stared at Patrice's lips, reaching out to touch them as he spoke.

"I can see this is making you uncomfortable. But we have to get you onboard that plane. The American government will make sure it gets all its citizens out. I know for a fact that your parents would insist you were on that plane."

I knew it, too. They would want me out of here. I wanted to ask "What about you and all the rest of the workers?" but I knew the answer, and it made me sad. Then I wanted to ask "What about Otto?" but I knew the answer to that, too, and it made me sick.

All I could do that afternoon was walk. Around the edge of the enclosure. Around the nursery, with the oblivious young bonobos pranking one another. Around the front walk. I kept moving, because if I'd stayed still for even a moment, I would have fallen apart.

At any moment, the UN truck would arrive. I, and only I, would get in and leave. They'd fly me to Miami, and I'd be with Dad in time for my first day of high school. I wished so much that I could call him.

I was worried about my mom, but wartime Congo was the opposite of fairy tales: The wilderness was the safe place, not the town, because hiding was the only way to survive. By now my mom was off in the remote reaches of a national park. She might not even know what was happening. She was probably fine, and would learn about our few days of crisis only when she came back to civilization.

Because I didn't need to worry about her, I worried about Otto. At any moment the UN vehicle would come, and I would have to leave him. As the political upheaval settled down, the mamas would take care of him alongside the other nursery bonobos — but it was only because he'd bonded with me that he'd pulled through and survived. I didn't think he'd make it through the loss of another mother, not when we hadn't yet transitioned him over. Even another week with me might make the difference. If I left now, he would fall into despair and give up. Saving myself would mean destroying him.

I kept thinking of those two little bonobos on the back of the bike. Could I doom Otto, too?

SEVEN

The big white UN van came rumbling by in the midafternoon. Otto and I were already on the front step; when the rest of the staff heard the noise of the approaching vehicle, they came out to join us. Their expressions were hard to read. Knots of relief and envy and fatigue. They'd been through situations like this a few times in the last twenty years. Some people got rescued, and most didn't. There were no screams, no attempts to plead their way into the van.

Two guards in light blue camouflage uniforms and flak jackets got out. An officer stood in front of them, a slender man with a blue cap that somehow looked both rakish and sloppy on his head. When he spoke I recognized an Italian accent. Like my dad's parents. Unconsciously, I put my hand to the silver chain around my throat.

"Are you Sophie Biyoya-Ciardulli?" he asked. "Your father called central command and said you were here."

I nodded.

"You are allowed one bag."

I pointed to the large duffel at my side. I'd filled it with clothes and food, figuring I couldn't count on in-flight meals on a UN plane.

The officer stalled for a moment, like he was mentally searching his protocol book for how to handle this particular situation. "Miss, is that a monkey on you?"

"He's an ape. A bonobo," I said slowly. I'd prepared my words ahead of time. "They're an endangered species, and I know that means they can't legally be taken out of the country, but you have to understand that he's fragile and will die if parted from me, so it's actually his best chance for survival, and maybe once we arrived a zoo could take him and . . ." I lost words. I knew there was no way they'd let me fly with Otto. Only my desperation was making me even try.

The officer let me cry for a few seconds. "I'm sorry, there's no way you can bring him. You'll have to leave him here."

Patrice stood forward. "We'll take care of him, Sophie, don't worry," he said, reaching for Otto, who batted him away, gripped me harder, and bared his teeth.

"Otto," I said through tears, stroking his little head with its wiry hair, "you have to be good and stay here. They'll take good care of you. Soon this will all be over and I'll be back, and . . ."

Otto's arms began quivering, he was holding on to me that hard. I pulled at his hand to loosen him, and each time I managed to get a few fingers up he'd switch his grip somewhere else.

"Patrice, could you help me?" I said. "I can't . . ."

It took the combined efforts of Patrice and one of the gardeners to get Otto off me. He kept making these high-pitched cries and reaching his arms toward me. Seeing that I wasn't going to take him back, Otto fought fiercely, biting Patrice's forearm so hard that after he finally released I saw spots of blood. But Patrice held fast.

"We need to leave," the UN officer said. "We have another stop to make before we go to the plane."

"I can't go," I choked out.

"Look," the officer said, "your parents will be very worried. They need you to make the right choice."

"Go now, Sophie," Patrice called. "The quicker you make this, the easier it will be for Otto."

I believed him. I got into the van.

It was full of scared white people. From their nervous frowns I could tell that the situation in the capital was grim. I found an open seat and sat down.

Once the officer got in, the van began to move, backing down the driveway until it reached a space wide enough to turn around. An elderly stranger next to me held my hand.

But all I could do was stare out the side window.

Patrice was struggling to hold on to Otto, who was shrieking piteously, clubbing around with his hands and feet. Seeing Otto thrash made it hard to breathe, so I cast off the stranger's hand and put my head between my knees. Otto began to screech louder. The thought of not getting a final glimpse of him was too much to bear, so I raised my eyes.

With one big thrash, Otto fought his way out of Patrice's arms and was on the gravel path, running after the van. He was soon so close to the door that I couldn't see him out the window anymore.

He could go under the wheels any second.

"Stop!" I cried. "Stop the van!"

A mother with her arms around two children protested that we couldn't delay any longer, that if we did the plane would leave without us. The officer nodded and looked at me sadly.

"I'm sorry. He's just an animal, and we have to get out of here. We're not stopping."

"But you're going to run him over!" I shrieked.

I threw open the door. We were going so slowly that it was easy to jump out with the duffel. I looked back through the open door as the van continued to move away. "I'm sorry!" I called to the people inside. "My name is Sophie Biyoya-Ciardulli. When you get out of here, please get in touch with my dad and tell him that I'm okay and that I'll call him once all this is over!"

None of them could pull it together in time to say anything back. One of the evacuees slid the door closed.

Then I saw Otto. He'd flung himself at the front of the van and was clinging to the grille, staring at the moving ground and murping worriedly. I called his name. He turned his head, saw me, squeaked, and let go. He bumbled in the gravel, dodged a rolling wheel, then ran to me and leaped into my arms.

Patrice had his hands to his mouth in panic. "What are you doing?" he asked. "You have to be in that van!"

"I'm staying," I said. I told myself that soon the van would be gone, and they'd have to let me remain in the sanctuary with Otto. That it was the right choice.

Which was when the van stopped.

The officer and the two peacekeepers sprang out and started running toward me. "Young lady," the officer called out, "you're a minor — we will get you out of here, even if it means arresting you."

I threw my duffel bag over my shoulder and ran, Otto bouncing against my chest.

"Sophie!" Patrice called. "Stop!"

I ran headlong around the side of the administration building, focusing on speed and keeping Otto safe and not giving a thought to my direction. Only once I was past the nursery did I risk looking back.

The peacekeepers were running after us.

I dropped the duffel, hoping the obstacle would slow them down, and kept sprinting. Once I was past the nursery, I came upon the tall electrified fence of the enclosure and ran heedlessly along it. The fence would branch toward the pond soon, so I'd be penned in, and the guards would catch me. I couldn't keep this up for long.

Unless.

Farther down, embedded into the base of a tree and hidden by palm fronds, was the delay switch for the enclosure's entrance. It worked on a timer: When a code was entered the electricity went off for a few seconds, long enough for an attendant to get inside. The same code, when input on the other side, deactivated it temporarily so the person could come back out. I pulled back the fronds hiding the box and typed in the code. The familiar buzzing sound of the fence stopped. Then I opened the chain-link gate to the enclosure and went inside, shutting it behind me.

A moment later, the buzzing of the electricity started back up. It would take the peacekeepers a few minutes to get the code from Patrice, enough time for me to hide away.

Otto and I hurtled through the overgrowth.

Into the enclosure.

With the bonobos.

Part Three:
Enclosure

EIGHT

Otto and I had gotten only a short way in before the jungle shrouded us. I slowed, crawling over thick branches that arched through the air like tentacles before diving into the fertile soil and becoming roots. I pushed back giant ferns and leaped through the open space before they snapped back. Branches and fronds kept smacking poor Otto, but he seemed to take it in stride. All part of being a bonobo.

After a few minutes I stopped and listened. There was no sound of pursuit, no crashing of the underbrush. They must have decided against following us into the enclosure. We were safe.

Which meant, precisely, that we were *un*safe. I'd chosen not to escape a country heading into civil war. And for the time being, at least, we were stuck in a paddock with wild animals. Animals that had almost killed Pweto. The enormity of what I'd rashly committed myself to set in.

Young bonobos were mischievous and charming, but the adults were a different story. The only person who could safely enter the enclosure was my mother. Even Patrice always had assistants to back him up, and a tranquilizer gun.

The ground was muddy everywhere, so for the sake of my pants I stayed standing with Otto, rocking him back and forth and humming. I heard, from somewhere distant, the calls of the adult bonobos coordinating their foraging. I listened for something approaching, either peacekeeper or ape, but the jungle was quiet — well, as quiet as it could be, what with the constant squawks of birds and the repetitive ringing of the insects, like a demented show choir with sleigh bells.

After a few minutes Otto fussed to get down from my arms and started exploring the overgrowth. He peeled back pieces of rotting bark and delighted at the beetles and grubs he uncovered beneath, some of which he chose to crush and some of which he chose to eat, through some mysterious bonobo logic.

I couldn't get my mind to calm, not without knowing what was happening on the other side of the fence. It had been years since I'd climbed a tree, but I figured that if I got high up I could see whether the van had left. There was an ancient tree nearby with many well-placed branches and rough bark that should give my feet traction between the slick patches of moss. It also had thick foliage for hiding in case someone came in to get me. I started climbing.

At first Otto stayed at the bottom of the tree and called up to me. I worried he wouldn't follow, that he'd cry and I'd have to go down and get him. But then he started up and was soon way above me, reclining at the top of the tree and killing time until I arrived. Huffing, arms aching, I finally swung around the final branch. I was covered in a fine green film and tiny ants, which I brushed off as best I could. Bracing my feet against two branches, I looked out.

The driveway was empty, two brown tire tracks streaking through the white gravel. The UN van was gone.

I hoped the evacuees would remember my name long enough to get word to my father.

Then I realized I was smelling smoke. I pivoted and saw whorls rising from the village next door. A curling and greasy black, curiously sweet, pluming from burning homes.

The village was on fire.

Nearby was a cluster of men wearing mismatched uniforms, the greens, grays, and blues almost indistinguishable from my distance. They walked through the center of town, stepping over piles of clothes.

No, not piles of clothes. Bodies.

I squinted, trying to see anything more, even as a surge of fear made it hard for me to process anything. The men had blades at their sides and were sifting through abandoned homes before setting them on fire. One had a piece of burning thatch in his hand and was carrying it from home to home.

Barely aware of my own hands and feet, I hurried down the tree. I had to warn Patrice and the rest of the staff that whoever set fire to the village might be at the sanctuary next.

The fighting had come nearby after all. And I hadn't taken the UN vehicle. *Idiot!*

After hitting the ground, I ran toward the enclosure exit, Otto springing to my back, riding jockey-style.

I pulled up short. A shot had rung out.

Then another.

Directly on the other side of the fence.

I became acutely aware of the enclosure's impassable boundary all around me, the sensation of being in a jail cell; it became all the more important to get out. But I had to stop, because Otto wasn't on my back anymore. At the noise of the gunshots he must have leaped off. I finally spotted him quivering under a bush. I got on my hands and knees and picked him up. He was shaking so hard that I instinctively curled around him in the mud, forming a barrier like he was a fire about to go out.

More shots rang out from the sanctuary, and then another sound, a sort of wet slam that ended in a hush.

The screaming started. Some cries were long and full of panic and the labor of running, others were cut off almost as soon as they began. Otto shook even harder under me. I kept him inside the shell of my body and stroked him. I sang nonsense to him as my terrified mind skipped around.

I recognized Mama Brunelle crying, then heard a man yelling back at her, their voices fading and then getting stronger, a rush and a crash and a scream cut off. I was too far away from the enclosure fence to see anything — or to be seen — but I could hear it all.

The combatants must have made it to the nursery. I heard the young bonobos patter and make high-pitched calls as they fled. I looked up long enough to see branches of trees on the far side of the sanctuary shake as the young bonobos disappeared into the surrounding jungle. They wouldn't be able to get into the enclosure, but I hoped they at least made it out into the woods, and that the soldiers would be too busy to notice the meaty little bonobos until they had already escaped.

Too busy killing to notice.

I crouched in the mud with Otto, smelling filth and listening to the slaughter and unable to stop the *flash flash flash* of imagined images going along with the voices of the people I'd grown to love as they were silenced, witnessing their last moments in my mind until the familiar voices were gone, leaving only the unknowable Swahili of the rebel soldiers, occasional gunfire accompanied by laughter, and the crashing ruckus of pillage.

Throughout it all, I cradled the heartbeat beneath me and prayed the pulse wouldn't beat so hard that it tired and stopped, that I wouldn't lose Otto, too.

When I heard unknown voices nearby, I broke out of my paralysis. I was only a short way in — would they be able to spot me? A *zap* and then shouting, then another *zap*. The *kata-kata* had discovered the electrified fence.

I gingerly pushed up from Otto, who stayed on his side, breathing shallowly. He turned his head upward so his eyes could search out mine, the soft brown irises huge and rimmed in white in a way I'd never seen before. When I lifted him, Otto wrapped one arm and then the other around me. I laid him over my knees and blew stiffly into his face and belly, trying to convince him nothing was wrong. He refused to smile and only stared back, searching my eyes for reasons to calm.

Every time a *kata-kata* shouted, Otto would bark and bury his face. Eventually the rebels would realize that there were apes back here, but it would be best to delay the realization. If Otto was going to keep making noise, we had to go deeper into the jungle.

My blood thrumming in my throat with each step, we picked our way farther from the human world. Somewhat recovered, Otto took to the branches while I scrambled through the overgrowth, making sure to shuffle my feet so I wouldn't step on any wasp nests or vipers or millipedes. Not that I'd have been able to feel the sting in my state; pain didn't matter anymore, but all the same I wanted to stay alive.

Given their fear of loud noises, the bonobos had probably fled to the far side as soon as the gunfire started, so I didn't expect to come across any for a while. Though I was intimidated by the prospect of facing the apes, I was far more willing to risk my life with them than with the *kata-kata*. I figured I'd stay in the enclosure for a few hours, until the men had left, and then I'd go back out, forage what I could, and head with Otto . . . somewhere. To risk the capital, in hope I could make it to my aunt's house?

I couldn't think about that stage, not yet. I had to keep the scope of my situation as narrow as possible or risk falling apart. *Make it over this branch. There — see the fence on the right? Turn.* Having Otto to care for helped; if I'd only had to worry for myself I'd have broken down, but my mission was to keep him safe, and my own survival could come along for the ride. As if to convince me that life was totally normal, Otto stood on the edge of a branch and took a long pee.

I felt pretty sure that the fence would hold the *kata-kata* out, at least for a while. My mom had had it all reinforced a year ago, after she discovered that one of the night guards was snipping away bits of wire to sell in the scrap metal markets. Now it had redundant solar panels, whose frequent bursts of coordinated electricity were strong enough to knock back an elephant. And it was tall, over twenty feet. Though its purpose was to keep bonobos in, not people out, I figured it would fulfill that new need fine.

It was impossible to live in Congo without growing a thick skin for bugs, but even so, trudging through the jungle was almost more than I could take. Whenever uneven ground thrust me against a leaf or a tree trunk, I'd accumulate a new zoo-worthy creature: a roach-sized ant, a mantis fat as a crayfish, a centipede with pincers that could have bitten through a ruler. I stopped every few steps to brush the bugs off, and when I did I'd see Otto, dozens of feet above me, dealing with his own problem insects by eating them.

Eventually we came to a narrow clearing created by a recently fallen tree. I swept a space under its shelter, dusted dirt from my hands, and sat. Otto hurtled down from the canopy, swinging around the fallen trunk and landing hard in my lap. He reached his arms in his signal for me to play the airplane game, and I did, though I kept my anxious gaze on the surrounding jungle and what might stalk out of it at any moment.

Otto had barely any weight, but my legs unexpectedly buckled during our game and he fell. He landed on his head, sprang to his feet, and looked at me in confusion. I whispered that I was sorry and drew him toward me. My whole body was trembling; I'd kept the tension inside me stilled for too long and now it was coming out everywhere. Even my vision seemed to quiver. I squeezed my eyes shut and began to rock.

"I love you, I love you, oh God, I love you," I said. Though I said it to Otto, I was talking to my parents. I missed them so much, and my hysterical lost feeling was even stronger than six years ago when I'd had to say good-bye to my mom and my home. I thought back to the look of sorrow and odd surprise on her face when I actually got on the plane. We'd lost something then, something that we never got back. She wasn't first in my life anymore; she slid to the background after the divorce. "I need you," I said. "Oh my God, I hope you're okay."

An image came back to me, unbidden, one of the earliest of my life: Dad insisted I be sent to preschool at the Catholic school in the posh Gombe district, and when my mom dropped me off I bawled and bawled, begging her not to leave me alone. Eventually she left, and I stopped crying after a while. But when the teacher brought us outside hours later, my arms around two new friends, I saw my mother standing at the fence. She'd stayed all day, in case I'd look her way and be reassured. I imagined her in the distant release site, hearing word of the attack and worrying about me from afar, and my father waking up in Miami to terrifying news. I bet he was on the phone with everyone he knew. Though I was probably the one in the most danger, I was scared for them. I wanted to let them know I was alive. And I wanted them to rescue me.

I felt a hand in my hair, stroking me. Otto was standing tall in my lap and peering at me with those deep eyes. He stared at me harder — more without embarrassment — than any human had ever done. Then he found a termite in my hair and got distracted, not returning his attention to me until its brittle waving legs were crunching between his teeth.

This little creature, who needed me so much, could also care for me. I put my head between my knees and let Otto caress me.

Until I sensed we weren't alone.

NINE

I looked up and saw three adult bonobos at the other side of the clearing, muscular and nearly as tall as people. The one in front was young, with well-groomed, glossy black hair, somewhere in age between Otto and the adults farther in the background. A teenager. He stood upright, alternating between offering his hand in greeting and exposing his teeth in fear. To make myself as nonthreatening as possible, I put my head down submissively, laying my hands open-palmed on the ground. Otto buried his head in my chest.

All I could see was a tiny patch of Otto in front of my eyes, his wiry hair and a few fingers of his good hand where they curled on my shirt. I heard seconds tick by on my watch as I waited for the bonobos to decide what to do with me. My breath mingled with Otto's as I stayed frozen in that position, desperate to know what the other bonobos were doing but scared to look up and have it be interpreted as an act of aggression.

There was a touch on my knee. Now on the other knee. A touch much heavier than Otto's.

My thighs tensed as the weight grew more substantial. I raised my head and saw the young male fully on top of me. He smelled pungent, and I could see impossibly long toes curled around my thigh, like I was a branch. I couldn't figure out whether I was being attacked until I felt fingers against my scalp and knew the answer for sure.

He was grooming me. A sign of friendship.

The bonobo's weight, which I guess would be no big deal for another bonobo, was crushing me into the ground. I had to let my legs flop open, and he stumbled. I felt a tickle against my forehead as he lifted my hair with two long fingers to peer into my eyes. I closed them. I knew from my recent reading that if I didn't look at this bonobo, he would know I wasn't going to challenge him for dominance. Otto ignored him, too, burying his head into my shirt.

How long was this guy going to sit in my lap? I felt more hands on my head. The other bonobos were grooming me, probably trying to get to the root of this bizarre and virtually hairless female who'd invaded their enclosure. I cracked my eyes open and saw there was nothing like affection or welcome in their expressions, only cold curiosity. That was fine. I could live with cold curiosity.

Finally, the teenage bonobo eased off me. He ripped up a shoot growing out of the rotting trunk and started peeling away its bark to get at the green pith inside. The other bonobos came over and prized up their own shoots, biting into the pith eagerly. Food had been discovered, which meant the weird naked ape girl had become old news.

Thinking it would help me fit in, I tried to rip out a shoot of my own. The stubborn stick wouldn't come away, though, and slipped through my sweaty palms. The male bonobo looked at me quizzically and went back to his snack. As if to rub in my ineptitude, Otto handily pulled away a shoot and munched away. He offered me the inedible castoff bark.

Thanks, Otto.

One of the female bonobos shrieked, the other replied, and then the foraging group wandered out of the clearing.

With no more warning than that, Otto and I were alone again. I settled deep into the shelter of the tree, my body going limp as tension drained. I gave Otto a kiss on the top of his head and held him close. I suspected that part of the reason I wasn't attacked was that I was a girl — Mom always said the bonobos had a harder time with men. It made sense, given what they'd all been through at their hands. At that point I, too, didn't feel like seeing any human males for as long as I lived. As the adrenaline left my body, it left an unexpected feeling behind: loneliness. It had been nice to have more company.

Otto and I were still in the same position come sundown. I'd hoped to be out of the enclosure by darkfall, but during the late afternoon I'd heard another burst of rapid gunfire from the sanctuary, followed by laughter — the *kata-kata* hadn't left. The possibility opened up in my mind that they might never leave, that these were rebel soldiers with no loyalty or source of pay who were going to take advantage of the sanctuary's solid walls to make themselves a home. If I were part of a lawless band marching in a thousand miles from the east, wouldn't I pull my legs under me and stay here awhile, where there was shelter and supplies and plenty of food to harvest from the fields of the slain villagers? If they really were here to stay, I'd have to wait for the war to be over for them to leave.

And who knew how long that could be?

I'd figured I would wait until night and then sneak out, using the cover of darkness to slip past the sanctuary. At the first opportunity I'd steal what provisions I could and hit the road with Otto. Toward the capital or, if that route looked too dangerous, wherever took me away from the soldiers.

But when night actually arrived, when the world blackened and chilled and the jungle filled with unrecognizable sounds and I could barely see what was in front of me, I couldn't bear the thought of putting my plan into action. I felt almost safe where I was, but I could imagine all the fanged creatures that would be under my feet as I wandered blindly, could imagine rounding a bend and finding the eyes of a hostile ape staring back. So instead Otto and I climbed on top of the fallen trunk and sat there, where the sun's warmth lingered in the wood beneath us. Otto was too wound up to sleep, so he kept crying and walking up and down my body. He was probably starving. I was, too, now that the havoc of the last few hours was fading; my stomach kept growling and it seemed like I wouldn't ever fall asleep.

Even in August, nights were chilly. I tucked my shirt into my pants, planted my palms in my armpits. The warmest parts of me were those covered by Otto. I lay back in the wet night air.

My thoughts unspooled and my breathing got quicker rather than slower. What was going to happen to me? The UN plane was gone. I assumed everyone who worked at the sanctuary had escaped or been killed. My mom was hundreds of miles away, my dad much farther than that. Even if Otto and I made it out, how far would we get? With the government fallen, hostile soldiers would be scrambling over the countryside. I'd have to stay here with the bonobos. If I survived them.

My thoughts picked up speed. How could I be both panicked and exhausted?

I must have finally been able to ignore the occasional dropping leaf or the tickle of insects on my skin, because I fell asleep. I woke up to a loud crashing sound and the light of day. I snapped to a sitting position, my hands instinctively going to my belly to check on Otto. He was missing. I jumped to my feet.

The bonobos were back.

At least ten of them were across the clearing, all staring at me. I recognized the one in front from that one morning in the nursery. Anastasia the Queen. She bent a sapling over, as if to pluck a choice fruit from the top. Then, her eyes never leaving mine, she ripped up the entire tree and brandished it at me, shrieking.

I did my trick from yesterday, making myself small and lowering my head in submission. I shook my head, trying to clear the sleep from it. My eyes darted; I was desperate to find Otto. I spotted him on the other side of the clearing, standing and worrying his hands, making the murps that meant he wanted me to come pick him up. I couldn't afford to be submissive anymore, not with Otto unprotected. I stood tall, only just maintaining my balance with my sneakers on the slippery mossy log.

Anastasia grew more agitated, waving her weapon and barking. There was such strength to her movements — she swung her arms as if she were holding nothing at all, certainly not a sapling in full leaf.

Then she rushed me.

At the sight of her mass bearing down, I jumped off the fallen tree and bolted across the clearing. Anastasia came crashing after me. I made it to Otto first and threw my body over his. We rolled in the mud together, Otto grunting as the breath was pressed out of him when we slammed into a trunk. I waited to feel Anastasia's weight on us, to feel teeth in my shoulder or hands ripping at my leg. But there was nothing. I looked up.

Anastasia had dropped the sapling and was staring at us, the remaining bonobos — probably the aggressive Pink Ladies Mama Brunelle had told me about — again flanking her. Her breath came out in loud snorts. Her attitude seemed to have softened from hostility to mere distrust. Something about Otto, about the fact that I was protecting a bonobo infant and was therefore somehow like her, had changed our chemistry.

Another female, this one nearly bald on her head, approached me. She kept looking sideways and all around, but despite her nervousness she reached a tentative hand forward and patted me twice. Then she lay back and stared at me. As if to demonstrate what I should have done, Anastasia sat on top of her and rubbed their bodies together, staring into my eyes the whole time. It's often said that bonobos constantly have sex, but this wasn't erotic; it seemed more of a way to express goodwill and reduce tension. But I wasn't ready to go rubbing strange bonobos, so instead I sat down where I was.

I recognized the male nearby as the one who sat on me yesterday. As the females greeted one another, he got a good running start and re-created Anastasia's charge. It wasn't quite as dramatic a showing, though, since instead of a tree he'd armed himself with a leaf. Barking, he hurled it at me. Seeing how unimpressed I was, he lost passion and sat down heavily. He let out a sigh and kicked at the leaf that had so let him down. When it finally came to rest, he smiled at me in unexpected pleasure at what he'd accomplished.

I found myself smiling, too. Big mistake. The moment I showed my teeth, all the bonobos tensed, backing up and pounding the earth. Anastasia charged me again, and I fell to the ground and curled up, making sure I again had Otto beneath me. As we lay still, Anastasia put her lips right against my temple and barked. Ear ringing, I scrunched my eyes closed. She leaned heavily into me, and I felt a crushing pain on my forearm. Crashing sounds became quiet rustling as she departed.

I opened my eyes once I was sure Otto and I were alone again. A row of divots dotted my arm, in the shape of Anastasia's teeth. Two spots had already begun to well with blood beneath the skin. Otto prodded the blossoming bruises and murped. His touch hurt, and I shook him off. He took his comfort position around my torso.

I'd have a big bruise, but the wound wasn't too bad. If Anastasia had meant to really hurt me, she easily could have. She could have killed me. What she'd done was give me a warning.

She'd left me alive.

And here we were again, all alone.

As the adrenaline from the encounter ebbed, a thirst dry as salt came over me. The more the feeling increased, the more I couldn't get out of my mind a tall plastic tumbler full of club soda, ice tinkling inside. On Friday nights, my family would go to the Centre Culturel Belge. Dad would usually be entertaining clients, with my mom beside him. Me, I'd snuggle myself away into a nearby *paillote* with the latest installment of my book series of the moment, taking advantage of the concealing thatch of dry fronds to watch my parents during page-turns.

My mom had this gift for putting people at ease, treating each person she met like she'd known them for years. My dad was the opposite, gliding past everyone like a car passing pedestrians, but what he did have was this quiet focus. He was a man who listened. I loved those evenings, because I got to simultaneously read about a made-up world and revel in how well my parents worked together in the real one. But I also loved Friday nights because the waitress knew to bring me club soda after club soda. All I could think of now was the almost bitter taste of the bubbles popping against my tongue, the crunch and numb swallow of ice cubes, condensation accumulating on textured plastic until it dripped.

And if I was thirsty, I couldn't imagine what Otto felt, used as he was to getting milk every couple hours. Remembering that there was a pond in the center of the enclosure, I headed out, encircling Otto with my unwounded arm.

Once we reached the pond, Otto sprang from my arms and scampered to the edge, cupping water in his hand and gulping greedily. The water looked awful and murky and the very embodiment of disease, but once it was cupped in my hand gave the impression of overbrewed tea. I took a sip. It tasted earthy. I took another sip, and was soon drinking mouthful after mouthful. Our thirst satisfied, Otto and I lay back in the grass.

Though the sanctuary staff had worked hard to keep the bonobos healthy, I didn't like the idea of drinking from the same source as they did. There were loads of waterborne diseases in Congo, and a thousand different paths that all led to the same destination: diarrhea. It was how most of the kids who died here ultimately went. I'd grown up boiling even the water I used to brush my teeth. If I'd had iodine, I'd have used that to purify it. But I didn't, and letting Otto and me get dehydrated was no alternative.

Now that our thirst was taken care of, there was food to worry about. Those green shoots weren't going to cut it, not if I couldn't even peel them open.

The bonobos in the enclosure spent their days foraging, but it was more out of habit than for sustenance; their main source of food was the massive mound of fruit my mom's staff bought from the local market and piled into the enclosure each morning. But the staff was probably dead or gone, and the village farmers were definitely dead or gone, so there would be no more food delivery.

My hunger was getting sharp.

My mind went to the duffel I'd packed for the UN flight that I'd thrown to slow down the peacekeepers. Figuring I couldn't expect Coke and peanuts on a refugee flight, I'd packed my last American granola bars, a liter of spring water, some powdered milk in case by chance they had let me bring Otto, a bunch of clothes, contact lenses, some pink girly razors, sleeping pills for the flight, American tampons and Congolese pads, and I forgot what else.

To eat, I had to get that bag back.

But it was on the other side of the fence.

TEN

Two in the nursery. Two by the shed. Four on the main steps.

Those were the soldiers.

One in the nursery. Seven by the shed. Two on the main steps.

Those were the bodies.

Mama Brunelle was closest, legs splayed, her corpse sprawled halfway into a ditch. I couldn't tell from here whether she still had a head, but judging from the amount of blood staining the ground around her throat I thought not. *Don't flip*, I told myself. I couldn't panic now, couldn't yell or make a sudden move.

I calmed myself by focusing on Otto. I kept him under my shirt, so he was both blinded and close to my body. I couldn't leave him behind, but also didn't want him to see what had happened out there.

The rebels had dragged the couch from my mom's office onto the back lawn, soda bottles and bits of paper and food scraps strewn around it. One of them, a kid who couldn't be much more than ten, was wearing a sanctuary gardener's uniform, the sleeves rolled up so they didn't swallow his arms. He was smoking with two other soldiers on the steps. Another, wearing a string of bullets over a bare chest, paced nearby.

They all had machetes. Two of them also had rusty automatic rifles dangling by shoulder straps of fraying twine.

Hidden behind foliage, I watched for a while. The soldiers didn't move much or even talk. They smoked and drank and sat. I got the impression that they'd been traveling for a long time and now were settling in for a rest.

I got the impression that they were here to stay.

If that were true, how would I ever get out? My options were shifting: My best hope now was to stay put behind the electrified fence and wait for my parents to come through and rescue me. But I still needed food, which meant I needed the duffel.

At least the enclosure's gate was shaded, so I imagined I could get through the fence without them seeing. They probably didn't even know yet there was a gate. But if I went more than twenty feet toward the main building, I'd be in the middle of them. If I were captured, the best I could hope for would be to die soon.

But. There, flung at the base of a tree, its black nylon blending into the shadows, airline baggage sticker just visible, was the duffel. The men hadn't discovered it yet, but it would be only a matter of time. It wasn't more than twenty feet from the gate — even if the fighters did see me, I could get it and get back, unless they were quick with their guns.

After humming to Otto for a minute to get him nice and calm, I approached the exit. Steadying myself, I input the code and disabled the electricity. I went through the gate, pausing at the far side until the electricity hummed back on.

No one had noticed me. I had a few yards to go. The only problem was that I would be in full view of the soldiers sitting on the couch. They'd be facing me.

I crept as slowly as my nerves would allow, keeping to the blind of the biggest trees. Otto squirmed under my shirt as I went, but mercifully didn't make any noise. I inched closer and closer, the whole time keeping my focus trained on the men lounging on the couch. One had his eyes fully in my direction, but didn't react. Now that I was closer I recognized him; he was one of the four I'd seen in the driveway days ago. I inched closer to the bag, closer to him.

Then I was on it. I reached from around the back side of the tree, hooked one strap, slung the bag over my shoulder, and started back to the enclosure, this time focusing only on the entrance and pretending the men no longer existed.

When I heard a murp.

At first I thought it was Otto. But the sound was coming from the nursery.

One of the young bonobos was still there.

I paused, torn: Head straight back to safety, or risk a detour to the nursery?

The murp came again, a shriek hoarse from prolonged suffering. A call like Otto had made back when he was being sold on that dusty road. Like those two young bonobos had made on the back of the trafficker's bike.

Cursing my own foolishness, I dropped the duffel behind a bush by the enclosure gate and skirted the nursery wall. As of my earlier spying, the nearest rebels were on the other side, so I paused every few feet to listen for a sign that they were onto me. As long as I heard them still chattering away, I knew I was still undiscovered.

There, on the far side, was Mama Brunelle's body. A dead body, a thing and not a person. To keep myself going, I didn't let my thoughts rest on that fact. She was facedown, her legs the only part of her that wasn't covered in dried blood. Bits of her were missing; I couldn't understand, or make myself understand, which ones. *Inhale, exhale, inhale.*

Next to the dead surrogate mother was a young bonobo.

She was murping, lifting Brunelle's lifeless hand and patting herself with it. She put the hand down, and then picked it up and stroked herself with it again. Her movements were restricted, since a piece of rope was around her wrist, leashing her to an iron stake in the ground.

I whispered quiet nonsense to get the bonobo's attention. When she looked at me, I recognized her: It was Songololo, Anastasia's daughter, who'd been brought into the nursery to be looked after once her mother rejected her. She looked at me and then returned her attention to Brunelle. I murped, or as close as I could come to it, and held my open hand out in greeting. She didn't take it.

I approached and examined the rope around Songololo's arm. It was knotted tightly, and her wrist was already bleeding from the chafing. I tried to untie it, but when Songololo cried out I had to stop for fear of alerting the soldiers.

Roused by the activity, Otto crawled out from under my shirt, hopped to the ground, and approached the other bonobo. They stared at each other. Otto was intensely curious about the rope, and Songololo let him examine it until he got to her wrist. When Otto put pressure on it, she bared her teeth at him. He retreated to a spot behind me, holding on to my calves like protective bars.

I couldn't linger here. I was already farther from the enclosure exit than I'd ever planned to be, and one of the soldiers could wander by any minute. At the same time I couldn't leave Songololo — who knew why they'd tied her up or what they had planned for her? But I couldn't untie the rope without her crying out and alerting them.

Brunelle was naked — I'd only just realized it. As far as shock went, nudity lagged far behind blood. Her *pagne* — a lavishly cheerful yellow wrap that I'd always admired — was wadded up a few feet away. I picked it up, at first thinking I would cover her body. Then I realized the militiamen would eventually take it, and I wanted the fabric as a memory of her. It would also be useful; a *pagne* could be worn as clothing, tied to bundle a baby — or a bonobo — onto your back, or serve as a ground cloth for sleeping.

Hers was especially durable, covered in a layer of supple wax. When I picked it up I found her cloth bag beneath. I plucked it up — it might have some of her personal possessions inside, and I wanted to keep some memory of her in case I found her family.

Otto and Songololo stared at me, wide-eyed, as I placed both hands on the stake. When I braced my arms against my thighs and pulled, it came away in my hands. I figured once I got Songololo and Otto back into the enclosure I could worry about getting the rope off.

As I started back toward the fence, Otto bounded up and assumed his favored jockey position on my back. Songololo lagged behind. What a sight we must have been, me running with an ape on my back, trailing another bonobo attached by a leash.

I input the code, and the buzzing of the electricity stopped.

I grabbed the duffel, dropping the stake as I did, and passed through the gate with Otto and the duffel. I turned just in time to watch Songololo hobble through. We'd made it.

But the long stake hadn't. It hit the opening crosswise and held. Songololo jerked backward when the rope yanked on her bleeding wrist, shrieking in full voice at the pain. After a few seconds the sanctuary was alive with shouts. Men's shouts. I dropped the duffel and grabbed at the stake. Songololo kept pulling on it and screaming, yanking her leash taut, which made it impossible to turn the stake so it would pass through.

Two of the *kata-kata* were running toward me, machetes at their sides. I had both hands on the stake and was still fiddling with it when I realized another danger: At any second electricity would start surging through the fence.

Straight through the iron stake. Straight through me.

I was tempted to drop it, but I screamed and wrenched the stake. It dented the fencepost and came free. I fell away with it as the fence started humming.

The two soldiers were running at me, only a short way away. With the enclosure gate still open.

I knew I couldn't touch it now that it was live, so I looked for a branch on the ground. There weren't any, so I swung the duffel against the gate. A burst of sparks splattered as it impacted the metal, then the gate was closed, with the soldiers stuck on the other side. They shook their machetes and shouted at me. If they'd been the other soldiers, the ones with the guns, I'd have been dead by now. Even so, I could see movement at the main building and knew the men with the guns were on their way. I dragged the duffel, now sizzling and smoking, toward the jungle line. Otto bounced against my back as Songololo followed us, the stake in her hand so it wouldn't tug on her wrist anymore. We crossed the black border of the jungle and disappeared.

ELEVEN

That lunchtime we ate like kings. Well, kings in a land of granola. I figured I'd ration the bars later, but for now we were going to enjoy them. Otto preferred his mashed into milk and I had mine as is, gulping down three cinnamon-flavored bars in as many minutes. Songololo looked longingly at us while we ate, but refused to come near. She'd cried in torment while I'd removed the rope from her wrist and sat rocking for a few minutes by the edge of the pond, one hand in the other, staring into the water. Once he'd eaten, Otto sat beside her, his feet against hers. He delicately took her hand and traced his finger over the red wound. She winced, but tolerated the attention.

When Otto returned to me, Songololo trailed him. She picked at the bits of granola left in the cup I'd fashioned from half a water bottle that must have blown into the enclosure long ago, and when I poured some more milk in, she drank it willingly. Once finished, Songololo moved a few feet away, sitting on her haunches and staring at us.

She didn't remain there for long. As I was dozing off, I heard a rustling and sat bolt upright. Songololo had rummaged through my pack, grabbed a handful of granola bars and a pair of socks, and was now running across the clearing. I stood, but knew she would be long gone before I'd ever catch her. She was probably off to find her mother.

My stomach had felt a little off ever since we'd drunk the pond water. I had no idea where to go next, and had equally no idea whether anyone had managed to follow me. I spent the afternoon in the same spot, alert to every noise, every possible threat. Staying still felt as exhausting as moving.

We perched on a large rock beside the pond to watch night fall, wrapped up in layers of my clothing. Otto figured out how to work the duffel's zipper and seized on a vest I'd bought in Florida. The adorableness of the little black ape wrapped up in fuzzy white cashmere almost distracted me from my anxiety. The last time I'd worn that now-ruined sweater had been to go mall shopping with friends. A couple months ago I'd been arguing over food court bourbon chicken that colored denim was a sin. Now what I wanted most in the world was to manage to fall asleep on a rock with an ape snoring in my face.

Come morning, I marched with Otto to uncramp my legs, and when I returned to the pond I found a handful of bonobos on the opposite edge, sipping at the water. Anastasia was at their center, flanked by the Pink Ladies. Songololo must have located her during the night, and now kept near her side, her grip on whatever tuft of Anastasia's hair she could reach at any given moment. Occasionally Anastasia would bark at her daughter in irritation and Songololo would run away, only returning once her mother had calmed down.

They stared for a while, but once they got back to their foraging none of the bonobos seemed at all interested in Otto and me. Otto played in the dirt by himself and shot occasional longing glances at Songololo. I sat on our sleeping rock, watching the bonobos forage while I puzzled how to get out of my predicament. The granola bars would soon be gone, and I'd have to find another way to feed us.

I made mental notes of everything the bonobos put into their mouths. A lot of shoots, and the occasional hard purple-green fruit plucked from the trees. One graying bonobo had a rock with him, which he brought crashing down on nuts, occasionally breaking their shells, but more often than not just making a big mess or slamming a finger.

Anastasia waded through the pond, pulling shoots up from the muddy bed and eating them. Songololo followed until the water went over her waist, then shrieked and climbed her mother, clinging to her skull. Anastasia suffered the indignity, slapping Songololo only when her fingers went into her eyes. They made it to the far side, where Otto and I were. Anastasia continued foraging, but Songololo broke off and joined us.

She squealed and rubbed her body against Otto's, the way young bonobos will when they're anxious and want reassurance. Otto rubbed back, something I'd never seen him do. Songololo climbed a nearby tree and murped at Otto until he joined her. Soon they were playing in the branches. I watched them like I'd seen mothers do at playgrounds, with the same mixture of pride and loneliness.

Anastasia started picking fruit off a nearby bush. I worked my way over, keeping my eyes downcast. She noisily turned her back on me. I tried a plum-berry. Tart, but not too bad. I ate another and made a pouch out of my T-shirt to place some inside for Otto to share.

I called his name to get his attention, in case he was hungry. He stood on two feet to locate me, then went back to playing with Songololo. They were on a low tree branch, taking turns leaping onto each other's heads. Songololo was playing rough and Otto, though smaller, was giving plenty of rough right back. After one particularly fierce Songololo dropkick, Otto countered with a swipe at Songololo's ear that knocked her off the branch. She fell to the ground and squealed in shock.

Anastasia came bounding over, barking. Songololo watched her mother with astonishment. Anastasia was up to Otto's branch within two fierce arm-pulls. He cowered, murping in fear. Before I could do anything, Anastasia had snatched him from the branch and bitten his foot. Then she threw him down and watched him fall.

Otto tumbled through the air, arms pinwheeling. I couldn't react in time to catch him before he crashed into a bush.

He was still for a moment, and then groggily raised his head and called for help. I reached him as Anastasia dropped from the tree. I turned on her, out of my mind with fury. She had her teeth bared and arms out to strike, and I bared mine right back. Before I knew what I was doing, I'd pushed her. She rocked back an inch, surprised, then shrieked back right into my face.

It hit me how dumb I was being. Though no more than four feet tall, Anastasia was much stronger than I was, and I could see out of the sides of my vision that the other females were closing in to back her up. *Do not cross the Pink Ladies.* I turned defensive, plucking Otto into my arms and backing away. When my heels struck the edge of the big rock, I whirled around.

I was surrounded. Anastasia feinted at me, hurling sticks and leaves and dirt and whatever else she could manage to grab. Songololo stood a few feet behind her, looking shocked and more than a little pleased at the commotion she'd created.

One direct swipe from Anastasia would be enough to do me or Otto in. Shielding him with one arm, I backed up a few feet. Anastasia advanced on me as I retreated. I worked my way toward our stuff and leaned back with one hand to grasp the metal stake. I swung it in a wide arc, glancing Anastasia's shoulder. She shrieked, outraged. One of the other females reached for the stake, and I tapped her on the head as her hand came near. She staggered and recoiled; I hadn't hit her hard, but the metal — its hardness or smell — had her spooked. All but Anastasia backed away. She advanced on me, lunging for the weapon, but with a new wariness.

Twice she grabbed, and twice I dodged her. The third time, she connected. The stake was knocked out of my hand, into the pond.

It hit the water's surface with a loud splash. Startled, the bonobos leaped and ran around, climbing over one another and shrieking. They crowded the edge of the pond, slapping at the ripples. Having lost the focus of her audience, Anastasia retreated.

I turned to Otto.

He had his foot cupped in both hands, groaning. I lifted him and tried to move his fingers so I could see how bad the bite was, but he refused and struggled to get down from my arms. I tenderly lowered him to his feet. As soon as he put weight on it, the injured foot buckled and he crumpled.

The other bonobos remained fixated on the pond, but Songololo came over. She put her hand on Otto's ankle, and he released his hands to let her see his foot. I felt strangely jealous. *She's the one who caused all of this!* There was no blood, but Otto's toes had curled up and refused to straighten. She tugged at them, and though Otto scrunched his eyes up at the pain, he allowed her.

They stared curiously at his injured foot. She kissed his heel.

I knew Otto had to be in pain, but he wasn't whimpering anymore. After a few minutes, Otto was able to uncurl his long toes and teeter to his feet.

He was going to be all right.

By then the rest of the bonobos had given up on the mystery of the missing stake and returned to foraging. Songololo went to join her mother, but when Anastasia refused her pleas to be picked up, she walked a few paces back toward me. Then she changed her mind and returned to Anastasia. She climbed onto her mother's back, only to be pushed off. Songololo tried again, and this time Anastasia let her stay. Being someone's child was always tough, always in its own way.

I foraged along with the bonobos, making sure to keep clear of Anastasia. Most of what they were eating they found in the trees, but since I couldn't get up there easily I joined two bonobos on the ground, the teenage male I first met and the nervous female. When I approached, she made room for me to sit with them. I copied their technique of pulling up yellow-green stalks, removing the outer layer, and crunching on surprisingly tasty chives. I looked at my new bonobo companions, puzzled. They wouldn't let me forage with them before. Something had changed, and I suspected it had to do with swinging that stake. Without ever quite meaning to, I'd entered the troop's pecking order.

When the bonobos wandered out of the clearing, I would have been happy to let them go and stay a duo with Otto. But he'd started playing with Songololo again, and I didn't know how to break up their budding friendship. So I wandered into the jungle with the group, staying a ways back and foraging whichever berries and plums and shoots I recognized. Otto broke off from Songololo and joined me after a while, copying my movements and eating whatever I ate.

When the sun got its hottest in the midafternoon, the bonobos sprawled in the grass and relaxed. When Anastasia lay down, Songololo tried to curl up beside her, only to be pushed away. After Songololo gave up, she came over to Otto and rubbed her body against his to make herself feel better. Then she curled up with him. He looked at me, confused about what to do. I shrugged. *You're on your own, kid.*

I reclined on the rock and closed my eyes. I was nowhere near sleep, though. Much as I tried to drag them away, my thoughts slid to the bodies I'd seen in the sanctuary. Had my friends suffered before they died? Were the soldiers ever going to bury the bodies, or leave them to rot in the open?

I still had Mama Brunelle's cloth bag around my shoulders. I pulled it off, placed it in my lap, and stared at it. It smelled like her, and like bonobo, and like blood. I opened it and pulled out the contents. Of course the soldiers had taken any money, but there were still precious things inside: an almost-finished lipstick whose color I could easily remember on Brunelle's lips, and a pen wedged into a beat-up spiral notebook. Inside were pages of notes with photos stapled alongside. The bonobos. Names and histories. She'd been observing them and noting when they ate, who they interacted with. She'd never mentioned a word of it, and none of that was officially part of her job. She'd just been interested.

The friendly teenage male was Mushie. The nervous and nearly bald female was Banalia. The old one who did a terrible job of opening nuts and occasionally bumped into things was Ikwa.

I recognized Anastasia's photo from years before, and everything clicked together. She was the first bonobo my mom had ever met, but it had taken years for her to arrive at the sanctuary. Some family friends had rescued her from a market years ago and had decided to raise her in their house. Anastasia had her own bedroom and the run of the whole place, including full permission to get herself a soda from the fridge or use the toilet. Whenever I'd go over to their house as a kid, I had to leave the bathroom door open after I'd used it so that Anastasia could get in — she wasn't good with doorknobs. Eventually she stopped being cute and started being strong, and had to be kept outside because she kept breaking things. When my mom founded the sanctuary, she finally convinced Anastasia's owners to let her live there.

She hadn't been around other bonobos for years. When Anastasia had first arrived, she'd sat by the fence and cried, wondering why she'd been locked away with stinky apes. Slowly she'd adapted, though, and had become part of the bonobo society. Her time with people might have explained her hostility to me, how she seemed to look right through me and find me lacking. She was deeply familiar with humans, those creatures who had once accepted her and then locked her outside in the jungle. But she was in charge now.

I read and reread, finding out more about this place I would have to make myself think of as my home. At least for a little while.

TWELVE

Toward dusk, the foraging group I'd been tailing began to call out and move to the center of the enclosure. Otto and I followed a short ways behind, careful not to lose sight of them. They made locating calls to keep track of one another, and Otto would hesitantly call back, though not loud enough for anyone but me to hear. Eventually the first foraging group joined with another, greeting and rubbing and chattering. I tried to keep at a distance, but as soon as the new group spied us, they came over to investigate. Mushie stayed near me and worked like an ambassador, rubbing against Otto to demonstrate that we'd earned a place in the group. They'd seen my mother in the enclosure before, so they took my presence in stride. I was thankful that they seemed more interested in one another than in me.

Except for Anastasia. She studied me from a treetop, Songololo begging for attention at her feet. Seated in a ring of branches around her were four females, one of whom was nervous Banalia. I figured I was seeing the Pink Ladies.

I had an idea about the order of their hierarchy by who was grooming whom. Anastasia only received. Banalia only gave.

Sometimes a bonobo would come over and sit in front of Otto and me, back turned, expecting to be stroked. I wasn't sure what to do, so I'd make a few lame attempts to pat their hair until they wandered away in disgust. Mushie was always grooming ladies, never receiving. Since even he never tried to groom me after we joined the other groups, I figured I was still at the bottom as far as the hierarchy went.

Minutes before darkness plunged, rain started to fall and I had barely enough time to pack everything I had into the nylon duffel and hang it from a tree branch to keep it dry. August was in the dry season of Bas-Congo, and normally we'd go months without a drop, but it was like the weather had decided to join in the political upheaval. I stood in the driest spot I could find, clutching Otto and wondering what to do. The main building would be nice and dry, but the *kata-kata* were in there. Within the enclosure there weren't any caves or rock overhangs to shelter under. The ground would soon become wet, and sleeping in a puddle would be a surefire path to pneumonia, without any hope of a doctor or medications.

So I studied what the bonobos did.

The rain quickly went from a sprinkle to a downpour, thundering against the leaves and trenching water through the soil. To save my shoes and socks from getting soaked, I did like the bonobos: I found a tree and climbed. Otto rode on my back, occasionally reaching out to grasp a leaf or twig whose beading water interested him.

I stuck near Mushie. He took one branch in hand, reached for another nearby, and skillfully tied the supple ends together. Then he found another and tied it to the first two. Within minutes he'd made a springy platform, sheltered by the branches above. Only a little rain made it through, and what did funneled right down the leaves and to the ground. I was impressed: Mushie had been able to choose any position he liked in space, all by selecting which branches to use and where to tie them.

This task was made easy for Mushie, of course, by his long arms and grasping toes. It's like bonobos have four hands. With my relatively worthless feet, I didn't find making a nest quite as easy. Tottering high over the jungle floor, I braced against the trunk and got one branch into my hand. When I reached for another, though, the rain-slicked first branch slipped right out of my grasp and I wound up on my butt, nearly falling to the ground. I was down to one branch again. When I reached back for another, both of them slipped from my hand. I cursed. Otto, curious about what was getting me so upset, got off my back and sat in the next tree over to get a better view.

Finally I managed to get two branches limply tied together. They didn't look like they'd hold any weight, but it was a start. I'd need a third and, ideally, a fourth branch to make the nest stable. Those would have to come from the next tree over — I'd have to climb back down, go up the other tree, and hope I could reach across in the rain without plummeting to my death. All in the darkness, which would be nearly absolute within a few minutes.

I flopped down, sighing in frustration. Otto joined me, huddling his wet back against my side for warmth. I rubbed a hand up and down him, and he crawled inside my damp sweatshirt, shivering against my clammy belly. As I sulked in the fading light, I noticed Mushie staring at me from his nest. Suddenly the tree shook as he leaped to my side. Nearby bonobos cried out in surprise and I cringed. But he didn't mean me any harm; he focused immediately on my nest. Mushie undid my pathetic knot and, leaping easily to the next tree over, efficiently made a new nest, using eight branches instead of his own three, maybe because he knew I needed a far safer nest than the average bonobo. Without another glance at me, he returned to his own nest and lay down to sleep.

Cautiously, I eased along and settled into the bed he'd made me. It was unnerving to be suspended high above the ground, but the nest felt sturdy — surprisingly sturdy, as good as a store-bought hammock.

Once we were out of the rain, Otto crawled from under my sweatshirt and snuggled beside me. Now that I was in the security of a nest, the sounds of raindrops against the broad leaves and the good-night cries of the other bonobos became soothing instead of alarming. I drank a little rain that had collected on a broad leaf, figuring it was more sanitary than the pond water, and enjoyed the cool sensation on my lips. Otto followed suit. Although it was totally new to me, this life was routine for the bonobos. This was an evening like any other to them, and from here I could fool myself that the massacre at the sanctuary had never happened. As Otto's breathing slowed, I realized an unexpected miracle: *I might sleep tonight.*

I knew I was falling before I knew I was awake. As soon as my eyes opened I stopped being me and started being a body — I was a bag of meat, soon to splatter. Bonobos screamed above me, and branches thudded against my back and then my face as I contorted through the fall. Then my belly came down hard on a branch. My arms swung out in reflex and I held on.

I couldn't breathe; there was a sharp pain in my gut, I was wet and in shock, and all I could think about was keeping my arms around the branch. Then I realized that all my weight was on the part of me that Otto had been clinging to when he fell asleep. I reached under my belly, terrified of what I'd find. But he wasn't crushed. He wasn't anywhere. I listened for Otto's cries, but heard nothing.

Still struggling to get my breath back, I wrapped a leg over the branch and tried to get my bearings. It was still nighttime. The rain was still slapping the leaves and running down my arms. I could barely make out the shapes of other sleeping bonobos around me.

"Otto?" I called.

From far below, I heard a murp. Then it was closer and closer, until Otto swung up onto my branch and flung himself into my arms. I held him and clung to the wet branch, only slowly becoming aware of slight burning feelings on my arms and legs. My nose was tender and smarted when I touched it. I was intact, but I'd been scratched up pretty badly by the branches I'd passed. I'd be looking great come morning.

I'd fallen out of my nest. I was such an amateur bonobo.

I slowly made my way back up the tree, pressing sloshy, squeaky sneakers onto branches until I was up high again. I edged past Mushie, still snoring away in his nest, and relocated my own. The branches he'd tied were still attached. I cautiously got in, thankful for the brief but intense exertion: I might be wet and a little bloody, but at least I wasn't shivering.

It was going to be impossible to calm down enough to fall back asleep, not when I might wake up plummeting to the ground. I stared up at the stars, feeling my thoughts slow and my mind grow calm as the bonobos around me stopped shrieking and dozed off.

There was movement above me and I saw, like in a grainy movie, a humanoid figure silhouetted by the moon. Anastasia.

I watched, horrified, as she turned her attention to me, so we stared at each other through forty feet of vertical space. Then she was hurtling through the air, her mouth open in a scream, canines gleaming white. Her shape grew larger and larger until she was on me with a shriek and a rush of wind. As the nest pitched downward, my mouth filled with wet bonobo hair and my gut dropped. My nest didn't give, but the branches sprang, slingshotting Otto from me. He screeched as he and I and Anastasia plunged through the night. I glimpsed him as he grabbed a branch and clung to it while I kept falling. I was in the air for another second before sharp leaves raked my face as I hit the upper fronds of a bushy branch, sinking in until I stopped, panting, mired in brambles.

I heard a loud cry and scrambling sounds as Anastasia returned to her nest.

Now it all made sense. I hadn't fallen out of my nest before — it had been her both times. I picked my way out of the brambles and climbed to the ground, ankles wounded and creaking. I called Otto to me. He bounded down, and I rummaged through the duffel for a few moist shirts to use as a mattress. I laid them down in the mud at the base of the tree, positioned Otto on top of my belly so he could sleep without being directly on the ground, and got ready to wait out the night.

I'd started a war with the queen. And I was losing.

I woke up soggy and congested, my nasal cavity smelling faintly of blood. When I sat up, my pants squished. I warily laid a finger on my nose; I didn't think it was broken, but it was close. It was hard to get a stable reflection out of the pond's surface, but I could see enough to know I was heavily bruised. My primary task would be to keep Otto's curious fingers away from my wounds. He, too, was doing none too well. His wet hair stuck out in random directions, he was limping slightly from his wounded foot, and he wheezed through obstructed nostrils. At least the rain had stopped with the morning, but the sky was cloudy and it seemed likely that the bad weather would be back. If we spent many more nights sleeping on the ground in the wet, I might not survive. Little Otto definitely wouldn't.

I skinned a papaya with a sharp rock and removed the seeds. Then I unwrapped the second-to-last granola bar and mashed its bits into the sweet flesh. Using the curved peel as a plate, I fed it to Otto and me. We got a drink of tea-brown water, and I rummaged through the duffel for the driest change of clothes I could find. Even though the morning was warm, Otto was shivering, so I wrapped him up in a cardigan. Its musty fabric pooled at his feet.

Having suffered the rainstorm, the bonobos appeared to be taking the day off, draped around the clearing like damp towels left to dry. When the rain started back up that afternoon, it was even harder than the night before. Some of the bonobos got back into their nests, but most hunched around, holding elephant-ear leaves over their heads to keep the water off. Otto and I used my rain poncho the same way. Banalia kept clutching her leaf-stalk so hard that it would bend over and let water flood in. She would sulk, then go find a new stalk, and the same mishap would repeat. Finally she came over and tried to pull my poncho away. When I refused, she joined us instead, crowding in with me and Otto.

Anastasia was hunched over a safe distance away. She held her leaf in such a way that water streamed right onto Songololo's head, where she sat shivering in her mother's lap. Songololo would move so she was out of the rain, at which point Anastasia would shift position and expose her daughter all over again. As far as Anastasia was concerned, there was no child in her lap, and it was driving Songololo insane.

In one of the books Patrice gave me, I'd read about an American scientist who'd experimented with monkeys in the 1950s. He'd taken babies away from their mothers and offered them two fake mothers instead. One was made of wire, but provided food, and the other was made with snuggly cloth, but didn't offer any food. The babies would always choose the cloth mother, even if it meant they didn't have any nourishment to live on. Then the scientist went a step further and installed a device in the cloth mother that would make it kick out and hurt the baby monkey. When it was hit, the baby would run away in fear, then try to win the fake mother back. It would flirt and coo and risk curling back up against it. The baby monkeys would ignore their friends, concentrating all their energy on winning their fake mothers over.

Watching Songololo brought all that home. She could have given up on her mother, but she was obsessed with trying to get Anastasia to love and take care of her, even though Anastasia acted as though she didn't have a daughter. Songololo was the most insecure of all the bonobos, and for good cause — she was the only one, after all, still getting soaked in the downpour. Finally giving up, Songololo slid off Anastasia's back and hunched in the rain.

Banalia seemed to take great pleasure in Otto, toying idly with his hair as she took cover with us. At one point, as an experiment, I slid snoozing Otto into Banalia's lap. She squealed and looked down at him with a mix of confusion and delight, like I'd given her a pound cake. Freed of Otto, I motioned shivering Songololo to come join us. She looked at me, and then peered up at Anastasia, her mouth opening and closing but no sound coming out. Songololo was in full despair mode. Leaving Banalia with Otto and the rain poncho, I crept over. Anastasia looked at me and then looked away, but I could feel her focus. I came right near. The runoff from Anastasia's leaf splashed against my ankles.

Songololo startled when I placed my hand on her back. I opened my arms, and she looked at Anastasia, looked back at me, then slowly climbed up. She burrowed under my sweatshirt. My heart pounding, I watched Anastasia's reaction. Sighing, she turned her back as I crept back to Otto and Banalia.

When I sat down with Otto and Banalia, Mushie bounded over and joined us. It was getting to be quite a crowd under my little rain poncho. Old Ikwa wandered over curiously and, when he couldn't find any room underneath, sat near us with his elephant-ear leaf held up.

That night, Mushie made me a nest even nearer to him, Banalia, and Ikwa. Songololo slept in it along with me and Otto. Whenever I'd look over toward Anastasia, I'd see her eyes trained on me in the moonlight.

THIRTEEN

Every morning I would climb the tallest tree to check out the *kata-kata's* position. After ten days, it was almost a routine. Usually I'd find the core dozen or so that I was coming to recognize on sight. Other times their numbers swelled, and I'd see men hanging out of the windows, relaxing on the roof, urinating against the nursery's mural wall. One day a truck appeared in the driveway and never moved again; if the region really was at war, there was probably nowhere to get gas.

Sometimes they shouted loud enough for me to hear — they spoke Swahili or some other language I didn't recognize. Once, though, I watched them get drunk on some foul brown corn brew, stand at the enclosure gate, and shout for me in accented Lingala, their eyes dancing mad. I was glad they were too far away for me to make out most of the words. I'd been careful never to go near enough to the fence to be seen, and of course didn't reveal myself then. So they switched over to calling to the bonobos: "Animals, animals, give us meat, meat!" Maybe they figured apes spoke Lingala. They chanted the phrase over and over. In Lingala, *animal* is just the plural form of *meat* — which tells you a lot about the state of wildlife conservation in Congo. *Banyama, banyama, pesa biso nyama, nyama!* It stuck in my head for some time. *Banyama, banyama, pesa biso nyama, nyama!*

I took pleasure in how scrawny the rebels looked, while as far as the bonobos were concerned it was as if the attack had never happened. Realizing that the soldiers were starving was small consolation when, one morning, I smelled an awful sweet smoke as they burned corpses somewhere. Then I hoped the *kata-kata* starved until there was nothing left.

With the soldiers there, my best option remained the same: stay with the bonobos while I waited for my parents to get through and rescue me. We were fairly secure in our position. The protective fence was humming away, and the bonobos stayed clear of the front half of the enclosure — they had a long memory for gunfire.

I knew there wasn't any electricity running to the sanctuary, because at night there was never any light from the buildings. Once the *kata-kata* had run through the gas for the generators, they were in the dark as much as I was. At least it didn't mean the fence, with its solar panels, was out. Thank God no rebellion could cut off the sun.

I was sure my father was doing everything he could to get me out, once he realized I wasn't on the evacuation flight out of Kinshasa — but if the rebels had control of the airport, if they'd chased out the UN, there was nothing he could do to help me except wait for liberation. He might have assumed I'd been killed long ago. He probably feared I was in the hands of the rebels as much as he feared I was dead. But I couldn't possibly get word to him. I had to remain in the enclosure until someone finally came and chased away the *kata-kata*.

At least it didn't seem like food would be an issue; there was more to eat in the enclosure than I'd first thought. Every time one food source was depleted, the bonobos discovered another. They liked fruits the most, but once those dwindled they began selecting certain leaves and munching on those, too. It took a lot more greenery than fruit to feel full, so foraging went from a few-hours-a-day activity to a major occupation. Even the youngest bonobos began to help collect food.

I remembered my mom telling me that a big reason for the bonobos' peaceful society was how plentiful food is south of the Congo River. The Congo is so wide that it effectively splits the country in two. Chimpanzees live north of the river, where there are also gorillas. Since the bigger gorillas leave chimps only a fraction of the quantity of food bonobos get, each chimp must fight ferociously to survive, including killing other chimpanzees. Watching my bonobos groom and play, even as their mouths were full of leaves, made me proud. Kindness was a luxury that only the full belly could afford.

During my second week in the enclosure, giant green gourds began to soften and sag and drop from the trees. Each was nearly the size of an infant bonobo, and a few breadfruit were enough of a meal for the whole group. Within a few days of the first ripening, more of them were dropping than we could ever eat. The skins were too leathery to bite through, so old Ikwa used his sharp rock to open them. I joined him, using a similar rock, but lacking Ikwa's strength I had to use it as a knife, slicing rather than smashing. It worked better, though. Other bonobos started bringing their fruits to me and dropping them at my feet. I'd cut back the peels and hand them back. They'd rub against me as ape payment, and then lay back to enjoy their lunch. The air was full of a sweet, overripe smell and the high-pitched calls of fruit-sticky bonobos. I'll forever remember the image of muscular Mushie lying back, mouth hanging open, while Songololo picked out a morsel to eat from between his jaws, happily smacking it between her teeth.

We'd fragment into small groups during the day to forage and come back together at night. I was still terrible at making nests, so Mushie would dutifully make me and Otto one before crafting his own. Even though she hadn't attacked us since that rainy night, I couldn't get to sleep before seeing Anastasia fall asleep first. Otto had had a raspy cough ever since we'd been forced to sleep on the wet ground, and I wasn't about to let her subject him to that again. But ever since Songololo's breaking over to my side, everything had been remarkably peaceful — in fact, anyone who observed us during the days of the fruit harvest probably wouldn't have known the bonobos had a queen or Pink Ladies at all. The matriarchy revealed itself only at times of stress. Like when I first intruded into the enclosure and a hairy screeching bonobo dropped on me during the middle of a rainy night. Times like that.

Mushie may have been charming, but I found myself most often searching out the company of old Ikwa. I had no idea how old he actually was, since he seemed as strong and able as the other male bonobos, but he had distinguished silver whiskers under his chin, and one eye that was rheumy and blue-gray. Plenty of females displayed themselves to him or invited him in for a kiss, but he ignored them, keeping his focus on the horizon. I loved sitting next to him at sundown, high in a tree to get a better view of the gold and purple in the distance, swinging our legs as we watched the sun disappear.

I had more chances to get to know the other bonobos as Otto was growing increasingly independent. He still checked in with me, but in between times he'd range, playing with Songololo and the other young bonobos. He learned a game from them that everyone else enjoyed with gusto but made my heart stop: They'd climb the highest tree they could find and then, after a few minutes of goading, drop to the ground, saving themselves from splattering by grabbing a branch at the last possible moment. Otto would run up to me proudly, coughing his cough and rasping his laugh, all to scamper back up the tree with his friends and start the game all over again. *Don't forget,* I wanted to call after him, *that you have only eight fingers, and they have ten.*

Meanwhile, it was becoming apparent that Mushie had a painful crush on Anastasia. While she submitted to the attentions of other males and females, she wouldn't give Mushie the time of day. Apparently his rank wasn't up to her standards.

That didn't stop him from trying, though. He'd race around her in a circle, finally flopping to the ground in exhaustion. He'd come up behind her and drop a pile of leaves on her head, running away in surprise when she snarled back. He'd reach a hand out to stroke her palm, only to see it batted away. Finally he gave up and collapsed at her feet, his head turned away in misery. She ignored him. Slowly, he let his arm uncurl toward her. His hand landed right by her thigh and, building up his courage, he flicked his fingers so they toyed with Anastasia's hair. She moved over a fraction so he was no longer touching her. Mushie lay there, staring at her. Then, finally, Anastasia headed into the jungle and stared back, waiting for him to follow.

Mushie was in such a good mood when he returned that the other bonobos crowded around him to see what was the matter. But he didn't give up his secrets, just lay back, blissed out. Ikwa and I, old souls, watched the beginning of the love affair from our perch in the tree.

The other young males kept bothering Mushie, and like rowdy teens they engaged in some good-natured jostling, ending in all-out wrestling. They got so into it that Mushie was barely aware that he was rolling toward the fence. I called out a warning, but before he could stop himself, Mushie rolled right into it.

And nothing happened.

The fence was off.

Part Four:
What Remained
Outside

FOURTEEN

I never found out why the fence cut off. Maybe the *kata-kata* got creative and found a way to turn off the juice so they could finally have meat. Maybe something in the system shorted since there was no one maintaining it. It had been cloudy for a few days; maybe the solar panels couldn't muster up enough energy anymore, and without backup from the national power lines, they gave out.

Whatever the reason, the fence was down.

Assuming the *kata-kata* weren't behind the power cut, I figured I had a little time. The rebels had tested the fence in their initial days, had gotten shocked plenty, and had left it alone ever since. They seemed to be like the bonobos: once jolted and forever wary. The problem, though, was that the humming of the lines was gone. As soon as they walked near, the soldiers would piece together what that meant.

I considered waiting it out. Even once the *kata-kata* got in, the enclosure was large enough that I could secret myself away like the bonobos, taking to the trees. But hiding on high was no defense against bullets; the orphans all around me were proof of that. There was only the one entrance to the enclosure — I could imagine the *kata-kata* manning a guard there with a machete in case anyone tried to escape while the rest hunted us inside, pulling their net tight until we were penned. They'd slaughter the adults for food, keep the young bonobos as pets or for sale, and do who knows what to me. Or worse: I had a very good idea of what they would do to me.

Our best chance was to escape before they figured out that the fence was off. They were wary of an attack from another rebel group, or of official forces arriving. That meant their attention would be focused on the front of the sanctuary; they wouldn't be ready for something to emerge from my side. Certainly not a girl with an ape.

It seemed wisest for Otto and me to leave during the night, but with clouds shielding the sliver of moon, the dark was near absolute. I'd be lucky to find my way out of the enclosure without breaking a leg, much less successfully navigate the main sanctuary and the front driveway. It would be better, I decided, to leave at first light. I'd noticed that the rebels tended to sleep in, only emerging from the main building a few hours after daybreak.

I knew to avoid the roads in times of war — any child knew that. I didn't have an exact plan of what to do, but since the capital was about thirty kilometers away, basically west, Otto and I could walk away from the morning sun and get there in maybe two days, taking trails or following streambeds and foraging as we went. I knew the assassination had happened in Kinshasa, but my hope was the capital would be the first place the UN would secure and that once I was there I could try my aunt's house. I really wished I could head straight for my mother's place, but there was no one there. It had probably been looted clean by now.

I didn't sleep much that night, hashing and rehashing the next morning's strategy. As soon as dawn came, I nudged Otto awake. He groggily sat up, snorting back the mucus that had accumulated during the night. I'd taken to wearing socks on my hands for sleeping to cut back on bites and rashes, and as I peeled them off, I used one to wipe his nose. He yawned and curled against me, nodding back to sleep. *Perfect*, I thought as he clutched me. *I would love for you to sleep through this.*

I tried to extract us from the nest without waking Songololo, but that would have been hard enough in a bed, even worse in an

improvised hammock that tipped and rocked with every movement. She was instantly up, peering down over the side of the tied
branches as Otto and I descended, her eyes open wide.

Don't follow, please don't follow, I prayed as I worked my way down,
branch by branch, unhitching the nearly empty duffel bag at the
bottom and tossing it over my shoulder. But there was Songololo
standing in front of us, wringing her hands and glancing back at
Anastasia, then back at me. She had two moms, a real one and a
surrogate, and she'd chosen the surrogate.

Now we would be three.

Part of me was frustrated, because having Songololo along
lessened our chances of escape, but I was also relieved that I
wouldn't have to live with the guilt of leaving her yet again in the
hands of the *kata-kata*. We picked our way through the pale yellow dawn jungle, Otto dozing on my back and Songololo walking
beside me, her hand in mine. I felt something in my chest, both
sharp and sloshy, that I first thought was anxiety, but then realized
was guilt. Major guilt. The bonobos snoozing above me were
pretty well doomed. But what could I do? I knew that I didn't
have a great chance of getting myself out of this alive, less with
Otto and Songololo, and much less with thirty bonobos herd-
ing alongside me. Not that they would follow me to Kinshasa,
no matter what I did — bonobos weren't pack animals, they were
social foragers. There was no leading them anywhere, unless it
was to a nearby clearing for fragrant leaves. Even if they did freak-
ishly decide to follow me to the capital, what would I do, parade
with them down war-torn streets and hope people would be
nice to us?

I'd done the best I could. And though I didn't like the feeling
of leaving them behind, I'd be able to live with the guilt of aban-
doning the other bonobos if it meant keeping Otto, Songololo,
and myself alive.

We passed the central pond, then the fallen tree where Otto and I had spent our first night. When we finally came to the enclosure gate, I peered out between the wires. There was no one in the yard, and no movement in the buildings' windows. So far, so good.

I kneeled down to input the code, and panicked when the panel of buttons didn't work. Then I laughed at myself. *You moron. The power's off. You don't need a code.*

I pulled on the gate and it swung free. I closed it quietly behind me.

I avoided the nursery, whose murals were now partly obscured by rubbery black stains where the rebels had burned the corpses of my friends. I took the other path instead, which led alongside the administration building. It was my first chance since the attack to see it up close: Garbage overflowed out the back door, one wall was sprayed with bullet holes, and a couple of black circles were on the grass where the men had inexplicably burned tires.

Some of the windows had been busted out of their frames. Otto was on my back, but to protect Songololo's feet, I swung her over the sprays of glass shards that swirled through the grass. She seemed to know that she needed to stay quiet. The scene was too strange and anxious for her, though, and she made a stream of whispered murps. I squeezed her hand as we cautiously walked forward.

We'd have to avoid the gravel in front, because of the noise our feet would make crunching on it, and instead skirt the grassy edges of the driveway.

I'd made it to the front of the building, where the UN van had once been, when I heard rustling behind me. I stood stock-still.

Songololo was the first to turn and look, and she shrieked exuberantly.

There, at the edge of the administration building, was Anastasia. She'd followed us. She'd followed her daughter.

Songololo shrieked again and ran to her, climbing up Anastasia's back and wrapping her arms around her mother's neck. Anastasia didn't move. Keeping her eyes on me, she plucked a rake from the side of the building and started using it to gather the garbage into neat rows. She was mimicking what she'd seen the gardeners do — after all, she'd spent more of her life with humans than with bonobos. Performing the chore was just a place to put her anxiety, though; she raked the same spot over and over while she stared at me.

Songololo's jubilant shrieks were very loud. Though the guards must have become accustomed to bonobo calls, they wouldn't be expecting them from this side of the building. We had to get away.

Clutching Otto to me, I continued down the path.

There was rustling behind me, and foot- and hand-steps on the gravel. *Fine,* I thought as I kept walking, resolutely not turning around. *Go ahead and follow me, Anastasia.*

But something was wrong. There was way too much noise for it to be only Anastasia and Songololo following.

I allowed myself to turn around. I was right: It wasn't just Anastasia anymore.

The front lawn was dotted with black shapes. I quickly stitched together what had happened. Songololo had followed me. Anastasia had followed Songololo. Mushie had followed his crush. Like any dutiful Pink Lady, Banalia had followed her queen. And Old Ikwa, nearly blind and an easy victim to peer pressure, had ambled along behind. Five bonobos out on the lawn.

They greeted loudly, calling and rubbing against one another to purge the anxiety of their new surroundings. Even as Otto and I crept down the driveway, I watched them, glad they were out of the enclosure, but the thought running over everything else in my head was *We're dead we're dead we're dead*.

I gave up on creeping and started running down the path with Otto. I hoped Anastasia would follow like she had before, but now that I didn't have her daughter with me, she stayed. Which meant the other bonobos did, too.

When the *kata-kata* woke up and looked out their windows, they'd find bonobos grooming one another on the front lawn not twenty feet away, perfect shooting-gallery distance.

I shouted, "Come on! Move!" and waved my hands in the air.

The bonobos froze in mid-rubbing and stared at me. Which meant they were all looking the other way when one of the second-story windows opened and the muzzle of a rifle poked out.

"No!" I shouted. "Go, everyone! Now!"

The man behind the rifle started shouting, and more windows opened.

There was a flash of light, and all I could think was *Why are they taking a picture?* but then I saw Banalia turn gracefully with one leg splayed out, like a ballet dancer, only her head was open and a cloud of red mist framed it, and she was down on the ground, twitching in a way that I knew meant she was gone.

I heard the shot and the bonobos' answering screams all at once. They were suddenly creatures of pure energy, blurs of black jetting across the clearing and into the trees. Only Otto was stiff and unmoving, stunned and heavy at my back. The living bonobos were gone and it was only Otto and me facing the men at the windows.

I crashed into the trees surrounding the sanctuary. The bonobos had taken to the branches and were already far ahead — I could see fronds waving in the distance. Leaves and spiderwebs lashed my face as I pushed through, and fat panicked birds took to the sky. I couldn't spare time to plan where I was going, and wound up in a stream up to my knees, pitching forward into the muck. Otto cried in terror at my back as I foundered, but I regained my footing, and we were back to running through the trees.

I was much slower than the bonobos, but after a few minutes of frantic fleeing they took a break, Anastasia and Mushie assuming a high perch and scanning the group, then shrieking for us to continue. I lost sight of them a couple of times, but then I'd glimpse a black blur leaping between trees and I'd regain my bearings. Inevitably the first bonobo I'd manage to catch up to would be Ikwa, who was slower than the rest. We became two halves of the troop: Anastasia and Mushie and Songololo high and in front; Ikwa, Otto, and I lower and in the rear.

By then there were no more gunshots behind us, or sounds of pursuit. I figured the *kata-kata* had realized that the enclosure was open, and they'd headed in for the rest of the bonobos. It wouldn't end well. All great apes were naturally wary, but, because of my mother's painstaking work, these bonobos had become accustomed to seeing humans as allies. I tried not to imagine them descending from the trees to investigate the new humans in the enclosure, as they had once done for me, tried not to imagine them running forward, arms outstretched and excitedly calling for food, and getting a machete in response.

I knew at least Banalia was dead; that had happened right in front of my eyes. They would either eat her now or smoke her body to sell the meat. It made my stomach turn — the DNA in that meat was almost 99 percent the same as human DNA; it was nearly cannibalism. But the men were hungry.

It was cold comfort that the massacre of the remaining bonobos would slow the *kata-kata* and aid our escape. It made me feel bad, but in an abstract, numb way. I was tired of living for the memory of those who'd been lost, for the memory of Otto's family and that of those twin bonobos, gripping the bars of their cage as the trafficker pedaled away.

Now that the immediate threat was over and seemingly forgotten, Anastasia stopped moving and began to forage, taking advantage of the plentiful fruit in an area that had never seen bonobos. The others followed her lead. There was a lot of dithering and stopping to groom or rub, but despite their stress everyone got a fair amount of food in. Otto descended from my back and began to forage, too, following Mushie for a while before coming to find me and leading me to a papaya tree. I crashed one papaya with a rock to slit it open, gave half of the fruit to Otto, kept half for myself, and settled down to eat. When Songololo came to join us, I cut open a papaya for her as well. What she didn't eat went to Ikwa.

It was barely afternoon, but it appeared the group was settling in here through the evening. After the morning we'd had, filling my belly with papaya and sitting in the grass and staring at nothing sounded fine. As long as we hadn't been followed.

The bonobos went about their foraging with a single-mindedness that made me jealous. Was it possible that, for them, the morning's events hadn't happened? No. I knew their emotional intelligence, their delicate minds so near my own. Ikwa kept picking at the same spot on his back, where there was no bite or scab. Mushie had gone from tenderly soliciting affection from Anastasia to standing on his hands and falling into her, running away, and shrieking his head off when she responded angrily, then starting all over again. Things weren't normal for the bonobos.

That afternoon I didn't let Otto out of my sight. He'd wander a few feet and I would call him and he would bound back, his mouth full of grass. I held on to him and rocked him and kissed him and tried not to think of Banalia, spun so violently by the bullet entering her head.

FIFTEEN

After the havoc of the morning, Mushie neglected to build me a nest that night, so I slept on the ground. It hadn't rained for days, so the earth was dry, and Otto and I slept on a mossy flat rock in the next clearing over, using the emptied duffel and Mama Brunelle's *pagne* as ground cloths. I woke up to a cricket chirping near my ear, and when I sat up, a horde of them skipped away, like a handful of clay pellets hurled into the tall yellow grass. Otto exacted a minor revenge by eating the two he could catch.

I stood up, yawned, peeled the socks off my hands, and shook the duffel casing. More crickets and a pair of inchworms fell out. I stuffed my spare clothes back in, shaking each piece first in case of snakes or centipedes, and slung the bag over my shoulder. My still-sore nose scrunched while I forced my feet into my sneakers. They smelled so bad; if feet had taste buds, I'd be puking. It wasn't only my sneakers that stank; all my clothes were dingy and mildewed — but at least everything was holding together. The sleeping pills that had been for the plane were still in their plastic cylinder, and also in the duffel I had a liter of pond water and a handful of for-aged nuts. That was the sum of my possessions.

I made special note of which two trees the dawning sun appeared between and set my sights for the opposite direction. Kinshasa was a sprawling city of ten million, and if we headed west we'd be sure to hit some part of it. If by some chance we came in too far north we'd reach the Congo River instead, and could follow that downstream.

The bonobos were still asleep. Not about to sleep on the

ground, but rejected by her mother, Songololo had crowded into Ikwa's nest. I heard her stirring and murping, but Ikwa was still snoring loudly. Mushie and Anastasia were in nests higher up. I felt bad to desert them all, but bonobos don't range more than a kilometer a day, and Otto and I needed to go much faster than that. Besides, these bonobos were free of the sanctuary *kata-kata* now, and in a jungle rich with food — they might make it for quite a while, and with a little luck could last out the war until Mom and I were able to come back and track them down and bring them to the sanctuary. If there was a sanctuary to go back to.

I placed my arms through the duffel bag's hand straps so it became a sort of backpack. Otto scampered up and settled on top of it, winding his feet through the straps and using them as stirrups. The air smelled fresh and loamy, and in the clean light of morning, I felt something like happiness, or at least hope. I knew the day was fraught and shapeless, and that anything could go wrong inside it, but with so many hours ahead, it seemed like there was an infinite space to work through whatever came up.

"I'll miss you, Songololo," I whispered, and headed out.

But she wasn't going to leave it at that. Discreet as I tried to be, Songololo spotted us and scrambled out of Ikwa's nest and down the tree. Ikwa woke up and was soon sounding his high-pitched call after her.

And then, suddenly, I heard a puff of air and smelled chemical smoke. A shot from an air rifle, almost silent. I knew hunters went after bonobos in the evening or the morning, taking advantage of the moments they clustered together and revealed their position by calling out. But this region wasn't natural bonobo habitat, so it hadn't crossed my mind that there would be any bushmeat hunters around. But here was the snap and recoil of a rifle firing, the hot smell. Here was Songololo shrieking, Anastasia and Mushie shrieking, Ikwa quiet and staring, sniffing the air.

I dashed behind a tree. I still couldn't tell where the shot had come from, and might have been revealing myself instead of hiding away, but it was the best I could think to do. I grabbed Otto's arm and whirled him to my front, holding him in the air and checking for wounds. Nothing. He murped to me, his eyes wide with fear.

I leaned around the tree to check on the others. None was bleeding. The hunter had missed.

As I frantically tried to find out where the gunfire had come from, another shot came.

He missed again. I spotted him, shooting from a bush from the direction of the sanctuary. He was one of the *kata-kata*, the short bald man who had pointed a rifle at Otto on the front walk so many days ago. He was firing wildly now, a line of bullets tocking into the gun, hot casings popping out the other side. He pointed the gun at Ikwa and then Anastasia. Teeth bared, the bonobos jumped and shrieked in the trees. Only the man's awkward angle and the height of their nests had kept them alive so far.

With a rising shriek, a shape dropped from the trees and knocked the hunter to the ground. The creature rolled and came to its feet, and it took me a second to recognize the bonobo. Pweto. He wielded his useless arm like a club, flexing his powerful shoulder muscles to hurl it against the ground while he barked. When he bared his teeth, the flesh of his maimed cheek parted and revealed a row of yellow and black molars.

The hunter raised his rifle at Pweto. Terror made the muzzle shake.

Pweto didn't retreat and didn't charge. He didn't want to attack the man, but neither was he going to back down until the man left.

I cringed, curling my body around Otto. I waited for the shot to come.

The man put his eye to the rifle sight, got a good look at Pweto's teeth, then thought better and fled, turning right around and crashing through the undergrowth. The bonobos still in their nests kept shrieking while those of us nearby gawked at Pweto.

He stood still in the clearing, his crippled arm lying in the dirt, and his chest heaving from exertion. He stared after the man. I tentatively lowered Otto to the ground.

Anastasia descended her tree, barking, and body-slammed Pweto. He rolled across the clearing, got to his feet, and gave a stricken cry.

Enraged, Anastasia paced around the clearing, beating against tree trunks, ripping up shoots, and hurling them into the air. Mushie joined her, devotedly mimicking her movements. Cringing, Pweto slunk into the bush and disappeared.

I wished we could speak, that I could convince Anastasia that Pweto had saved us by attacking the hunter and that she should finally forgive him. Of course bonobos didn't have language, couldn't trap thoughts and keep them to use on others. But beyond the language issue, that kind of reasoning was beyond bonobos, smart as they were. The simple fact of the matter was that Anastasia had been scared and adrenaline had surged, and once the hunter was gone, Pweto had become her next target.

Finally, Anastasia and Mushie calmed down enough to begin rubbing against each other to ease their tension. Ikwa and Songololo joined me and Otto, and we four sat on a log and stared at a nearby anthill. I don't know what their thoughts were, but once the excitement had passed all I could think about was Pweto.

He must have gotten out of his personal enclosure, during the attack or once the power went out, and hid out in the surrounding jungle until he saw us leave. Then he tailed us from the sanctuary, too afraid of Anastasia to present himself but coming as close as he'd dared. He spent the night a ways back, and therefore was the only one to see the approaching hunter.

Maybe he'd been harassing the soldiers ever since the attack. Maybe he was why the hunters, instead of swarming us, had stayed inside and shot from the second story.

After the excitement died down, Ikwa assumed his role as the wise man at my side, sweaty hand in mine. Songololo wrapped her arms around my waist and peered nervously at her agitated mother. Mushie and Anastasia did their courtship thing. There would be no quietly sneaking away anytime soon.

I'd have to leave them openly instead. I put the duffel back on, despite the hindrance of Songololo's grasping arms, and waited for Otto to climb aboard. As we headed from the clearing, I felt a hand work its way back into mine. Ikwa. With my free hand I tried to remove Songololo from my waist, and she took the opportunity to grasp my other palm, escorting me along on two legs. I tried to extricate my fingers from hers, but she held tight. I had one bonobo on each side, and another on my back. Each time I made a step forward, we all moved together.

I sat down, and so did Songololo and Ikwa. After a while they let go of me. Songololo went off to track down her mother, and Ikwa lay back in the grass. I waited maybe ten minutes and then stood up. Ikwa stared up at me with a penetrating look, like he was acknowledging my coming betrayal. His eyes, one a gentle tea brown, the other milky, both rimmed in silver whiskers, watched me with wistful sadness. How had he figured out my secret plan, that Otto and I weren't heading off to forage?

Ikwa started to follow me, but he passed too near a tree on his blind side and smacked into it. Disoriented, he staggered, trying to get his bearings. Otto murped, and Ikwa located us and walked in our direction again.

Could I leave him — all of them — behind?

I had to. I was heading into civilization. They had a much better chance fending for themselves here.

Please stay, I thought, beaming the thoughts to Ikwa. *It's better that you wait here. This is for your sake.*

But these weren't wild bonobos — they'd been raised with people, and had been cast out of their tiny familiar world and into a strange planet, where the hunters with guns, those mother-killers, were back. We'd left their world and entered mine, and I sensed that they knew that. As I walked into the jungle, Songololo kept by my side. I heard crashes as Ikwa lumbered after us. And from on high, Mushie and Anastasia called to each other as they passed through the trees.

Maybe, I told myself, *in a few hours they'll pick a spot and give up on following me.*

I went at the fastest pace I could manage through the thick vegetation. There was one moment when I thought I'd succeeded in losing them. Otto and I'd stopped to eat a fruit lunch, swatting at heavy flies and bolting down globs of mango before I filled my water bottle from a nearby stream. I hadn't drunk any water from outside the sanctuary, and hoped I wouldn't have to ever risk it; so far the fruit we were eating was juicy enough that my thirst hadn't become too nagging. Songololo had left my side a while ago to join her mother in the treetops, so it was just us. But then I heard bonobo shrieks nearing, and before I knew it, the group had descended on us, drinking from the stream and ripping away their own mangoes from a nearby tree.

Bonobos weren't supposed to act like this — we'd already gone a few miles, more than they would ever range in one direction in the wild. But these were extraordinary times, and they were apparently willing to make an exception for their leader. Me.

SIXTEEN

That afternoon we continued our progress through the choking green of the jungle, until it thinned out and finally retreated completely. Anastasia and Mushie descended from the trees and joined me on the ground as we came upon a field planted with short, weedy bushes. Manioc was common throughout Congo, and its starchy root kept millions from starvation. There wasn't anyone in the field and, judging by the thick weeds engulfing the manioc plants, hadn't been for a while. The bonobos were unsure of the change in terrain and stuck to the edge, calling out to me when I stepped into the greenery. Songololo made a few steps with me and Otto, then ran screaming back to her mother, her courage spent.

I pulled up manioc, knocking away clods of dirt and stuffing it into the duffel. I'd need fire to roast the roots, but until then the leaves could be eaten like lettuce. The idea of subsisting on greenery alone — of prolonging that full-yet-empty stabbing sensation in my stomach — was totally unappealing, but the leaves would keep me alive. Otto watched from my back as I harvested, squirming at the constant up-and-down.

As Otto and I continued through the field, my eyes on the horizon for any sign of life, the bonobos followed us as best they could from along the jungle line. Past the fields was a trail that skirted another abandoned farm, also overgrown and untended. An entire village appeared to have been abandoned. All that remained were the shadows of huts, rings of waxy charred black on the ground. There was nothing else: not a clay pot, not a fork, not a body.

All the structures had been burned, except a simple straw hut that had been only half scorched away. It fronted the jungle, and as I investigated it — hoping to find a pot, a lighter, anything — the bonobos joined me. Mushie and Anastasia shared the roof while Ikwa helped me sift through the trash that had accumulated against the wooden poles.

I found nothing useful. But the village got me thinking. The area had the alien quiet of a place that had been long abandoned, and was connected to the jungle by trails, not roads, so with the villagers gone, no new people were likely to pass by. With nothing left but a soon-to-wither manioc crop, it could hardly be a strategic advantage for the combatants to seize on. And the area was distinctive enough with its one remaining hut that I could track it down later, after I'd gotten out of Congo and come back after the conflict.

It was a good place to leave the bonobos.

But how? If Otto and I walked out, Songololo would tag along, and Anastasia after her, and then the whole group. I had to prevent them, but even if I found a way to restrain them it wasn't an option, since then they wouldn't be able to forage and keep themselves alive.

I removed the sleeping pills from my bag and rolled them out like dice onto a flat rock. With their love of novelty, the bonobos swarmed me, poking at the pills. Mushie immediately took one and stuck it in his mouth, and it was only by throwing my body over the pills that I prevented him from eating them all.

Songololo was the one I had to drug, but I had trouble judging her weight. I figured she was forty pounds, and if the pills were meant for me, then I should give her . . . two-sevenths? I found myself doing calculations I'd failed at in geometry class as I determined the angle to cut the round pill. After I finally made the cut and handed it to Songololo, she looked at my hand and kissed it, knocking the fragment to the soil. The wedge winked at us, pretty and pink.

Granola crumbs did the trick. I pressed the drug into their gooey center and then gave the morsel to Songololo. She gulped it down, licking her fingers and marveling at this turn in her luck. When the rest went up into the trees, she stayed on the ground, snoozily leaning her head against my knee. Soon she was snoring away. When Songololo was quickly followed by Mushie, Anastasia and Ikwa grew perplexed and settled down on the ground beside them. Anastasia prodded Songololo, pried her eyes open with her fingers, only to have her daughter, in a move that looked familiar from my own typical Saturday morning behavior, roll over, groan, and put her arms over her face.

Anastasia was clearly anxious about Songololo, getting up, walking in a circle, and sitting back down at her side. I wished I could tell her it was going to be okay, but all I did was maneuver to Ikwa's blind side, take Otto in my arms, and slink away. I didn't risk a second to say good-bye; I crossed the abandoned fields in the rapidly diminishing light and was alone by the time the Congo five-minute twilight began.

I got to business, arranging some thatch that had fallen from a ruined hut and laying clothes over it to make a sort of mattress. As I finished the bed, thinking it looked surprisingly comfortable, a terrible black feeling came over me and I shuddered, aching at the sudden loneliness. I missed my new family.

I sat on the mattress with Otto, splayed him in my lap, and gave him a good tickle. At first he resisted, looking around anxiously for the other bonobos. Then he finally gave in, and the raspy laughter he made heartened me a little. We had each other, after all. I blew a big raspberry into the sole of one of his feet and then the other, and he made the husky wheeze that meant he was truly delighted, almost losing his breath entirely. When I stopped he threw his arms around my head, indicating he wanted me to continue. So I tickled him more, even though by then it was dark and I had to go by feel. When I finally stopped, I felt him at my shoes, playing with the laces. I was going to leave them on for sleeping, anyway, to avoid bug bites, and figured I could tie them again come morning. I fell fast asleep, Otto at my feet.

When I woke up, I did my best to fill our bellies with manioc leaves. My feet felt clumsy, and when I looked down I saw that my shoes were already tied. Otto had not only played with untying my laces, he'd also tried to retie them by doing the same simple cross knot over and over. It looked more like a carpet tassel than a shoelace.

Once I'd retied my shoes, I regained my bearings from the sun and we continued toward Kinshasa. I was thirsty, my tongue a mixture of dry and moist patches, like a sun-baked pond bed, but I didn't want to hazard drinking the wild stream water unless it was totally necessary.

Within a few hours the jungle began to clear, and finally thinned out entirely to another field. It, too, was planted with manioc, and seemed recently tended. Whoever worked this land was probably still alive.

A farmer was not likely to be trouble, I decided, so I figured I would try to track him or her down and find out what I could about the war's progress. I put my poncho on over Otto, hoping whoever I came across would assume I was wearing a pack. He loved being blinded and hot under the plastic, and gave contented sighs.

I walked through the manioc, brilliant green parrots scattering before me. When I neared the far side of the field, an ancient woman emerged from a thatched hut to watch me. She disappeared inside and came back out with a young boy, no more than nine or ten. He rubbed his eyes sleepily. She hunched behind him, scowling, holding him forward with her arms. He was only a child, but he was her protection.

As I approached, the woman rubbed her hands on her dirty dress and then made shooing motions at me. She whispered in the boy's ear, and he began making shooing motions, too.

"I need your help," I called in Lingala, holding up my open hands to show I meant no harm, the same way the bonobos did. "Please."

Otto began to murp on my back, and I prayed he would be quiet.

As I continued to walk toward them, the woman got more and more agitated. "I don't need anything from you," I said. "Just information."

"What do you need to know?" the boy called back. I stepped closer. "You have to stop there," he said shrilly. "You have to."

I held still.

"What do you need?" he asked.

"What has happened?" I asked.

He conferred with the old woman. "What do you mean?"

"I've been away for a month. What has happened here?"

"They killed my parents and my sister," he said. The woman shushed him furiously. "She thinks you're a witch," the boy added.

"I'm not," I said quickly. In the villages, anyone unusual could be thought a witch. And witches didn't survive very long.

"They're taking children," the boy said, "so that means they have witches with them."

"They?"

"The combatants."

"Is the capital safe?"

The boy conferred with the woman. "We don't know."

"Can I stay here for a day?" I asked.

She shook her head savagely.

"Which way is the capital?" I asked.

She pointed in a direction, the same one I'd been heading. At least that was confirmed.

"You can take as much manioc as you can carry," the boy called as the woman pulled their grass curtain closed.

At first I wondered why they would give away their food and livelihood, but then I realized: There weren't enough people left to eat it.

I emptied my bottle and refilled it from their well. Otto and I gulped down cold, clean water straight from the pump, and then we headed back across the field. The trail joined an empty road, and I nearly shouted for joy. It was the N-1 capital road, the same one where, many miles farther along and many weeks ago, I'd first found Otto.

I'd be able to reach Kinshasa much more quickly over the road, but it was also more dangerous. Many kinds of horrible things could happen to me there if I ran into the wrong men.

Otto was getting heavy on my back, and wherever his weight rested my muscles were becoming tight cords. I tugged him down to the ground and we walked hand in hand for a ways. Otto's short strides meant moving slower, but my back needed the break. Nervous that someone might come down the road, I kept scanning the horizon ahead and behind. Otto copied my movements.

The road's dirt and pebbles weren't easy on Otto's feet, and after a while he stopped and refused to go any farther, giving me his *Why are you putting us through this?* look. The going wasn't easy on my feet, either, which had blistered in my ever-moist sneakers, but I picked up Otto and placed him on my back, which ached in familiar protest.

We'd gone a few more paces when I saw a low cloud of dust at the horizon. I scurried into the jungle growth, hiding a few feet back and out of view behind a briar. The dirt was kicked up by a truck, moving with extreme slowness. When it neared, I saw that the back was clogged with shirtless men with guns and machetes. The reason the truck was going so slowly was because an equal number of guys were behind it, pushing. It must have been out of gas or broken, but they weren't going to give it up.

The men in the cab — four of them, pressed shoulder to bare shoulder — were all wearing evening gowns. One had on a bright green wig. I'd heard that soldiers searched out fancy clothing from the women they'd killed, thinking it made them fearsome and magical. It would have been funny if the men hadn't had such severe, heartless expressions. I sighed in relief when they rolled past us. If they had seen me hide away and come after us, or if Otto had cried out . . . but that hadn't happened. I didn't have any fear to waste on hypotheticals. Still, the fact that roving gangs were free to travel on the main thoroughfare didn't bode well for the condition of the capital.

Otto and I returned to the road, and I took advantage of our moment of rest to lower him to the ground. We made a sharp turn, and when I rounded the corner I saw, not far away, a lone man wearing a military uniform. He was long and lean, sitting against a tree with a club at his side. When he saw me he sprang to his feet and approached. I froze. I could disappear into the jungle, but what if he followed? I'd rather confront him somewhere there was a chance of someone compassionate coming along.

A side road forked off, and though I had no idea where it went, I tripped along it, pulling a protesting Otto up from the ground as I went. I risked a look behind me and saw the soldier following and closing distance. I sped up, breaking into a jog. Otto barked at the man over my shoulder, and I pressed my hand to the back of his head, willing him to stop. Spread across the road was a metal bar, which we skirted. There was a sign on the other side, a big piece of plywood with the letters *S-I-D-A* scrawled across in red paint, French for *AIDS.*

The word gave me pause, but nevertheless I hurried down the road, and when I looked back, I saw the soldier stopped at the other side of the *SIDA* sign, staring after me. AIDS was such a warranted fear here that the simple sign held him at bay. I knew you couldn't get HIV by walking into an area, but maybe he didn't. I had no idea what I *was* walking into, but I knew one thing for sure: It was preferable to falling into that soldier's hands on a lonely road.

Around a bend was an aging colonial house, with two peeling white stories and a much-repaired tin roof in every variation of sun-bleached red. Its many doors were wide open, and I could see shapes moving around inside. I stood nervously at the far side of the yard, wondering whether to approach. If that soldier wasn't willing to come near, did that automatically mean it was safe for me? Or did it mean the opposite?

My feet hurt, I was light-headed with stress and bad meals, and the idea of perhaps eating real food and sitting in a chair — or even sleeping in a bed! — sounded like bliss. I carefully draped my poncho over Otto on my back, then made a step forward.

A man stood at the front door, a weary expression on his face. He was old, and leaned heavily on one leg, probably the result of childhood polio. "There is AIDS here," he warned.

"I don't understand what you mean," I said. "You have AIDS?" *So what?* I thought.

He stared down at my dirty clothes, my skinniness, the squirming bundle at my back. "Do you want to come in?" he finally asked.

There was something about his face, the sad fatigue of a good-will whose reserves have been exhausted, that made me start to trust him. But I wasn't ready to go inside yet. "What's the story with the sign out front?" I asked, not budging.

The man smiled with a hint of pride. "It's what keeps us alive. No combatants will come near. AIDS is the only thing that scares them."

I'd heard whispering, but it cut out when I approached the door. Against the far wall were a dozen stricken-faced boys, from probably ages three to nine. Some had bloated stomachs, others were lying down without the strength or will to look back at me. As I stood staring at them, one coughed, a deep rattling sound. He covered his mouth, eyes wide, as if he'd done something he should feel guilty for.

"Hello," I said. No one answered back. They stared at me as I crossed the room.

The man led me to the back porch and offered me a ladleful of grass tea from a cast-iron pot. As we sat, Otto squirmed out from beneath the poncho and sat in my lap. The man took a long look at him, then went back to stirring his tea. "This is a school as well as an AIDS clinic, and those are my students," he said. "The combatants seek out boys to fill the ranks. They make them take turns beating one another to death, and the ones who are willing to kill their friends they take as soldiers. They were all once boys like these. I did not want the combatants to take mine, so before the fighting came to the school's door, I painted that sign in front."

"What about their families?" I asked. "Are they all orphans?"

He shook his head. "This is a boarding school, and the boys are from the capital. Not a single parent has made it here since the attack started."

"So the capital . . ."

"The combatants are streaming in from the east, thousands a day. They've looted everything. There are bodies in the street. At least, this is what the *radio trottoir* says." *Sidewalk radio* was the popular phrase for the word on the street.

"And the airport?" I asked, scared that even posing the question would make my fears true.

"The combatants were smart this time," the teacher said grimly. "They started there, bombed holes into the runways. No one can fly in. They want to have their government installed before the UN or whoever else cares to help can get here."

"And they want to kill anyone who supported the president?"

"Yes. They thought he was a traitor to Congo and an ally of the West. That he's a puppet to American mining companies."

Companies like the ones my dad had worked for. "I assume that by loyalists, they mean Tutsis?"

He nodded grimly. "Anyone who looks like a Tutsi or a foreigner. I hear they're being very effective at searching them out."

"I look like both of those," I said, dazed.

"Where are you coming here from?" the teacher asked, apparently weary of the topic of the war.

I took a deep sip of tea to be polite, even though my stomach groaned at the taste of liquid leaf. I was desperate for bread, meat, anything that wasn't green. To distract myself from my queasiness, I dived into my story.

As I did, Otto got down from my lap and began to wander. He walked through the yard, slipping on a loose piece of bark, picking himself up and stomping on the treacherous thing, then sniffing the ring of ashy stones where the man's teakettle had heated. When he returned to the porch, he froze. Two of the boys had come outside to check Otto out. He hid between my legs, but resisted when I tried to pull him onto my lap; he was too curious to fully hide away. When the boys shyly neared, Otto stepped toward them, then sat down and watched them. The boys sat down and watched him. Otto stood up. The boys stood up. So it continued, a slow courtship on both parts, until within a few minutes, Otto was grooming them, the boys giggling as he ran his fingers over their scalps.

The man interrupted me while I was sharing my story. "I have to tell you how nice that sound is. I haven't heard laughter in weeks. Sorry, continue."

"What do you think I should do?" I asked. The question brought with it an unexpected feeling of release. It was a relief not to have to make my next decision alone. "Do you have a phone or a computer?"

The teacher shook his head. "I've got a cell phone upstairs, but the rebels have taken out the networks." He paused, scratching his chin. "Look. You can stay here as long as you like. But I don't think it's wise. As you see, we have little to eat, and I don't know how long the AIDS sign will keep the combatants away."

I told him where the abandoned manioc field was, and he thanked me. "I don't dare leave the boys alone to go there myself, but maybe I will send two of the older ones tomorrow. To answer your question — the combatants are not just trying to cause trouble, they are trying to set up a new government. The worst region is no longer far away in the east. It's right here near the capital. You should leave. Alone you have a chance of sneaking out of this area, and you should while you can. I think you should also leave the ape behind."

I rubbed my head. "That's not an option. Where do you think I should go?"

"The roads are so terrible that, unless they get fuel for airplanes, the combatants can't easily get around the country. Which means the revolution is happening only in the towns and cities that they happen to hit. The old government wasn't in touch with the rural areas, anyway — there, life is probably going on as though the attack never happened. Some of them probably think we're still Belgian. Some of them probably don't even know the Belgians ever *came*. Any undeveloped region would be safer than here in the middle of the revolution."

Revolution. A momentous new word for all of this.

Otto shrieked when one of the boys roughhoused him, then mounted a counterattack by standing on his hands and falling into his new playmate. They tumbled to the ground, the boy laughing and Otto making his pleased raspy sound as he got a gloppy handful of mud and smooshed it into the kid's thigh.

I watched, but my mind was far away. Four hundred miles away, to be exact.

"I think I know where I have to go," I told the man. "I know someone who's on an isolated island in the middle of the Congo River. About as far from roads and cities as you can get."

"That sounds perfect," the man said. "Who is this person?"

"My mother."

I stayed there four days, leaving the man to care for the boys each morning while Otto and I brought the two eldest to go harvest manioc from the abandoned fields, carrying it back in groaning bamboo-and-liana crates the man kept behind the clinic-school. By the time those four days were over, we'd built them up a good store of food. The man's fire pit was a blessing, and I ate manioc with a gusto I would never have thought I could muster. It didn't hurt that we roasted it with whole bulbs of fragrant wild garlic pulled from the yard. The combination of manioc and garlic and well water and a forest antelope caught in the man's snares made for the first balanced meals I'd had in weeks. By the second or third day, my insides were running normally, and I no longer had that bloated feeling from my greens-only diet. Otto ate a piece of the duiker, which surprised me since I'd always thought of bonobos as vegetarians. But I guess the circumstances were extraordinary for all of us. He enjoyed sleeping in a bed with me, and his lingering cough finally cleared up.

During a quiet moment it struck me that Congo was an easier country to survive in than most during a time of war. In peacetime the teacher couldn't afford to buy food at the markets, which meant he had a field, and snares for wild game, and a well for water since the government had never run pipes out here. I tried to imagine getting by if the same thing happened in Miami and couldn't. When a country was as primed for civil war as Congo was, when it came apart, the pieces weren't as heavy.

It was wonderful to linger in bed in the morning, listening to the sounds of Otto playing with the boys downstairs. I thought a lot about Songololo, and debated whether it would be a good idea to fetch the other bonobos and bring them here. Though I made sure during the manioc gathering never to go near the spot where I'd left them, because I wanted to keep their location a secret, I often scanned the jungle line for them. Only once was I successful, when I saw a distant Mushie and Ikwa lounging and grooming in the clearing of the burned-out house. I missed them so much at that moment and was struck through with concern for their well-being.

But I thought better of bringing them to the plantation house; they had a much better chance of staying alive in the abandoned village, away from people. It seemed unlikely the schoolteacher and his boys would turn to eating bonobos — they treated Otto reverentially, the old man once even calling him "our national heritage" — but if things got worse and they began to starve, everything could change. And there were those duiker snares. They were designed to capture antelopes, but I'd seen bonobos at the sanctuary with hands or feet missing from snares like those.

On the morning of the fourth day, I told the schoolteacher that I was leaving. He sighed, but didn't try to convince me to stay, and helped me pack my duffel with bottles of well water and garlic-greasy hunks of roasted manioc wrapped in their own leaves. My bag was heavier now than it had ever been, so I hesitated on the front step, debating whether to ditch anything. I could get rid of some of the water, but I was dreading going back to drinking from the river — I'd been fortunate that Otto and I hadn't gotten sick so far, and I didn't want to press my luck. The schoolteacher saw me wavering at the front porch and came over. "Come around here. I have something to show you."

He led me around the corner to the side of the plantation house and drew back a tarp. Against the wall rested a bike. No, not just a bike — it had a motor attached. Granted, a motor that looked the right size to run a home aquarium, but a power source nonetheless. "This is how I used to get to the school," the man said. "It's not like I'll be able to leave without the boys, so I want you and Otto to have it."

"Really?" I asked. "Are you sure you won't need it?"

He shook his head. "It's the least I can do — that manioc you pointed us to will keep us going for a while." He jimmied the bike so the plastic tank sloshed. "There's probably a third of a tank of gas in there. It won't get you all that far, but it should be enough for you to get to the river. Then maybe you can find a fisherman to take you upstream in a pirogue. You could offer the bike as payment. It might be enough."

"I don't know what to say," I said. "I don't know how to thank you."

"Let them know about us," he said. "If you find help, come here and get these boys out. Or get us antiretrovirals. Please."

I nodded solemnly. "I promise."

"I've got a wooden crate upstairs," the man said. "I could lash it to the back, and you could transport Otto inside."

"No!" I said quickly. "No, thank you. He'll ride on me."

The man looked bemused. "People first, Sophie. People first. Then you can help Otto."

I thanked the man, strapped my duffel on my back, and mounted the bike. Otto stood on my head, slapped his hands on my forehead to keep his balance, and murped at the boys, who had lined up in front to wave good-bye to their new friend. One of the younger kids ran forward, crying, and stroked Otto's foot. Once he was out of the way I kick-started the bike and nearly jumped off at the sound. The motor was ragged and loud — I was riding something the sound and speed of a lawn mower.

We puttered across the lawn, the boys screaming their good-byes. Otto got spooked at all the noise and wrapped himself around my skull. I peeled his long toes off my eyes so I could see where we were going, and we noisily putted off, to the *SIDA* sign and into the world beyond.

SEVENTEEN

The way I figured it, getting out of the Kinshasa area would be my toughest challenge. I hoped that if I kept to the narrow trail-roads running between villages, I could avoid any soldiers until I reached the river. The motorbike helped me, because I could get to the river in half a day. It also hurt me, as it restricted where I could safely travel because the noise broadcast my location.

When I was near the spot where I'd seen the lone soldier, I cut off the motor, sat Otto down on the seat, and walked the bike. The day was hot and dry, and I felt a headache forming behind my eyes. I didn't see anyone along the road, though the horizon was wavering, which made it hard to distinguish anything. "You ready, Otto?" I said as I lifted him up and got back on the bike. Otto climbed onto my front, and I started the motor. He barely startled — he was becoming such a hardy little bonobo. The whir and roar beneath us was the only sound in my ears — riding the bike was the only time I couldn't hear the constant insects and birds of Congo.

I was feeling something more than fear as I rode: It was fear with a purpose, fear devoted entirely to the task of being alert. It was fear that, in the context of survival, was doing what fear was meant to do; all my edges were left sharp. When I finally got off the bike in the late afternoon, the trembling in my legs and arms from the vibration was the only evidence that any time at all had passed since I left the plantation house. I had no memory of what I'd ridden by, except the concentration hangover.

I came back to being Sophie when the trail joined up with an abandoned railway and began to parallel the airport road. I could see people not thirty feet off through the foliage. A lot of people. I dismounted to see a sluggish train of women and children and the occasional man, slogging through the mud in their best clothes. Everyone was carrying something: Some women had massive nylon-wrapped packages on top of their heads, and some children had large plastic bottles — the thick dented type you usually see containing gas or chemicals — dangling from their hands. They were all heading toward the airport. The runway had been bombed out, so what were they hoping for? But the answer was another question, one I shared: What better option did they have to hang their hopes on?

They must have decided to dress up in hopes of increasing their chances of getting on a plane. One mother was in a gorgeous red-and-green *pagne* wrap, her sons drowning in suits whose shoulder pads hung around their elbows. I watched the elegant and bedraggled refugees drift along and wondered whether to join them.

Maybe there *was* some hope of salvation at the airport, some way out that all these people knew about. I could join the group, find out what was going on. But what would I do with Otto? To me he was a treasured traveling companion; to them he was food. As we sat there, eating a snack of cold greasy manioc followed by the slimy leaf in which it had been wrapped, I debated what to do. I could put Otto under my poncho like before and hope no one noticed, but if they did . . . if the mob wanted to take him from me — to eat, to sell — then they could. Not to mention the motorbike. It didn't have much fuel left, but that wouldn't stop them from taking it if they decided to. I had more to lose than the people in the crowd. I wasn't the same as them, not yet.

I decided I'd wait until there was a gap in the flow of refugees, then dart across with Otto. A dozen people stopped in their tracks and stared at the half-white girl emerging from the wilderness, wearing a bulky poncho in the afternoon sun and pushing a motorbike.

I smiled meekly and pointed to the far side of the road, trying not to make eye contact with anyone. Otto shifted on my back as I lugged the bike over furrows and puddles. The walkers didn't do anything to make my passage easier as I neared. As I got halfway across, a teenage boy stepped in front of my path. "Bonjour, *la blanche*, where are you going?"

I didn't answer, only continued moving forward.

"Did you hear me, *la blanche*? I asked where you were going."

I had about twenty feet to go. Nineteen. Eighteen.

"The airport is not that way," another voice said. Now there was a crowd around me. I didn't dare look up to find out how many, but I could feel them surrounding me, on every side but forward. They weren't blocking that yet.

"If you are headed for the river, a bike won't help you," said another man. "You should give that to me!"

Now people were in front. But I couldn't let them stop me. I bumped into shoulders, said "excuse me" as I tried to push through. These were refugees, not fighters, and most kept a polite distance, but nevertheless hands were on my neck, and then a tug on my poncho became a yank and I fell on my back, right on top of Otto. I heard him cry out and felt him scramble against the plastic and squirm his way out from under me. The bike was ripped from my hands and passed into the crowd, instantly gone, and then the hands were back and voices were shrieking and the hands were on Otto. I tried to get up and slipped, and saw him pulled away from me. His fingers were in mine and then they were not, as simple as that. His eyes filled with terror, and then the crowd came between us and he disappeared.

I lunged in the direction Otto had gone and unexpectedly I had his three-fingered hand back in mine, and held on tight to his wrist as I felt him do his best to grip on to mine. The opposing force pulled harder, and on the other side I saw the teenage boy who had called me *la blanche*. Finally I found words. "Why are you trying to take him?" But the boy didn't answer. He was a creature who had nothing, trying to get something.

Then a woman was between us, scolding the boy in Lingala. Under the onslaught of her fierce, wagging finger he released Otto, who pressed himself against me, shrieking in terror. The woman and her three small daughters circled us protectively. They linked their arms to shield me, even the littlest girl. A group of boys faced us, but as more women joined my side, the males faded into the crowd. My attackers might have been gone, but the horde of onlookers remained. There was no ground to see; there were only people in every direction. I might be safe inside this line of women, but there was no escape. I held Otto tight against me.

The mother tried to get people to move along by shouting and shooing, but they held tight. Finally, she tugged our little circle over to the edge of the road. The same side I'd started from — I'd gotten nowhere. The smallest daughter found the process of moving as a group hilarious, giggled, and kept her dancing eyes trained on Otto.

Now that we were out of the center, most of the women started moving again. The mother released her daughters' arms and examined me head to toe.

"Are you okay? Did anyone hurt you?"

"I'm okay."

"You are not Congolese."

"No, *mama* — I am Congolese," I said.

"You can get out," the mother continued resolutely, pointing to the skin on my arm. "Look at you! The UN is here. They can get you out!" She had plump powerful arms and a vivid yellow dress. She was a third of the way to being my mom, and my heart ached. *Tell me what to do,* I prayed.

"Where is the UN?" I asked.

"Not at the airport. You do not want to go with the crowd if you can help it. The blue helmets have abandoned the capital, but they made a base near here to help the *mundeles.* They have cut a square of trees out for their blue helicopters to land and take them away. The helicopter landed this morning and is here — we heard it come in. They will not allow us near, but you they will. I can show you! Do you want to go there?"

I nodded, eyes wet.

The woman pointed to three men in the crowd. "Take this girl to the UN guard." They stared back sheepishly, reluctant but cowed by the woman's forceful manner.

"Please," I asked her, "couldn't you take me?"

The woman looked at her three daughters, indecisive. The youngest, no more than eight, said, "What's your monkey's name?"

"Otto. He's very scared right now, but if he weren't, I know he would love to meet you." Otto was hugging my front, pressing into me with everything he had, as if hoping to disappear into my rib cage. The girl extended a hand and gave Otto's foot a pat. Emboldened, another daughter patted Otto's other foot.

"Fine," their mother said. "We'll go with you."

The men, relieved, started back on their march to the airport.

"Stop! Didn't you hear me, *papas?*" the woman asked. "We need you to take us to the UN station." That maternal fire. I recognized my mother in her again, and a touch of the Pink Ladies, and it about made me burst with happy and sad.

The men unenthusiastically escorted us against the gaping crowd. Just as she'd said, there was a turnout a little ways along.

The mother and her daughters stopped before I reached the blue-helmeted guard at the end of the short path. "They don't want to see us," she said. "We have already tried. But go ahead. The blue helmets will take care of you."

"Thank you so much," I said. "Really."

"Ask them to remember us. My family and many others will be living at the airport." I thought of the Kinshasa airport — dark unlit hallways, one steel hangar — and shuddered. She gave me her name and, one by one, so did each of her daughters. "Good luck," she said.

I didn't know yet what I hoped for from the UN. But I knew they would at least give me advice and something to eat and drink. This woman and her children had a long way to go, with nothing to sustain them. "Here," I said. "I want you and your children to have this." I handed her the limp duffel. Inside there was still manioc and clean water.

The mother didn't protest. She took the bag and was on her way, the youngest daughter staring at Otto over her shoulder until the crowd poured in between us.

Once they'd left, Otto and I headed down the path to the UN.

We were stopped at the chain-link fence. The guard lowered his gun to block me and Otto as I neared. The sharp sight on the muzzle pressed into my arm.

"*Bonjour, monsieur,*" I said. "My name is Sophie Biyoya-Ciardulli. I was supposed to be rescued."

"You . . . were . . . supposed . . . ?" the man stammered, obviously unused to French. He looked Indian. I repeated myself in English. The man let out a long, frustrated sigh. "Good lord!" he said. "The evacuation was weeks ago."

In this case, a lie was far more believable than the truth. "I was trapped. I couldn't get free, and the van left without me. It took me this long to get back here."

"I have very simple orders," the man said. "And I'll tell them to you like I've told everyone else. Until the Refugee Commission is here, I'm afraid no one can help you. There is one helicopter, and four hundred things that have to be done with it. There is no space for you."

"What am I supposed to do?" I asked. I hadn't expected I would be turned away, not after what the mother had said. My thoughts went to my supplies, that little bit of food and water, so important to keeping me alive, that I'd just given away. Those little girls needed them, but I, I —

"Join them, go to the airport, try there," the guard said, waving me away.

"I'm an American citizen, does that matter?"

"No," he said flatly. "Not anymore."

I couldn't believe what he was saying. I was on my own. Really on my own. I didn't really believe it until now. *Of course, if things get very bad, someone will swoop in to help me.* Not true.

"I can't. . . . There's no way out at the airport. So there's no way out at all," I said. I sat down in front of the man. Otto got off my back and stood at my side. He was holding my hand but staring at the man, chirping worriedly, wondering what was happening that was making me react like this.

"Move along!" the man barked, peering at Otto nervously.

"I'm sorry," I said, wiping my eyes. I thought I could get up then and walk away, but my legs wouldn't do it. I tried again. Otto climbed into my lap and started punching my chest; I didn't know why, and he probably didn't, either. I cried out.

Seeing me and seeing Otto, another soldier came over and said something to the first that I couldn't hear. The Indian guard replied, "But look at her — she's black."

The second guard rolled back some of the chain link and waved me through. "Why don't we see if we can work something out?" he asked me, resting a hand on my shoulder, then rapidly pulling it away when Otto bared his teeth at him.

I stood up. Otto leaned into my calf, his finger in his mouth. "Can he come with me?" I asked.

"He's a bonobo, right?" the second guard said.

The men looked at each other. "Another bonobo?" the Indian one said. He shrugged in resignation. "Why not, sure."

I wanted to ask him what he meant, but then the second guard shouted for an officer and we were moving. I pulled Otto up and into my arms. We skirted around the helicopter and up to two large white makeshift offices the size and shape of shipping containers. Gas-powered generators thrummed at the end of each, and air conditioners hung out of the windows. On every face was emblazoned MONUC. The man opened a door and led me up two steps and inside.

Outside had been warmth and chaos and color, but here was the crisp sharpness of a newly split block of ice. The air-conditioning was strong enough that papers on the desk flapped and curled. Otto and I sat in a chair while the man behind the desk checked something in a binder. The only decoration on the pure white walls was a big map of Central Africa. Two flags were on the desk, the blue UN flag and another country's flag that I didn't recognize, maybe where the guy was from. He looked South American.

A minute ticked by. I was grateful to be away from the crowd, but I wondered what I would say to the man when he looked up. The UN had already told me once they couldn't bring Otto out of the country. I guess I was hoping that in the new upheaval they'd break a rule for me. And if not . . . it struck me that I'd leave. Without Otto. Now that the attack had happened, what I wanted most was another chance for someone to tell me I *had* to leave Otto behind, for a reasonable adult to make the decision for me and lead

Otto away and save my life. It was both the worst and best thing that could happen.

Finally the man looked up. "So, you're the American who skipped out on the airlift."

It took me a moment to find my voice. "Yes. My name is Sophie Biyoya-Ciardulli. Ciardulli is my dad's name. The American. I'm hoping — I guess I'm hoping you can get us out of here. He lives in Miami. My dad."

"Right. My name's Hector Carrizo. And I'd love to go to Miami, too. But I don't know if you've noticed, but the *mayi-mayi* are in charge now."

"I thought it was the *kata-kata*."

"Not familiar with that one. But take your pick, sure, them, too. Or the LRA. Whoever. Everyone wants to come visit the bar once the music's playing, you know what I mean? Let me tell you what we can and can't do for you. For starters: Do you have any paperwork, passport, anything?"

I shook my head.

Hector smiled. "How about the monkey?" He looked at Otto. "You have any documents, sir?"

"Him neither."

"It's okay, you speak English like an American, and that's enough proof to convince me. In any case, this little white box we're in is basically what passes for civilization in Congo these days. The capital is down and out for the count, except the Belgian and French embassies, and who knows how long they'll last. The only UN troops here are the same forty thousand guns that have always kept the peace in Congo. No reinforcements have gotten in, because they can't. We're outnumbered a few thousand to one. We're alive only because they have rifles and machetes and we have RPGs."

I didn't know what an RPG was, and didn't have space to ask. I sensed Hector was telling me more than I needed to know, but that these were things he wanted to get off his chest and couldn't admit to his men.

"Look," he continued, "you're clearly a bright girl. When I say that help can't get in, it's partly logistics — the runway was bombed out. But that doesn't mean the West couldn't send in helicopters or ships up the river if they wanted. If they wanted to put a stop to this, they could. But the imperative isn't there. Maybe the powers that be approve of the regime change. Maybe they enabled it. Maybe the president was starting to restrict the flow of minerals out of Congo, and for the love of all things Nintendo they're hoping the rebels will install someone who will want foreign aid and all the trade concessions that come with it. Congo can become a dependent vessel all over again, and people can get cheap minerals and cheap electronics. But what do I know? I'm a peon on the ground. Like you. Except I've got a gun. Nice monkey, that's a good little monkey you've got. What's your name again?"

"Sophie Biyoya-Ciardulli."

"I don't suppose you have a passport or anything on you."

"No," I repeated. "But I was registered at the American embassy. Do you have a list?"

"As I said, I'm going to take you no matter what, but it's easier if I have a number." He rummaged through a stack of curling papers on a clipboard, then switched clipboards and searched another. "Birth date?"

I told him.

"Sophie Biyoya-Ciardulli," he said, tapping his lips as he scrutinized the paper. "Sophie Biyoya-Ciardulli . . . oh yes! Looks like we have a message for you. From your mother."

The air conditioner whirred and clicked as my brain stuttered. "I'm sorry, what? Where is she? Is she okay?"

"She is . . . I'm sure she's . . . I've got no clue, tell you the truth. Let me find the message. That should settle things." The clipboard opened, and he rummaged through the compartment beneath until he found a note typewritten in blue ink on pale blue paper. He took his time reading it, and I resisted the urge to rip it from him as I scrutinized his face for a clue as to what was inside. "It looks like this came in during the week after the assassination. A month ago. The embassy put it in our hands when they evacuated." He handed the slip over.

> My dearest Sophie,
> We were a day out and heading toward the release site when we heard the news. I don't even know that it's news. Maybe it's wrong. I hope it's wrong. It's not safe enough for us to travel on the river until the unrest has died down, so our only choice is to continue to the release site. I'll be able to leave word with the villagers in Ikwa every few days, and if anyone heads downstream you better believe he'll be carrying a message for you, but otherwise I don't know how I'm going to be able to get in touch. I don't want you to worry about me. But know that if I could come right back to you, right now, I would.
> I'm comforted that everyone I speak to is saying that as usual the capital is the safest place to be. Patrice and the mamas will take good care of you. Make sure you do whatever they tell you. And your father will be checking in with you constantly, I'm sure.
> I love you more than I can ever say. Be safe, and I know this will be over soon and I'll be back and giving you the biggest hug you've ever gotten. Don't worry about me, okay? I'll be here, and will come back as soon as it's safe.
> All the love in the world,
> Your Mother

Hector studied my face as I read. "That was a few weeks ago. But I'm sure she's still fine," he said.

I nodded.

"She'll be glad to know that you're with the United Nations now and we're getting you out of here. As soon as we establish contact with Mbandaka, we'll get word to her somehow that you're safe and sound. That's a pledge."

"Thank you," I said numbly. "Does that mean you don't have any contact with Mbandaka right now? I thought it was supposed to be safer farther north."

He shook his head, then clapped his hands and shrugged, eager to move on to a new topic. "How about you tell me a story. Like what's the deal with the monkey?"

"He's . . . I'm sorry, can you give me a minute?" I put my head in my hands. I couldn't talk about Otto in my state, not when so much depended on what I said. If my mom was still alive, she would be at the release site . . . I thought her remoteness would keep her safe, but she was near Mbandaka. It was among Congo's most dangerous cities even in times of peace, and the UN had no contact whatsoever with the entire city of almost a million people. That radio silence was full of imagined monsters, like a broad empty space on a map.

Otto had a good ear for when he was being talked about. His arms around my neck, he turned his head to take in the man. I wiped my eyes. "Sorry. I needed a moment. Otto's a bonobo. I don't know if you've heard of them. They're relatives of the chimpanzees. And endangered." I was hoping that word would work some magic. Maybe there was a UN mandate that calling an animal endangered worked like clicking ruby slippers, and meant they'd have to drop everything and whisk us to safety.

"He's lucky he hasn't been eaten, is what he is," Hector said, eyeing Otto.

Ah. No ruby slippers. "Can you do anything to help him?"

He laughed. "Help a monkey? No. I've got my men doing tours to stop as many *people* as we can from being shot. You could say we're all out of monkey chow. I don't have the capacity to help another one."

"Another one?"

He looked at me quizzically. "I figured you were here because someone told you about the others. A starving man showed up a few days ago with two monkeys in a cage on his bike."

"A guy on a bike brought you two bonobos?"

Hector squinted at Otto. "I guess he did. Must have figured we'd be the only ones who could buy them. They looked like yours. Just not quite as healthy. Scraggly. Scabby." He screwed up his lips, as though some thought struck him, something he'd forgotten about.

"Where are they now? The bonobos?"

He flicked his pen against the desktop, leaving little blue pockmarks in the aluminum. I could read the thoughts running across his eyes, like a news ticker: *I've been clumsy. Young woman in my custody about to become a problem.*

"They're monkeys," he said levelly. "Animals."

"What are you trying to say?" I said, heart quavering.

"We took them from the trafficker. But we don't have the resources to take care of people, much less animals. We let them free out back."

"You let them go, right here near the airport, in the middle of all these crowds of people?"

Hector sighed, and I watched his estimation of me plummet. "Would you have rather I left them with the nice bushmeat trader?"

I'd made a mistake. Otto and I needed to have this man's goodwill, whatever he'd done. "I get it," I said. "What else could you do?" And I did get what he'd done. I just didn't feel it.

He nodded and shrugged. "What else could I do?"

"So," I said, shaking my head, "what do you think I should do?"

"Here's the plan: I've got the chopper doing a run to Brazzaville every evening to get supplies. You could go with us tonight. The war hasn't spilled over to that country, at least not yet. We can set you up with one of the embassies, and you can get a flight onward from there. You mentioned family somewhere? Besides your mother?"

"My dad's in Miami."

He nodded. "Good. Right, Miami. *Hace calor.* It's all settled, then." He stood and adjusted his gun belt over his gut. "Are you going to be okay sitting tight for a few hours until we leave?"

I nodded. Hector walked to the door. "There's rations in the bottom drawer of the cabinet, and the jug of water on my desk is iodine-treated. Those plastic glasses are clean. Ish. Help yourself." He paused, his hand on the handle. "Look. To answer your earlier question. We're in the richest country in the world as far as minerals. Some very fancy metals that go into electronics can be found only here. What's lying unused in the Congo soil is worth more than the combined yearly GDP of Europe and America. So: How did a bunch of impoverished scraggly Rwandan mercenaries overthrow the standing government of the Democratic Republic of Congo? With lots of help from rich friends. Rwanda is the biggest exporter of coltan, diamonds, and gold. Rwanda has none of these, but it's next door to Congo. Follow?"

"It's not about Tutsis. It's about access to the mines. These rebels have investors that want access to minerals."

"Right. The rebels enslave the people and get free miners. In turn, they use the billions of dollars they make to buy more arms and terrorize more people."

I sighed. "So basically you're saying that this war isn't going to be over anytime soon."

Hector shook his head. "No. It's not. You're lucky you're here with us." He opened the door, and I was hit by a moving wall of sun-hot air. "I'm sure those two monkeys we let out back are fine. Like I'm sure yours will be fine. There's lots of nice trees around here."

His tone turned my stomach. "I was hoping Otto could come with me."

"Absolutely not. That's against every protocol. Besides, the chopper will be full."

"Full? He'll stay on my lap. He won't take up any more space," I pleaded. "He's endangered, I can't leave him here."

"All the more reason. Transporting endangered animals across country lines is illegal."

"During a *war*? Please, I'll do anything —"

"There are millions of *people* suffering. Do yourself a favor and worry about them instead. He'll be fine. Lonely for a bit, and then he'll be happy as a clam. Make sure he doesn't touch anything. I'll be back for you in a bit." Hector left and slammed the door. The white bubble shuddered.

Otto got up and slapped the door handle curiously. He stood in the middle of the floor, swaying on his feet, and stared up at me. He'd met so many new people, seen so many new things. He must have been so overwhelmed. I opened my arms, and as he scrambled into them I wished we could stay in this clean white box for days, doing nothing but leaning against each other and not worrying about food and water and disease and machetes.

But we couldn't, because in a few hours Hector would come back and separate us. He'd throw Otto into the jungle. Into this narrow triangle of greenery between a road and a river, surrounded by starving people.

I imagined those two young bonobos tossed out back. I'd once have predicted that they'd scurry away as quickly as possible. But then I remembered Anastasia and Ikwa and Mushie, how they'd gotten used to me and, when their lives were upheaved on a scale bonobos were unprepared for, looked to a friendly human for a solution.

Those two little bonobos had spent many weeks with that trafficker. They didn't know how to forage on their own. So where were they right now? The answer seemed clear: right where they'd been dumped.

I cracked open the door to the UN pod and stood at the border of cool, soft-lit sanity and the vivid familiar chaos of Congo at war. A pair of guards was rushing toward the helicopter with crates in hand, and in the distance I heard commotion, heated complaints in Lingala. The guard at the fence was talking patiently to a group of old men who kept shouting back, pushing against his assault rifle, never pausing to take a breath or acknowledge the deadly weapon they were pressing against. This civilized space felt so small, a dry circle shrinking on the floor.

I took the pitcher of water in hand. If they were still here, those bonobos were probably thirsty, and I had a couple of hours to spare to care for them. Otto on my back, I stepped out of the door and let it click closed.

Making sure not to pass too near any of the peacekeepers, Otto and I headed to the far side. There was a pile of trash at the back, and then the clearing abruptly gave way to jungle. We went a ways in, until the ground went from clear to overgrown. Finding it difficult to pass, I set Otto on the ground and pivoted, peering into the greenery. Otto sat for a moment, then wandered away, investigating the trash pile and toying with a piece of old oily cardboard before I scolded him. Irked at me, he jumped up and down a couple of times, ran a lap around the open space, and finally, spent, plopped down beside me. I offered him some water and he took a few tired gulps, his hands keeping the pitcher's rim steady, and then he slumped, resting his back against mine. He remained that way for a few minutes, until something caught his attention.

He murped, then went to the edge of the overgrowth and stood there agitatedly, waiting for me to follow, glaring at me like I was an idiot who didn't know how to take a hint.

We didn't have to go far before we found them. There, in the lee where a fallen tree rested against a standing trunk, lay two little black furry forms. They were curled up, one inside the arms of the other, impossibly small. Their spooning bodies together barely amounted to the size of Otto. They were covered with sores. Flies hovered over the carcasses, landing in the creases of their closed eyes.

Otto started shrieking, scuttling to the two bodies and then scuttling back to me. I tried to shush him, tried to grab him whenever he neared me, but then he'd dart back to the bodies, shriek at them aggressively, kicking at them. I guess he was trying to protect me from those two pitiful dead creatures.

"Stop, Otto," I said, my voice full of tears. "Leave them alone."

The smaller bonobo had a wide sweet face and ribs stark, like pencils in a row. She still had a rope around her waist, frayed green nylon. I knew very well that her death was my fault, and that soon sorrow would swell in me like illness, but right then all I felt was fury at the UN peacekeepers, that they could cast her and her sister out back without even removing the rope around her waist. Her hips were covered with angry blisters, which oozed a fluid that had matted with the strands of old rope.

If I had taken a healthy young bonobo and shot her, I could repent and atone. But I'd become part of a system, as permanent and complex as war itself, made a dozen small choices that had led to these dead creatures with their wide faces and chapped lips.

Otto had calmed somewhat and was preoccupied with trying to bring the smaller bonobo back to life, lying next to her and murping, blowing on her mouth, trying to get her to react. Gently, gently, I picked at the knot in the frayed green nylon. I got one strand loose and then the other, and untied the loop. It fell open around her like a cuff, keeping the shape of a circle. When I finally got the rope untied, I tried to pull it away, but found I couldn't. The end was tight in her dead fist. In her last moments she'd curled over the rope like a sleeper around a pillow, clutching it to her cheek. It had been her treasure.

Otto finally lost interest in the smaller bonobo and climbed on my back, wrapping his arms around my neck and barking furiously at the dead sister. He sat in my lap and slapped my chest, trying to attract my attention. In my misery, I hated Otto for his jealousy. I threw him out of my lap and heard him hit the soil behind me. He murped in bafflement, then was back on me and barking angrily.

"Stop, Otto, please stop," I said. He got distracted by my tears, dabbed at the wet corners of my eyes. Once he'd seen that the dead bonobos weren't going to take all my attention away, he calmed.

I kissed Otto on the side of his head and pressed him close to me. Too close, and too hard, and I knew it. He yelped, and I softened my grip. I thought not only about these two bonobos but of the stream of homeless refugees, of my dead friends in the sanctuary, of the larger and yet-unknown tragedies elsewhere in the country, in the world. The creature in my arms wasn't an answer, but it did somehow make the question of how to keep going irrelevant. The weight of him, the prevention of his misery, was the answer that defied all logic.

As I re-entered the clearing, swiping at my eyes with the butts of my palms, one thing was very clear to me: I was *not* leaving Otto here.

I knocked on the mobile unit's window, relieved when no one answered, and went inside. Otto climbed down and clamped onto my leg as I opened the cabinet. There were foil-wrapped rations there, but what I was really hoping for was iodine; if Hector had treated the water, there had to be more, and — yes! — in the bottom drawer I found dark plastic bottles of it, with printed instructions on how much to use to purify water. I looked around for a container and found a plastic grocery-style bag lining the wastepaper basket. I pulled it out, dumped the contents under the desk, and filled it with rations and one of the bottles of iodine, tying the bag around my belt loop in case my only way out of the UN zone turned out to be running for it.

I wished there was a computer in the office I could use, but there wasn't. I didn't even see a phone — Hector must have carried his satellite phone with him. I scribbled a note on a pad on Hector's desk, saying I had to go and leaving my dad's e-mail address and phone number so he could let him know I was safe. Then I opened the door and stepped out into the sweaty, frantic afternoon. Figuring I could count on the base's chaos to ease my escape, I stole toward the fence, Otto holding my hand and toddling beside me. Hector was loading boxes into the back of the helicopter. Maybe he didn't notice me, or maybe he did and was quietly relieved to see one of his responsibilities disappear. I smiled at the guard at the fence and said I had to go pee in the bushes and would be right back. He seemed about to yell at me, then his attention returned to the latest batch of pleading refugees. We slipped past him. Otto and I were out.

EIGHTEEN

My plan from there was simple, if terrifying: Head up the Congo River to Mbandaka, and then skirt past the city to my mom's release site. Given the UN encampment was on the road to the airport, I knew I was beginning the journey north of Kinshasa, with half a mile of marsh separating me from the river. If I headed straight for the setting sun, I should be at the waterfront before dark. I retied the plastic bag to a back belt loop, rolled my sleeves up, took a steadying breath, and started.

Almost immediately the hard soil gave way to marsh, and I was glomping through muck up to my ankles. It was nothing new for my poor sneakers, which had spent the last weeks perpetually brown and moist. But as the sludge came up to my knees, I entered a new realm of worry. Carnivorous fish. Or snakes. Cobras love to swim, and I'd seen them often enough arrowing through water hyacinth, their wide flat heads spading up out of the water. I was going slowly enough now that I figured I'd startle one away before it would strike me, but as the sun rapidly descended I became less sure. Otto avoided the matter entirely by taking to the overhanging vegetation, but the reedy swamp trees weren't nearly sturdy enough to carry my weight. Not that I had the strength to do the kinds of acrobatic leaps Otto was pulling off, hitting a stiff reed and using the rebound to catapult to the next. He'd make it way ahead and wait at the top of a tree, lips anxiously pulling back over his teeth as he watched my slow progress.

Catching up to him kept getting harder, because the water was getting deeper. My pants were wet up to the thigh now, and I wondered how much higher the marsh line would get before I hit the riverbank. I knew the stretch of the Congo River north of Kinshasa was a big setting off point for fishermen returning to their villages from the capital's markets, and that a straight shot to the water should place me in their midst, assuming that fishermen were still trading in the capital.

The Congo is such a huge river that as I got closer it felt like I was approaching the seashore. Around me were seabirds, egrets, and herons, as well as species of murky fish, many of them probably unknown to science, the only evidence of them the occasional spiny fin rising from the surface.

I was still in water up to my waist when the sun went down. I steered myself toward a strip of solid land with the wide, flowing river beyond. Otto had already arrived there, standing on his hind legs and murping at me.

With moonlight my only guide, all I could see clearly was the occasional white curve of a wave. My goal became steering for the darkest space, where no river water could catch the light and I knew Otto was waiting.

As I neared, I heard a cry from the air and felt sudden warm arms around my head. A real bonobo mother would have been able to catch her son, but I rocked back and fell. We were both submerged, Otto flailing around. I pushed off the mucky bottom, hand sinking deep into silky mud, and came back to standing. Bonobos can't swim, and when I fished into the river and plucked Otto out, he was shaking and shrieking in fright. I was desperate to get us out of the water, but still paused for a moment, hugging him to me. Only once he had calmed down did we slog to the dark spot that meant land.

I crawled onto the sand on all fours, invisible creatures skittering away as I collapsed onto what felt like a pile of leaves. Otto, too, collapsed, panting on my chest as we lay flat and stared unseeingly at the stars. The plastic bag of supplies was a mound against my back, but I couldn't muster the energy to untie it. *Later. Now sleep.*

I woke up fitfully throughout the night, shivering before curling closer around Otto's wet body. The morning sun, when it came, was hot, and I woke up feeling baked. I smacked my dry lips and rolled Otto off me, groggily sitting up. I freed the container of water from the plastic bag and took a long swig. The bag was half-full of water itself, the wrapped packages of UN food bobbing. I drained it and retied it around my waist. As soon as I nudged Otto awake he was at the water's edge, lapping away. I wanted to give him some of the purified water, but he was drinking like the bonobos in the sanctuary did, and I figured his system was more tolerant than mine.

Almost as soon as our thirst was dealt with, I began to itch. I'd been sleeping in some type of vine, and wherever my body was exposed my skin had a sprinkling of pink rash. I couldn't resist the urge to scratch, and when I did the rash sprang back red. I lifted the hem of my pants and was relieved to see it hadn't spread up my leg. But there was a sort of black leaf stuck to my calf. I tried to pluck it away but failed.

It wasn't a leaf.

It was a leech.

I prodded at its middle, hoping it was done feeding and would drop off. But it didn't budge. The center came up, but the suckers on either end wouldn't lift. You're supposed to wait for leeches to fill with blood and drop away. But it was hard to sit and watch something suck my blood. Shuddering, I let the pant leg fall.

Where there was one, there were probably more. I resisted the urge to take off my shirt and pants and examine the rest of my body. It wouldn't do any good, because I'd have to wait for those to fill up and fall off, too. I ran my fingers over my face and neck, and found none there, and none in my ears. I examined Otto, and he made pleased sighs as I groomed his hair. He had two, one on each butt cheek. He tugged at them, but when a spot of blood appeared at the end of one he shrieked and ran up my torso. I tickled him for a few minutes, and after that he seemed to forget about the leeches, rolling around on the ground right over them. I wrenched his mouth open and checked his throat. That was the biggest danger, because as a throat leech filled with blood, it could cause suffocation. The only solution was to lance it and let the blood it had collected run down into your stomach. At least Otto didn't have any in there.

I withstood the urge to scratch my increasingly prickly rash, and instead dug some soft mud from the riverbed and wiped it on my ankles and wrists. It didn't take the itch away, but made it difficult enough to scratch that I hoped I'd be able to resist. Otto didn't seem to be scratching, so I assumed his thick black hair had protected his skin. He was much more suited to this journey than I was.

As I sat there, thoroughly miserable, waiting for the leeches to finish sucking my blood, I thought back to Anastasia and Mushie and Ikwa and Songololo, going about their daily lives as best they could. I smiled. Then I thought about the bonobos back at the sanctuary, the mothers with their wide-eyed, bald babies wrapped around their bellies, and hoped that by some miracle they, too, were okay.

Enough. If I didn't stay engaged with my present, I wouldn't be able to continue. The riverbank wasn't more than twenty yards away, and once I was there, I could somehow get a boat and make it to my own mother.

The vegetation closed in as I neared the river, making it impossible to avoid clomping through bushes and thickets. As Otto and I blundered through the bushes, we surprised a Nile Monitor, a sharp-fanged lizard that would have been fearsome had it been more than two feet long. Even so, I was happy to see it scramble away and plop into the water.

Even though the Congo is the second longest river in the world, its breadth is almost more impressive. I couldn't see the other side, just water and horizon. Normally it was thronged with boats — in a country with few paved roads, the Congo was the closest thing to an interstate. Though the stretch I was in seemed deserted, I could hear fishermen calling out to one another farther along downstream. These fishermen were headed in the wrong direction for me, but they gave me hope for more. I settled down at a clear spot by the water and waited for someone to arrive heading upstream.

After an hour or two I felt something fall loose and heavy on my sock. When I stood, an engorged leech fell into the mud and lazily wriggled away. I shook my clothing, but no more came out. Relieved, I settled in to continue waiting. Soon after, another boat appeared, this time a massive dugout canoe, a pirogue heading downstream filled with racks of drying fish, one of the rows still wet and glistening and breathing. A small bird must have had a nest behind one of the racks, as it sometimes zipped in or out. I let the boat pass around the corner.

The next pirogue was heading upstream, much more slowly, and I watched it go a ways before deciding whether to call out. If I reached out to the wrong person, it would be difficult to escape, and something about this man didn't feel right. His pirogue was empty, which made sense if he were returning from the markets in Kinshasa; but there weren't any containers or racks, either. It's like he wasn't a fisherman at all, and his shut-down expression didn't offer any explanations. I let him pass.

A few hours later another pirogue came by, this one with an old man inside, a tuft of grizzled white hair on his head like a dollop of cream. Punting against the river was tough work, but this guy was making good speed. I decided to call out to him once I heard singing. An old man singing to himself as he struggled against the river seemed like someone I might be able to trust. Maybe it was because the song he was singing was one I'd loved since childhood, *"Uélé Moliba Makasi"*:

Olélé olélé moliba makasi.
Luka luka . . .
Oya! Oya!
Yakara a.
Oya! Oya!
Konguidja a.
Oya! Oya.

Olélé olélé the current is very strong.
Row row . . .
Come! Come!
The brave one.
Come! Come!
The generous one.
Come! Come.

"*Monsieur!*"

He looked up, startled, and saw me. He stopped paddling and let his pirogue drift, taking up again only once the current dragged him backward. I watched him decide whether to respond to the bedraggled half-white girl wearing a nervous ape.

"*Mbote*," he finally said. "What are you doing on the river, daughter?"

"I am running," I said. "I need your help. Where are you going today?"

He shook his head. "I cannot take anyone anywhere. The current is strong, and I am just one. Is that your ape?"

The fisherman knew Otto was an ape, not a monkey. Encouraging. I wanted even more for him to be the one to bring us up the river. "Yes," I said. "Can you help us?"

He chewed his lip with gusto, like it was a strip of dried fish. It couldn't have hurt much, since he didn't have any front teeth. "I will make Mambutu by tomorrow. I will take you as far as that. For a cheap price."

"Price? What is the price?"

"I will do it for the ape."

My heart sank. "No. I will not give him to you."

"Do you have money, then?"

I debated whether to lie, than decided against it, since it might cost Otto's life once I was found out. "I don't have money on me, but I will pay you as soon as I find my mother. She will pay you in United States dollars."

"I need the money now," he said, though he was already steering the pirogue to shore. Not a great bargaining technique. It made me trust him, though, that he was that un-slick.

"Is Mambutu your destination?" I asked.

"No. In a month I'll have made it home, to Lulonga."

Terrific. That was as far as the release site and then some. "I need to go to a spot past Mbandaka. I will pay you fifty dollars," I said. It was a huge sum, half a year's work for this man.

"But you already told me you don't have fifty dollars."

"I will get it to you."

"What if you decide not to get it to me, once I have worked so hard to carry you up the river?"

I wished I had something to give him to show that I was good for it. Then I realized I did — Dad's silver necklace. It had been around my throat this whole time, but I hadn't thought of it much at all recently. I unclasped it and held it forward. "Would this help? You don't find workmanship like this around here."

I saw him appraise me, and had a pretty good guess what he was thinking. If I'd had purely black skin, he would have said no. But I was half-white. Any crazy thing was possible.

"Silver is not worth much. But I will accept this until you get me dollars. I'll need you to help with the pirogue," he said. "The current is strong. I had enough trouble when it was me alone. Now I will have two more."

"Okay!" I said. "And Otto is very light. He won't be any trouble."

He steered the pirogue to shore. I dropped the chain into his fingers; after pocketing it, the old man helped us in. Otto murped and clutched me as we stepped over the side into the rocking boat. I set him down on the floor, kneeled, and took hold of the long pole by my side. The wood was blackened and thumb-grooved by years of hands.

"You pull on the right," the man said. "I'll pull on the left."

I didn't see how I could pull with a pole, but nodded.

He pushed us away from shore, and once we were in open water I tried to punt. Otto gripped his hands on the lip, peering over the side. Then the water freaked him out enough that he climbed up on me, coming to rest on my back and making worried murps into my ear. It would make pushing my stick off the river bottom harder, but I knew it would be impossible for Otto to sit still on the rocking boat without holding on to me.

"What's your name?" I asked the man as I sloshed my pole in the water.

"Wello. And yours?"

"Sophie."

"That's pretty," he said. Not in a worrisome way, but more like we were talking about someone else. I smiled and glanced back at him. He was a funny-looking man, with broad puffy shoulders, thick wrists, and kind eyes beneath gray brows. Despite the fact that he'd suggested buying Otto and presumably eating him, I thought Wello was going to be all right.

I'd traveled the Congo this way once or twice in my life, but more for fun when visiting village friends. I'd always been a passenger. It was safe to say I was a terrible punter, and after a little while, Wello told me it would be better if I stopped. I let the pole drop from my stinging blistering fingers, pride taking a distant second to fatigue. I lay back in the pirogue, Otto scrambling on top of me, happy for some full body contact.

It was a magnificent boat, solid and heavy in the water, over twenty feet long and carved from the trunk of one giant tree. Against my back I could feel the lines and divots where the wood had been scoured away by Wello and his fellow villagers. When the sun went down I was still lying there, seeing only walls of wood and the open sky, blue-gray as a pool. We were punting in the shallow waters along the shore, and Wello told me we would pull over to the bank once it was fully dark. But it seemed like that might not ever happen; once the sun set the moon feebly took over, lighting the low thick clouds and setting them faintly aglow. Night was dusk.

As I listened to the thuds and laps of the river streaming against the wood hull, Otto wheezing little snores against my throat — his old congestion was back, though not too bad this time around — I found I wasn't able to sleep, or even keep my eyes closed. Though Wello was stroking at the pirogue's rear, the dug-out canoe was long enough that, lying on my back and staring at the stars, I felt like Otto and I were alone. Maybe other pirogues were passing us, but they had no lights and made no sound I could hear over the wave-slaps of the river. The Congo and its surrounding banks were plush-dark. All I could see were stars crowding above, fixed in space even as I moved. As the wispy charcoal clouds moved over them the stars throbbed, illuminating a vibrating halo of the darkness. I'd never seen them like this.

My skin buzzed, like it was crawling with microscopic organisms that had been accumulating steadily since my last shower weeks ago. I kept wanting to scratch myself, though my rash had subsided and I was pretty sure most of the itching was all in my head. I'd have loved some fresh clothes, though. I inventoried my missing duffel, mentally taking the clothes out and placing them on the broad soft rug of my dad's living room. The pale blue blouse with the pink ribbon threaded through the collar. Well-oiled moccasins. The striped socks my friends had made fun of me for, from pastel green-and-yellow to sharp black-and-red. The white cashmere vest, impossible for Congo, but which I'd wanted to show off to my mom and so had carted home. The one Otto had made his favorite, and was now probably serving as a blanket for one of those little girls sleeping in the airport. Assuming they'd made it there.

I stroked Otto's belly. I knew by now not to touch his legs or head when he was sleeping, as that would wake him. But a belly rub made him sigh contentedly in his sleep.

It was strange, but I missed those clothes. Not missed them like I wished I still had them to wear — though that, too, was true — but missed them like I missed my classmates. I didn't just want that cashmere vest back; I felt guilty for the cashmere vest, that it had been run through the muck and cast off by its owner. Maybe I was tired, and feeling bad for lost clothing served as a place to shove a bunch of feelings: fear and stress and that nagging remorse over two furry bodies holding each other beneath a tree. But it was crazy to be sorrowful over things when I'd lost people, too. I thought about that girl fascinated by Otto outside the UN encampment and realized her mother would have gladly pressed her into my hands if she'd thought getting to my mother's island meant reaching safety; I could just as well be taking her with me as a bonobo. Wouldn't that be the better thing to do? Wasn't it my duty to protect my own kind first?

But that simply wasn't the way I felt. I loved Otto, which made all those facts hardly relevant. The moment he'd come under my care, it hadn't been a question how much I would do for him. Though I knew there was human suffering out there, it wasn't like there was a tragedy scale where some things outranked others, or that care given to a bonobo meant less left for people.

I peeled the foil back from one of the UN ration packets to examine the contents by moonlight. Inside were a tea bag, water purification tablets, sugar packets, tissues, bandages, a can of tuna fish, another of chili con carne, and a package with BISCUITS printed across the foil wrapper. I opened those and gasped when I saw the same brand of cookies that were in the dining hall at school. American cookies in Congo! *Thank you, United Nations.* I munched on one. I used to love these, with their mixture of nutmeg and molasses, but now all I could taste was the weird rush of sugar, the tang of chemicals. It wasn't unpleasant, but only added to my sense of being overwhelmed. I tucked the second half of the cookie back into its foil wrapper to give to Otto once he woke up.

"Wello?" I called out. "You want a cookie?"

He grunted a negative reply, his voice nearly lost in the *thuck* of the waves against the hull.

"Otto?" I said softly, dragging him up around my neck. I hoped he might open his eyes for a moment, so I could look into them. But he stayed asleep.

NINETEEN

Eventually we pulled ashore and spent a quiet night; Otto and I offered our rations and Wello shared his ground cloth. Wello didn't say anything more than "over here" or "over there" or "good night" — I figured he was very tired. But our wordlessness hadn't changed in the morning; he got up and settled back into the pirogue without a sound. I scrambled to get Otto and me in and arranged before he pushed off from shore.

After a while, I asked him how things were in the capital. At first he didn't answer. Then, a couple of hours later, while I was making a few lame attempts to stir the river with my pole, he spoke up out of nowhere.

"There are more of us than them. I would think it would be better than this."

I sat up. "What?"

"In Kinshasa. It is truly very bad. I hated to do it, but it was only the *mayi-mayi* that I could trade my fish to. No one else would come out of their homes to buy. They have all fled. I do not know if they are locked in their homes or in the jungles. I had many friends there. I do not plan to go back again until after this war is over."

"You think it will happen? That the war will be over someday?"

There was no answer beyond the suck of the pole through the murk of the river bottom.

• • •

We didn't go ashore in the villages we passed; if the villagers had anything to sell, they would run up to the Congo's banks, offering it in outstretched arms. Often it was familiar fresh fish like tilapia, but sometimes it was long unnamed beasts, still gooey from the sludge at the bottom of the river, fangs and whiskers drooping; clusters of snails suckered to broad leaves; honey so fresh that it was swimming with bees; chunks of bushmeat, smoked to black, animal origin unknown. Wello would manage the transaction from the boat. He'd gone to Kinshasa with a pirogue full of fish and traded it all for three bags of salt and a hunk of soap. The salt he kept for himself, but from the soap he would shave thick peels to trade for food. He was deliberate with his measurements, somberly weighing each pale pink peel in his hand before offering it in trade.

Nervous about attacks, we took whatever food we bought upriver a ways before pulling into secluded reeds to eat. Dinner would be whatever strange thing we'd been able to buy at the side of the river, but breakfast and lunch were always limp cassava bread and fish wrapped in banana leaf.

Wello bought much more food than we needed. I saw his reason when, after leaving one village, we didn't pass another for a week. We lived sparely, but it wasn't too bad. We ate a fist-sized piece of fish meat at each meal, accompanied by dark green leaves, rigid as cardboard, that Wello foraged for us out of the underbrush. Otto refused the fish, but he did love whatever snails I found for him on the leaves. He'd take them in whole, crushing the tinkly shells under his sharp teeth, smacking the gummy creatures down with his mouth wide open, giving me a terrific view of the whole process.

Otto's favorite position in the pirogue was at the prow, on his hind legs with his arms hitched over the side, dragging his hands in the water. Once he got bored of that he'd slump down, his back against the hull, and stare at me as I paddled.

I got the punting stroke down eventually — it was more of a pull with the lower hand than a push with the upper — and I was able to help Wello out more often. I could see where he got his boxy, top-heavy shape, and I imagined my own body starting to do the same.

Wello told me that in normal times he operated the pirogue with an outboard motor hitched over the flat stern, but he ran out of gas soon after the war started and was unable to locate any more. So he was back into the old mode by which the Congolese economy had operated for centuries, sticking near the shoreline and punting the pirogue. He had hopes of hitching it to one of the gas-powered barges that usually traveled up and down the river, but none ever passed, yet more evidence that fuel was nowhere to be found. Wello complained, but I was secretly relieved; if there had been fuel, the rebels would have taken those barges for their own use, controlling the Congo or launching attacks on the riverside towns. Though we were slow making our way up the river, I was fine with that. My mom was up there waiting for me, and if going slower meant getting there alive, I could deal with the delay.

The next morning we saw the first signs of Mbandaka. Right where the banks of the Congo turned marshy and indistinct, a cluster of pirogues appeared. They dragged parallel in the current, like as many pencils in a desk furrow.

"Here I take the right branch, the Ruki," Wello said. "So now is when we part ways. Once you are past the city, you will see the river split once again. Then you, too, will take the right branch. It is smaller still. Once you have reached the village of Ikwa — not the big village far away, but the other one, a little one that is near here, it is easy to miss, so you will need to ask which one it is — you can ask how to get to your reserve."

"Any advice on how to pass through Mbandaka safely?" I asked.

"Avoid everyone," Wello said.

He gave me the name of his village; if I sent the money to the chief there, he would get it. Not to worry if I forgot, he promised me — he would track down my mom's sanctuary after the war. I had Wello memorize my father's e-mail address so if he ever came across Internet access he could send him a message to let him know I was alive. Wello memorized the letters solemnly, like the syllables of a spell. After we'd finished negotiating, we went to shore, said our good-byes, and then he was gone. It was just me and Otto on the bank, the empty pirogues marking the start of the city before us. Otto had his hand in mine, staring up at me.

I squeezed his hand tight and lifted him onto my back. "Don't worry," I told him. "We'll get through this."

Part Five:
Everything Is
Raining

TWENTY

I had spent nearly two weeks in that dugout canoe with Wello, and our sudden parting left me at a loss. After he dropped us off at the shore of a sheltered inlet, I sat in a tight ball on the hot hard earth, knees to my chin. While I steeled myself, Otto devised a new game, digging into the dry dirt with his fingers, tilting his head back, dropping the whole pile onto his face, and proceeding to lick up whatever dirt his tongue could reach. His face gradually became lighter and lighter shades of brown, his pink mouth the only part of him that wasn't filthy.

I couldn't see much of Mbandaka from where I sat, only the canoes needling the water. But I had to get my mind around the fact that a city at war was there out of sight, and I'd have to get past it to make it to my mom — past it without ever going near it. But I'd never been to Mbandaka, had no idea how far I'd have to go out of my way to circumvent it.

While I puzzled through what to do, Otto climbed onto my lap and pulled my arms up and over so they covered him. He rubbed himself against me to comfort himself, then pursed his lips and exposed his small sharp teeth when I blew on him. Eventually bored, he climbed down and wandered into the foliage.

Don't go far, I said. Or thought I said — without quite realizing what I was doing, all I did was make a couple of head bobs and grunt.

Normally I'd wait for Otto to wander back, but I was feeling antsy and directionless, so I followed him, ambling after him into the undergrowth. I found him in the lower branches of a tree, play-ing by swinging from side to side, oblivious to the bright green shock of a praying mantis walking across his knuckles. He dropped to the ground and raised his arms to be lifted. My pirogue-weary biceps protested as I picked him up.

Immediately Otto struggled to get back down. I released him, figuring he had to go pee, but he stood on his hind legs and raised his arms to be lifted again. Strange behavior. It was like his per-sonality had shifted sideways a few inches. There were all sorts of possible reasons, from our days cramped in the pirogue to our proximity to an unfamiliar city.

From what Wello had told me, Mbandaka dominated one side of the river, blooming along it for quite a ways. Because the city was crisscrossed by water, clumps of buildings were interspersed with overgrown jungle, all muddled together with occasional sprints of broad avenues. Though I could cut my way through the jungle and go around, that could take me days out of my way, and with-out the Congo River to follow, I was likely to lose my bearings. Maybe instead I'd approach the city as long as I could reasonably keep hidden, and see if I could spot a way to make it through while keeping under cover.

Simplest would be to pass right along the shore, but I'd be too exposed. So I eased into the bush, Otto at my back. The ground was striped with streams of fast-moving ants, which I tried to step over. When once I failed, I felt a flurry of starbursts on my ankles. I soon had my ratty sneaker off and was banging it against a trunk, big fat ants raining down. Not to be left out, Otto imitated me by thumping his palms against another tree. I examined my ankle. I had at least five bites, each of which would throb for days and rise into a teacup-sized ring with a blister in the center. A good start.

My shoulder against a nearby tree for balance, I examined my smelly moist sneaker, doing my best to ignore its odor. Once I'd decided it was clear of ants, I put it back on over my dingy socks and continued on my way. Otto once again took his usual position on my back. Presently we came upon a circle of straw huts, intact but abandoned. Otto and I stole between them, arriving at the far side to an empty phone card stand, with its colorful umbrella intact but looted of all contents. I kept to the back sides of buildings as I crept forward, checking for people before advancing, Otto's hot nervous breath at my back.

We passed more buildings — huts and shacks and gray, peeling businesses — all abandoned. I couldn't figure out why everything was so quiet; it was hard to think the rebels would have killed everyone. Whatever the reason, no one was around.

Or so I thought.

I heard a rustling and turned to the house across the street to see two rusty gun barrels in a glassless window. I dropped to my belly, Otto squealing at my back, and scrambled behind a ruined wall. For a while we stood there while I listened for someone giving chase. Hearing nothing, I risked a look out and saw two teenage girls, one my age and the other a little older, expressions hard and weapons gripped in trembling fingers. Seeing me, the older girl lowered the barrel of her gun and croaked out, "Do you have any water?"

At first I shook my head, intimidated by their guns. But then I saw their dull eyes, their dry lips. These two girls were *bapfuye buhagazi*, walking dead. I had a half-bottle of iodized water. I took it out of my tattered plastic bag, holding my free hand high to show I was unarmed, and slowly approached. The older one took the bottle and gave it to her sister, who drank nearly all of it, and then the first one finished what was left.

"I need the bottle back," I said.

Reluctantly, she handed it over. She and her sister ducked out of view, transaction over. I cleared my throat and asked if they had any advice for getting to the other side of the city.

The older one raised her head and tilted it in my direction, though she didn't meet my eye. "They've taken everyone who is able to work to the gold mine in the east. Or the other men from before, they took our parents to dig for diamonds in the forest. Everyone who can't work is dead."

I felt stuck. What could my problems matter to her? But I had to press on. "I need to get east to find my mother," I said. "Can you help me?"

She ducked out of sight but kept talking, telling me about a hunting trail that skirted the edge of the city and stopped at a riverhead. If I forded the river, I'd hit a tributary that would lead me to Ikwa, the village nearest my mother's site.

I thanked the girls and ducked down the street, hiding in the shadows. The plastic water bottle was light and empty in my bag. I had two goals now: getting to the hunting trail and replenishing my water.

The hunting trail began where they'd said, between an abandoned haircutter's hut and a cluster of charred bed frames marking a looted furniture shop. I followed the trail for a ways, until it was crossed by a brook. I kneeled and took some of the water into my bottle. Holding it up to the sunlight, I saw it was muddy and full of mysterious particles, but I put iodine in until it was cast purple and hoped for the best. It tasted like liquid sea urchin. Otto refused the bottle when I passed it to him, so I took a big gulp, pulled his head back, and let the water fall through my lips. I was glad to see him suck it down.

We were back in the equatorial forest, but at least this time we had a trail to follow. Though there were plenty of flies and mosquitoes, I had a chance of avoiding ants and snakes and leeches.

As I continued, the trail became less traveled, turning from a corridor of beaten dirt to a line of trampled grass. Then it became more subtle, minor disturbances — a broken branch, a ring of flattened leaves — that I had to piece together to find a direction. Once the light waned and I grew unsure where I was going, I stopped for the night. I scratched an arrow in a tree trunk marking the direction I was heading in case I woke up disoriented, found a spot of thick grass that didn't appear to have any ant colonies near it, and prepared to wait out the night. We'd sleep if we could. There'd have been a much better chance if I could have built us a nest, but I'd never figured that one out on my own.

As I lay back, Otto sat on my belly and stared at me, alert. I sensed huffiness, as if he were disappointed that this was the best sleeping spot I could muster. I bounced him up and down a few times, and he squirmed away, his eyes on the trees. I sighed, taking in his perfectly made little ears, his smooth flat nose, the wrinkled brow over thoughtful eyes. *I need you, Otto.* My desperation to see him calm and content gave me extra inspiration. When I gave him a thorough tickling session and some tremendous raspberries on his belly, he cheered, cuddling up to me.

"Don't turn weird on me now, Otto," I whispered. "Please." My voice came out teary.

Fatigue surprised Otto, soon sprawling him out.

I watched the unfamiliar world go dark while Otto snored in my arms. The air was heavy, like everything was raining. Moisture thickened the air and hung there, always present and never getting it over with. Because it never rained, nothing was ever dry; and because nothing was dry, nothing had a chance to freshen. My white T-shirt glowed in the twilight, banded in modern art speckles of fungal reds, yellows, and blues.

I gingerly repositioned Otto to my lap so I could sit up and use the last moments of daylight to take stock of my supplies. As I was opening my sack and taking out everything I'd gathered during the river journey that wouldn't putrefy — some nuts and hard berries and a couple strips of dried fish — I heard the sound of heavy drops hitting the leaves above us. It was like my thoughts about rain had brought it on. The rainstorm in the enclosure had been strange enough, but another shower in August?

But I realized with a jerk that it wasn't August anymore. It was September. Or even October? Not October, surely . . . Could school have been going that long already? Did life go on in America when I was hiding from militias in Congo? Did I make it into the morning announcements? *No green elephant notebooks this year, kids.*

The first giant drop fell through the canopy, hit Otto on the forehead, and bounced off. Otto was instantly awake, outraged and murping loudly. He leaped off my belly, his bony heels nearly knocking the breath out of me, danced a jig, then peered up at the leaves. He climbed a tree, dropped back to peer into my face, then climbed another tree, holding on to the trunk with his feet while his arms flailed in the air.

"Otto, calm down," I cried.

The bouncing rainfall continued, and it took me a while to realize we weren't getting wet. Sprays of dirt flew up from the soil, like we were being strafed by gunfire. I investigated a nearby pockmark and saw, in the ring of impact, the fat coil of a caterpillar. By now they were raining down by the thousands. Otto scampered here and there, seizing the fallen coils and cramming them into his mouth. They must have been in the trees all along, and by natural mystery dropped at the same time.

Otto ate until his belly was full and then fell against me like a contented drunk. He lazily plucked another living bracelet from the soil, held it between thumb and forefinger, and let his hand drop open on my chest. The caterpillar thrashed. Otto looked up at me and looked away, his hand holding still, and I realized he was presenting food for me to share. Hesitantly, I lifted the caterpillar. I wasn't really a bonobo, but could I eat like one? Then, without even thinking, I put the caterpillar in my mouth. It tasted like a sausage made from frothed soil and grass. I ate another.

Otto and I sat up and stared out into the near-dark clearing like we were watching a sports game on TV, the caterpillars a bowl of popcorn we chowed through without looking. When the sky went black, we brushed our spot of grass clear and lay down. Though I could feel small flies land on me and was distantly aware of mosquitoes drilling the air around my ears, they'd stopped bothering me much. A mosquito bite meant a bit of itchiness, that was all. If I got malaria, it wouldn't show for another week or two, so for now I was safe. If I started batting them away, like I'd once have done, I wouldn't sleep a wink. Tomorrow I had to make it past Mbandaka, and I needed energy.

My thoughts grew illogical and fuzzy, and I distantly realized that I might actually succeed at falling asleep. Otto was being a total brat, though, sitting on my face and pulling at my ears, then ignoring me when I tugged his ears back. Finally I shoved him away so I could sleep. I didn't feel too bad — if I'd been a real bonobo mother I would have struck him a whole lot harder. He didn't come back right away, and I figured he was having a caterpillar dessert and would come snuggle in later, ideally not waking me up in the process.

TWENTY-ONE

It was still dark when I woke, all around me the rush and hum of crickets. I sat up and swiped at my face. Something felt off.

I swept my hands around in the blackness and whispered Otto's name. The continuing thrum of the crickets was my only answer.

My voice rose each time I said his name, and soon I was screaming. I became aware of how vulnerable I was making myself, though, and held still, waiting to hear from Otto. Nothing.

What I wanted most was to go charging into the bush to find him. But I couldn't see well enough to do it, so I swiveled, shouting.

No response.

I would have to wait.

As his absence sank in, I said Otto's name less and less frequently, finally calling only every minute or so. For the despairing moments in between, I was left in my personal darkness. I'd always thought of loneliness as a slow, ocean-wide thing, but it came over me like a sharp and sudden blow. I needed Otto to be the one constant thing in my life, and I was ready to cry from confusion. "Please, Otto!" I whispered. Had he left me because I'd shoved him? He loved playing rough; I couldn't imagine my casting him off was enough to anger him. Had he gone to collect caterpillars and gotten lost? Had some hungry rebel or Mbandakois come and taken him during the night? I had to believe I would have woken up.

I stood there for a lifetime, carved out and desolate, and kept saying Otto's name. If there had been just one response from him, even a little squeak, the world would have had light in it. But it stayed quiet, and so it stayed dark.

I would have to wait for the sun to come up and the world to lighten the normal way. First the sky turned the palest green-blue at the horizon, like the bottom of a petal. It wasn't enough to see by yet, so I waited. Finally the light was gray enough that I could see shapes. The clearing was as I'd left it the night before, my bag hanging from a branch, the arrow I'd carved into a tree still glistening.

"Otto!" I cried. I crept a little ways back toward the edge of Mbandaka in case he'd gotten lost and headed for the more familiar. I hoped to find a few bonobo-crushed caterpillars, but I could see no sign of Otto's passing. As I returned to the clearing, I imagined finding him there on my tarp, lying back with one foot in one hand, the position he so loved; but it was empty. I packed my supplies away, retied the plastic bag onto my belt loop.

The forest was thick on either side. Knowing Otto — though how well did I really know him, apparently, if I'd been unable to predict this? — he'd prefer going along the trail. So I continued forward along it.

Something big moved deep in the trees, and I froze, stopping and calling Otto's name. There was no response, though; it had been more of a skittering sound than one that a bonobo would make, probably some reptile escaping into the ferns. I wished I could see better; walking in semidarkness left me helpless. But dawns here came on as suddenly as sunsets, and it wasn't too long before the trail was bright enough for me to walk at normal speed.

Everywhere I looked, I could see small creatures moving. I called out Otto's name again.

This time, I thought I heard a bonobo call over the breeze rustling through the trees.

I sped toward the sound, tripping over ruts and roots but always scrambling ahead, sometimes on all fours, pushing against the ground with my knuckles. The calls got easier to hear, and I recognized the high-pitched, pulsating sound: Otto in distress.

The trail narrowed to pass through a thicket, and as I folded myself through I saw Otto at the far side of the clearing, dangling between two trees. A length of rope was wrapped tightly around his ankle: a snare. He swayed in the air, a good eight feet above the ground, revolving slowly, the green vine rope creaking.

The moment I saw him, I said his name. That instant I saw a black shape startle, turn, and crash into the brush. It had been a bonobo. A wild bonobo female, infant on her back.

Otto saw me and shrieked. He jerked in the air, then reached up and tried to grasp the knot in the snare. He failed, his arms again pointing to the distant ground. I didn't know how long he'd been up there, but his foot was swollen and purplish and the white of his eyes was replaced by red, like the vessels had broken. "Oh, my Otto," I said. "I'll get you down."

But how? Even raising my hand as high as I could, I wouldn't be able to reach him. So I took to the trees like a bonobo. I dug my fingertips into the little variations in the bark and, fully outside of my rational mind, pulled myself up high before I knew how. I plucked at the snare's tight rope, and it twanged like a guitar string. I'd hoped to haul Otto up, but the material was too slick to get a grip.

I craned into the open air, had my teeth around the plant fiber, and was about to start gnawing when voices made me freeze. Low, terse voices. I would have ignored anything and anyone to get Otto free, but if I were captured, there would be nothing I could do to help him. I pulled back into the cover of the tree's lime-green leaves.

A man and a woman crept into the clearing. Their movements were purposeful, and I realized either Otto's cries or my own had drawn them here. The man exclaimed when he saw Otto dangling, and they both took positions under him. Otto stared down apprehensively, quietly murping. If they bothered to look closely, they'd see me farther above; they were peering straight at me, though their vision was focused a yard closer. They each had a string of bullets worn across their chests. She reached her rifle tip up and prodded Otto's forehead, causing him to shriek and stare imploringly in my direction. They laughed.

She was gorgeous, with glossy short hair and crazy-long legs, but with a massive scar across her face. The man had a head that had been scoured by acne long before war scars had been layered on top. He drew a short knife and jabbed it at Otto's hand. Otto brought his pricked palm to his mouth, whimpering in pain and fatigue and confusion. He tried to curl his body up and away, but he was too weak after the hours spent struggling against the snare.

I resisted the urge to hurtle out of the foliage to Otto's defense, tried to calm my mind enough to reason through what to do. These weren't typical hunters; the strings of bullets told me they were combatants, probably hungry and unpaid and setting traps for extra food. They had likely set the snare for smaller game, like macaque monkeys or antelope, but they'd be happy to eat a bonobo.

The combatants discussed for a minute, and then the woman took to the tree on the other side of the trail, knife clenched between her teeth. She could as easily have chosen my tree, and then I would have had to risk fighting her one-on-one. Once she came up to my level she crept forward, intent on the snare's knot.

She was only a few feet away, and I could see sweat dotting the base of her neck, could smell stale clothing and body odor. I could lunge at her. I could sink my teeth in her neck and throw her off the tree. It was what I most wanted, but what would that do? She'd fall to the ground, and she and her companion would have their guns out, and Otto and I both would be dead.

So I watched her shimmy down, watched her raise the knife. My muscles tensed. If the blade got within a foot of Otto, I would be on her.

She cut the rope.

Otto fell onto the man's chest and immediately reached his arms out to be held. Instead the man shrieked in surprise and dropped Otto heavily into the dirt, holding the cut rope at arm's length, like he was handling a snapping turtle. As Otto's swollen foot was dragged upward, he was forced to stand on one hand. He cried and flailed his free hand while the woman descended the tree, laughing at her startled partner.

The man handed her the rope and they left the way they'd come, the woman hauling Otto behind. As he skittered along the soil, he scrambled to stay on his back, pressing his coarse palms into the ground to avoid turning over and having his face dragged through the dirt and rocks. He cried hoarsely as the trio disappeared around the bend.

I slid down the tree, landing in a rough heap on the ground. Springing to my feet, I willed my breaths to keep coming against the sharp constriction in my throat.

I guess they saw no need to be quiet, and I was easily able to follow them as they made their way into the city, Otto bumping and shrieking behind. *I'm here,* mon petit. *You don't know it, but I'm here.*

The hunting trail continued through the forest for a ways, until buildings began to appear. First it was huts, as silent and barren as the ones I'd seen earlier. I saw no one aside from a little boy, sitting all on his own in the dusty street. I was sure he noticed me, like he had to have noticed the hunters and Otto, but he kept his eyes trained on his knees, hoping to be ignored.

I heard crowds ahead, though, and knew I'd soon be spotted by someone who cared if I continued tailing along so obviously.

We passed a simple concrete building, the faded paint of LA POSTE barely visible on top of the vivid black and green of rotting concrete. The letters must have been painted during the Belgian occupation over fifty years ago. I made the reluctant decision to hide away before I was discovered, and slipped into a space between two wooden planks nailed to the entrance.

Inside was all must and dankness — like a shut-up basement, only more so. I had to get to the roof before the combatants disappeared from view with Otto. The stairs had long ago rotted away, but I was able to press a foot into a divot in the lacey concrete wall and leap upward, my arms just clearing the second floor. Mushie the acrobat would have been proud. I passed from the second floor to the third the same way, and finally made it to the roof. I rushed to the edge, just in time to see Otto and his captors hit the city center.

The market was teeming. There were only a few vendors, and all were engaged in harried negotiations with rebels, lean and sullen and above all bored, jostling and shoving and bilking as a way to pass the time. I had no idea if it was money being passed or favors and the right to stay alive. Along the near edge, rebels sat against the road, sharpening their machetes on the chunked remains of what had, at some point in the last hundred years, been a paved thoroughfare.

There were immediate shouts of interest when the hunters entered with Otto, and they were soon surrounded. The crowd circled so thickly that I couldn't see him anymore, and I was stuck through by my horrible imaginings of what was happening.

But soon enough, the crowd thinned and I could see Otto again. He was intact, wrapped tightly around the leg of his female captor, head buried against her shin. She moved forward stiffly, her gapped mouth open wide as she guffawed. Otto refused to let go of her, even when she shook her leg violently. Helpless on the roof-top, I felt a many-edged combination of anger and fear and jealousy that came out as rage, rage, rage. I kicked at the crumbling cement of the roof's low wall, and a spray of bits fell to the ground below. I dropped out of sight in case I'd drawn anyone's attention.

When I dared emerge, I saw Otto had changed hands. His new owners had tied his leash to the leg of a plastic restaurant table, and he was sitting on top, holding his hurt foot in his hands, lips pulled back over his teeth. I couldn't make out much else of his expression from the distance, but there were men sitting all around him, loung-ing about and smoking. I resisted the urge to kick out at the roof's ledge again. How would I ever rescue him? I'd hoped I could sneak up and snatch him, but it would be impossible in that big crowd.

All I could do was wait for things to change. I'd give it an hour, I decided. Maybe by some miracle the market would clear by then and I could creep over.

So I crouched, watching Otto test the radius of his leash as he circled the table. A laughing teenage boy in a soiled tank top handed Otto a cigarette and, when he didn't take it, pressed a beer into his hands. Probably remembering the many times I'd given him water to drink from my bottle, Otto took it readily and drank.

He dropped the beer as soon as he tasted it, but the boy caught the bottle and pressed it against him. Staring into the boy's eyes, Otto drank again. He had counted on me to take care of him, and now he was surrounded by soldiers. At any moment they might begin to torture him, and I was powerless to do anything about it. My outrage, without outlet, was quickly turning to despair.

Once he'd finished the beer, Otto sat down heavily on the table. The empty bottle fell from his fingers and crashed onto the ground. He twiddled a toe, his eyes downcast.

I watched in silence as an older soldier walked by and started to untie him, stopping only when the teenager who had given Otto the beer complained loudly. As the afternoon burned into evening and the crowds dissipated, the teenager was one of the few who remained at the plastic tables. He opened the door of the former restaurant — maybe he had taken control of the space after the previous owner was killed — and stood there for a while, chatting with the soldiers who passed.

I raged at my helplessness. This wouldn't have happened if only Otto hadn't wandered off. What had gotten into him? But while I waited it struck me that we'd returned to native bonobo territory. That bonobo mother probably heard Otto's juvenile cries of distress and came to investigate, fleeing when I arrived. Did Otto remember — or ever really understand — that his real mother was dead?

Finally, as night began to fall, the teenager untied the leash. Otto looked up, but seemed unable to stand. The teenager wrapped his arms around him and carried him inside the restaurant door, Otto lolling in his hands.

It was past dinnertime, and I hadn't seen the boy eat anything. A new fear struck me: Was that what Otto was for?

I no longer had the luxury of waiting for an opening. I had to act now. Twilight had begun, which meant I had only minutes to get to the bottom of the building and over to the restaurant. I threw myself down to the second floor and then to the bottom, gave a quick glance between the boards on the doorway to see if the coast was clear, and slipped out.

I was discovered almost immediately. A shout came from my left. Not risking the time to find who'd seen me, I dashed right,

195

turning the first corner I could and then another, hoping to lose whomever it was as quickly as possible.

In a dark corner I caught my breath and listened for sounds of pursuit. When there was nothing, I wiped the sweat from my face and walked out toward the marketplace.

It was terrifying and energizing to be among the soldiers, after watching them from hiding for so long. I forced my head high and my eyes wide open, tried to look like I belonged even as I yearned to cringe away.

I very quickly discovered that blending in wouldn't work, I guess because a girl on her own had no reason to be alive and intact. Very soon there were whistles, then soldiers with red eyes and prominent guns jostling my shoulders, grabbing their crotches and shouting at me in languages I didn't understand. The crowd was clotting around me, and I knew the only way this could all end. Men would turn to mobs, words would turn to actions, someone would grab at me, and then another, and the end would begin.

Fear pushed so hard on me that I was beyond thinking of anything else, could do nothing but fight to get out from under it. Words were impossible so I said nothing, only pointing at the restaurant door where I'd seen the boy disappear. Getting to Otto was the only goal in my mind, and pointing toward him was all I could think to do.

As swiftly as I could, I pressed through the corridor of groping arms to the restaurant door. I avoided the leering eyes, ignored the spit that struck my cheek, tried not to see the man who momentarily stood in my path, coolly tossing a grenade like a juggler's sack before his comrades pulled him back.

My mind raced as I pushed forward. Why was no one touching me yet? Apparently the boy who'd taken Otto was something of a figure among the soldiers. And since I'd indicated I was his, no one was stepping forward to interfere.

After an eternity I was at the door, soldiers hooting at my back. Someone snatched at the seat of my pants, and I felt the plastic bag with its few crude treasures rip away. I wasn't about to risk trying to retrieve it. I pushed the door and stepped through confidently, like I was returning to a home I'd known for years, like there was no place I'd rather be than trapped inside with the armed militant who'd taken Otto captive.

TWENTY-TWO

Almost before I was inside, the boy had sprung to his feet, knocking back a plastic chair. He shouted words I couldn't understand, and in the face of it I bowed my head and shut the door. When I turned back to him, he'd calmed somewhat.

Otto was alive. He murped when he saw me, staggering up from the soil floor and lifting his arms to be held. He fell down as soon as he got to his feet, knocking over empty beer bottles. They made hollow pinging sounds when they rolled against one another. Otto tried to get back up but didn't make it to me; again he staggered, heaping on the floor and staring at me in dull confusion, wondering at his body's betrayal.

The boy again shouted at me, but I couldn't understand his language. "Excuse me," I responded in French.

He surprised me by switching to rough French; he must have gone to school at some point. "This is my room."

I looked at him as much as I could with my head bowed. I avoided the eyes, which were bloodshot and angry. His frame was delicate, his wrists as narrow as mine, with knobs of bone that looked like they could be broken off like hard candy. The nails were brown with tobacco. Slowly I let my gaze rise, immediately realizing again the horror of his eyes, drugged and cloudy. But his face was unlined, his chin weak like a boy's. He couldn't have been much older than I. Not that that meant anything as far as my safety.

"I'm sorry," I said, hands out in a stand-down gesture. "I'm really sorry."

"Did Lukila send you in here?" he barked.

At the sound of his raised voice, many fists banged on the door. I was terrified to see Otto's captor go over to it. "Please, no, I —" But it was too late. He threw the door open.

Noise and flashing light streamed in. A crowd of men and boys was pressed against the entrance, grinning and leering, arms so entangled that no one of them could fall inside. While they ogled me, they spoke incomprehensible words. The feeling behind them wasn't hard to interpret: Something like "Are you going to share?"

The boy looked for someone that he obviously couldn't find, then barked back at the crowd and swung the door closed, whirling on me. "Who gave you to me?"

I couldn't give an answer. Partly because I didn't have one, and partly because I was transfixed by his necklace. At first I'd thought it was strung shells with shriveled black seaweed, but it wasn't — it was a chain of mummified fingernails, a black and curled strip of flesh dangling from the base of each.

Seeing my focus, he plucked his necklace between thumb and forefinger and flicked it into the air. It fell silently to his neck, one of the nails falling free and fluttering to the ground. Where the necklace had lain, his skin was powdery red and white.

I inched my way over to Otto. My plan was to go along with whatever the boy believed. I was safer if he thought someone had sent me — otherwise, he might call in the others.

"You're ugly," he said, looking me up and down, "but at least you're too young to give me AIDS."

He thought I was younger than my actual fourteen. The light was dim in the room; maybe it was too dark for him to mistake me for a *mundele*. I wasn't sure whether that helped me or hurt me.

Once I'd moved closer, I could get a better look at Otto. He was staring at the ground, beer matting his hair. One palm was curled in the other, and he occasionally gave it a mournful lick. There was a blister the size of a pencil eraser on it; someone must have burned him with a cigarette. As I crept nearer, he leaned into my shin for comfort. It was for the best that he was in too much of a stupor to reach up; if Otto had been sober, this boy might have seen that we were close, and that would raise all sorts of questions.

I snuck glances around the room while the boy stood there appraising me. In the feeble light cast by a lantern on a table, I could see a couple of chairs; some weathered plastic bags in the corner; a couple of guns in another, looking rusty beyond use; and a charred spot near the door where someone had started a fire, on purpose or accidentally. If this boy decided to assault me, it would have to be against the walls or on the floor.

As far as I could tell, my best hope of getting out of this room intact lay in the boy's unlined face. He was clearly respected here, and had probably killed many people judging by the number of fingertips on his necklace, but he also looked too young to have been doing this for long. Maybe I could get him to see me as another human being?

"My name is Sophie," I said, finally looking at him fully.

"I didn't ask you for your name. You bitch. Take your shirt off."

I stood still for a moment, but when he reached for a gun my hands instinctively went to the bottom of my shirt. Before I knew it, the shirt was up and over my head. It was the first time I'd stood in front of a boy this way. I was wearing a bra, but it was nearly tattered away. I reached my arms around my chest, my palms fear-slick against my ribs.

The shirt fell on Otto, and the familiarity of it stoked something in him. He rolled in it, then looked up and really saw me for the first time. He got up on wobbly legs and lifted his arms. I leaned down and picked him up, wearing him like a shirt. "I like your ape," I risked saying.

The boy looked ticked off for a moment, then a smile grew. "He is my new friend."

I rubbed Otto's bottom, and we did our blowing-on-pursed-lips move. The boy looked impressed by our connection — I decided to roll with it. "He's a bonobo, you know," I dared continue. "Not a chimpanzee."

"I know that. You can teach me nothing," the boy said. "My captain is from Bolobo. The name *bonobo* comes from his village. Years ago someone spelled it bad on a crate, and the stupid *mundele* didn't realize. The bonobos are warlocks, like me — in the wild they don't need to drink because the air is always raining in the forest. They know that everything is raining. That is what gives them their power."

Otto pressed himself hard against my bare skin, his soft little cheek rubbing against my shoulder. I stroked the back of his head. The boy started to look less proud and more jealous. "He likes you," he said.

I nodded. "I like him. He will be a good friend for you. You were smart to choose him."

Some of the tension went out of the room. The boy sat in his chair and, hesitantly, I lowered myself to a squat on the floor. I kept Otto wrapped around my chest; having him there made me feel less naked.

"My name is Bouain," the boy said.

"My name is Sophie," I repeated.

"You are from Mbandaka?"

"No." I took a deep breath. I didn't know enough about anywhere else to lie convincingly, so I told the truth. "Kinshasa."

"Kinshasa," he said, lips pulling back in a smile to reveal perfectly straight and yellow teeth. "That is the capital. My brothers have taken Kinshasa. That is far away."

"Yes," I said. "I ran away and came here."

"Then you are an idiot and deserve what you get. Mbandaka is no safer for you than Kinshasa." He waved Otto near, but though Otto stared at him, he wasn't about to leave me. *Please, Otto,* I willed, *help me keep this boy happy.*

It was such consolation to have Otto's body against mine. Everything he covered was sacred and safe. I saw the exposed parts of me through the boy's eyes: the scrawny waist, loose pants moldy and spotted, bug bites up and down my arms, bruises from Anastasia's bite still healing. I was not a pretty girl these days. Thank God.

"Come, dirty monkey," the boy said. "You want another beer?"

I bit down the hatred that swelled. "Ha, ha," I said. "Yeah, do you want a beer, monkey?" *I will get you out of here.*

Otto definitely did not want another beer. All he seemed to want to do was fall asleep. He sighed, and his breathing slowed against my neck.

By now the sounds of the men pressing against the door had died down. All was quiet, and our only illumination was from the lantern. The room felt curiously intimate. "Come over here," Bouain said.

Though my heart clenched, I obeyed, inching a little closer along the floor.

He took my hand in his. That was all he did. We sat like that for a few moments, I doing my best not to shudder. He wanted my sympathy, I guess. He took Otto's injured foot into his other hand. Otto kicked, but he was too sleepy for it to amount to much. I doubted Bouain even realized Otto had tried to be hostile, until he gave Otto a retaliatory pinch.

"That is the way of the world, no? To fight. For us it is like the animals," he said.

I hoped his affection for Otto could save me, that my knowledge could make me useful. "You know the chimpanzees?" I said.

Bouain nodded.

I swallowed against the foul taste of fear. "They war with one another. They rape and kill when they meet chimpanzees they don't know. For a long time, everyone thought they were our closest relative. And so everyone thought this was our nature, that we came from chimps and so we fight like chimps."

"You see?" he said.

"I'm sure you know more about this than me. But I like that the bonobo is as related to us as the chimpanzee. And they squabble, but they don't kill and they don't rape. The women are weaker but they come together and help one another and become stronger than the men."

"I do not like this idea," Bouain said, frowning hugely, almost comically.

I laughed, and was heartened to see him smile a little in response. I knew I'd taken a risk, but I had to try to shock him into seeing me. "So," I started, "it's another way to think —"

"No person has protected me," Bouain interrupted.

"No," I said. "They didn't." He was probably right, but I refused my heart its loosening, kept it tight and impervious to him.

"It is cold outside tonight," he said. "If you want to put your shirt on, you can. You will stay with me tonight, keep us warm as two, yes?"

I was baffled by this turn in his behavior and didn't get what he meant — put my shirt on and also sleep with him? But I immediately took advantage of the chance to cover myself. Maybe Bouain was tired by all the months of posturing to his men and wanted an actual companion. Whatever the reason, something had made me human in his eyes.

I pulled Otto's arms from around my neck, he making quiet complaints, and set him on the soil floor. I picked up my shirt. I had it half on, one of my shoulders still exposed out of my stretched neck hole, when I realized that in my nervousness I was putting both arms through one opening. Bouain laughed, and in the few moments it took me to rearrange, I found myself unexpectedly thinking of my mother. I got why she'd spent so many years charming boring men. To survive. The position I was in, playing some disgusting politics with this boy, was awful. But it wasn't the end of the world. The end of the world was that crowd of men on the far side of the door.

He made no move to take my hand back in his. "You speak good French," he said. "Maybe you could teach me some more words." He was eager to learn, and suddenly I could see the small boy who had once sat in a classroom. He reached down and stroked Otto.

"Yes," I said. "I could. Or English. I go to school in America."

He cocked his head. "Do not lie to me."

"I'm not."

"If you left Congo, why did you come back?" he asked.

"To be with my family."

"You are not a normal Congo girl."

I nodded. That was certainly true.

"The war started when my teacher dropped the chalk," he said out of nowhere. "They killed my teacher and my friends and tied me to a tree for hours."

"I'm sorry," I said, and didn't feel it.

"I thought they left me as dead, but they really went into the forest to hunt. We had many bonobos in our forest before the combatants came. The bonobos, they ran away as soon as the attack happened. Except one. She was in a tree. I wanted her to run, but she did not. And then I knew the reason, the reason was she gave birth, in front of me as I was tied to the tree. The baby fell out of her . . . it hit the end of the cord and — *pop!* — bounced back. The attack must have made her give birth. You see? She bit the cord and disappeared into the woods. But the combatants were everywhere by then. I did not have many hopes for her. That little bonobo baby was stuck, and probably was captured by the rebels. Like me, you see? I wonder what happened to him."

I did the math in my head: how long Bouain had probably been a soldier if he now wore those fingernails so coolly around his neck; Otto's age; the unlikelihood a newborn would survive any time apart from its mother, much less a trip downriver from the east to Kinshasa. But still, I could see the passion spring up in Bouain's eyes as he lifted Otto and laid him on his lap. This wasn't the actual infant he'd once seen, but it felt that way to him. "I take you from my comrades because you are to be with me. You and I . . . are two halves of the same soul," he said to Otto.

No, I thought, *you're not.* "He looks three years old, do you agree?" I said. "That's still very young to be separated from his mother. We have to keep him healthy for you. Has he eaten?"

Bouain shook his head.

"I could try," I continued. "I bet I could make him eat. Otherwise you will lose your friend."

Bouain shook Otto by the shoulders to wake him up. "No. He will eat when I tell him to eat. He respects my power."

The lantern flickered and dimmed. Bouain tsked in irritation and shook it. "You can go back out and tell them that they made a mistake to give you to me," he said.

My face burned. Relief was the overwhelming feeling, but also combined with worry over how to get Otto out and fear at what waited for me on the other side of the door.

I couldn't leave now, not without Otto. Before Bouain could stop me, I pulled Otto into my lap and pinched him hard. He shrieked and opened his eyes, almost as soon half closing them again. Bouain grinned — the hard pinch had earned me points. Setting Otto on the ground, I put my foot in his lap.

Despite his drunk sleepiness, or maybe because of it, Otto couldn't resist. He started untying my shoelace.

Bouain watched disinterestedly, like a king with failing jesters. Once Otto had my laces undone, he looked at them, then at Bouain, then at me. I willed him to begin tying. Instead, he closed his eyes to take a nap. *Oh no, you're not, Otto.* I pinched him again, and his eyes flashed open, staring at me in outrage.

Then, with furious exactness, he started tying. The last time he'd started this I'd eventually stopped him, but now I didn't. He made a simple cross knot in the lace, again and again, until it became a big mass of chaos that I'd never be able to undo. Bouain sat up excitedly and scrutinized the bramble of shoelace. "But how . . ."

"I have magic," I said quickly, "and this is my familiar. I can control him." With that, I clapped once and raised my arms in a big *V*, our sign for *come and hug*. Popped out of his stupor by relief that his mother was no longer an evil pinching stranger, Otto leaped and put his arms around my neck, pulling close and staring intensely back at Bouain.

"You tricked me! The French, the magic . . . you are a *touri!*" he said.

Now that he had used that word, I got nervous. A *touri* was a *mundele* with sinister, supernatural ends. A sort of foreigner witch. In the small, isolated villages, even local people suspected of sorcery were ostracized or killed — the punishment was even worse for a *touri*. But I was a witch who had power over a bonobo Bouain liked, a bonobo that he felt linked back to his home, so I hoped I might be safe.

"Can you cure me of a disease?" he asked, his hands to the drawstring of his pants.

"No," I said. "My magic supplies are back home. All I have is my spirit connection to this bonobo. I stole two of his fingers, but have promised to give them back once we are in the next world. In return, he is my servant in this one."

"I have seen that fingers are missing." Bouain sighed. "I hoped you could heal me." He looked crestfallen. Whatever disease he had was big on his mind.

"But if you remain in his good favor, he will bless you. Otto can cure you that way."

"Otto?"

"His spirit name. It means *Demon Vengeance* in a European language."

"I knew you were different. Your French. Your hair. Your skin. You will give me some of this magic."

I thought quickly. "I told you, I do not have my instruments with me. My demon spirit called me and compelled me to fly to him."

Otto looked at Bouain and then at me. His expression was a mix of *What do you think you're doing?* and *It's time for me to eat a peanut.*

"Why do you not fly away with him right now?" Bouain asked, his eyes narrowing.

"He wanted to meet the immortal hunter who calls himself Bouain. Now he has. If you will help him get free, he will make you immune to bullets."

"I am already immune to bullets," Bouain said thoughtfully. I wondered how to respond. Bouain continued before I came up with anything. "But another shield would not harm me, and is helpful if the other one stops working."

"He has met you now, and is satisfied. But he does not like to be trapped in one place. If he decides to give you this magic, it will be on the condition that you let us go free."

Bouain tapped his nose. "I would like this magic. But I cannot release you or the bonobo. You are a gift from my men, and they will not be happy to see you set free."

I tugged at Otto's ear and he, in response to the improvised game, swung his hand in the air, making a random Z. Bouain froze.

"If he gives you a gift and escapes, your men will see that you didn't release him. You will have been honored, and that will satisfy them."

Bouain continued to tap his nose as he considered my plan.

"Let him give you some of his strength," I pressed. I tugged at Otto's nipples, and he gave a complex confused grunt. *Good boy.* "The transfer will only take a minute."

Bouain shifted off his chair and sat on the floor across from us. He closed his eyes and nodded.

Once Bouain's eyes were shut, I tickled Otto's armpits so he'd continue his grunting throughout the spell. Once the minute was up, I told Bouain he could open his eyes.

"Do you feel different?" I asked.

He nodded blearily. He'd fallen a little asleep. I felt a crazy urge to take this murderer's shoes off and put him to bed. This all would have gone much differently, I realized, if Bouain hadn't been drunk.

He lay down on the ground, a hand outstretched to Otto. My bonobo, of course, was having none of it. He looked at the hand, then up at me. *That's not a peanut.*

Bouain said sleepily, "I must not release you, you see." His eyelids slid closed and stayed that way.

The padlock that hung on the back door was open, barely balancing on its hook. Whether he'd intentionally left us an escape route or simply fallen asleep without remembering to lock the *touri* and her bonobo in, I didn't know. But there it was: an open door.

PART SIX:
WHAT REMAINED
INSIDE

TWENTY-THREE

I opened the door just wide enough to slip outside, and shut it silently. I couldn't see anything in the still night, so I waited, hoping my eyes would adjust and that it wasn't actually pitch-black out. As I hung there, I listened to Otto's hungry groans at my back. Eventually the black became charcoal, and I decided it was worth the risk to start moving. I could orient myself only by the surfaces moonlight frosted: the rim of an old bicycle tire, a crumpled water bottle, the aluminum arc of a grenade handle.

I needed to get to the southern edge of the city, where I could locate the river and trace along it until I reached the village of Ikwa. What I feared most was a man's yell, and what I feared second most was barking. All it would take was one dog to alert everyone to the girl out on her own in the middle of the night. But the street remained quiet as I crept forward. It seemed the dogs of Mbandaka had all been eaten.

The time I'd spent on the roof of the post office had given me a pretty good sense of the city's layout, so I kept along the roads I suspected would be easiest. Occasionally I'd step on something that clattered, and once I stumbled into a crate that crashed into the night. I'd sometimes see red eyes shining at me, soldiers or their victims, too drunk or sad or tired to care about the girl slipping through their city.

I heard running water. On all fours, I passed down a steep, grassy ravine to the river, Otto bumping against my back. Some insects or plants stung my arms, but I couldn't see them and I couldn't care. Once we were a few inches past the edge, I heard Otto slurp greedily. I wished I still had the iodine so I could drink, too, but of course it had gone when the street soldiers had stolen my bag. I wasn't too thirsty yet, so I decided to hold off.

We trudged away from Mbandaka. It would be foolish to tromp much farther through the river's edge in the dark, with the risk of snakes and crocodiles. Once we were a few hundred feet along, I could no longer detect the silhouettes of any buildings near the water's edge, so I hoped we would be hidden if we lay out until the sun came up. I settled in a few feet onshore, held Otto to my chest, and rocked him through his complaining hunger while we waited for the dawn.

I'd thought the lumps along the river that had tripped me were logs, but as the light improved I saw they were bodies. Some had hit the water and sunk up to their throats in mud, and others looked like they were crawling, caught in bizarre motion. Some were men and boys, but most were women and girls, their wraps still in beautiful colors, undone and spread along the ground like butterfly wings.

On the far side I could now see the mine. There was nothing official about it, just a wall of crumbly earth surrounding a pit. No one was standing guard, because there was no fancy machinery to protect. It was no more than a sore in the earth, broad and chaotic, gouged out by human fingernails, ounce to pound to ton.

These corpses couldn't have been more than a day or two old and weren't visibly decomposed, but I still shuddered to think of Otto last night, drinking water steeped in rotting flesh.

We got moving quickly, before the day's soldiers and slaves arrived. With the morning came the flies thickening on the corpses. They gathered on me and probed my bug bites and the muck in my hair, batted against my face. My stomach was growling now, and I could feel Otto, desperate to eat, grazing his teeth on the back of my neck. I realized he was probably suffering from a hangover to boot. But where would I find us food and safe water? Everything around here had to have been well picked over.

I tried to remember the map of Congo hanging on the wall of the UN station. Ikwa looked so close to Mbandaka, like it almost adjoined. But in such a huge country, a millimeter could mean days of travel.

Thinking of the town made me think, too, of its namesake. I imagined old Ikwa once again sitting on a branch next to me, quietly watching the sun set. Then my imagination provided Mushie, lying next to Anastasia with his arm out, hoping for the smallest touch; Songololo sitting on her mother's belly, dreaming up ways to make trouble. Did they wonder why I had left? Had they figured out that I had something important to do? I wish I could have explained it to them, but explanations were something the bonobos had no way to understand. There was no telling their children they were sick and that was why they didn't want to tickle. There was no saying they had to go up the river to stay alive. There was no saying "Pweto saved our lives, so don't attack him." There was no saying "I'm only going to be gone for a few weeks, take good care of one another and don't think I'm dead." There was no saying "I love you."

That thought, that bonobos saw only behavior and not reasons, had always made me sad. But maybe being able to say "I love you" was just smoke and mirrors compared to having a living being under your fingers. I'd rescued Otto, and hugged him when he needed it and more. That didn't lie. I held myself to the standard of my thoughts and ideals. Otto held me to the standard of my actions. It was something I could learn from, especially in the context of the last few weeks.

Somewhere around midday I was hiking along, singing a lullaby and rubbing Otto's foot, when he unexpectedly tumbled from my back. I saw him squatting on the earth, grimacing apologetically. Beneath him a puddle of loose diarrhea was forming. A lot of it, and very liquid, like someone had poured out a pot of tea. His legs trembled as it continued, then he came back to me and lifted his arms to be picked up, murping. I stroked his head and kissed it, but held him at arm's length as I took some broad leaves and cleaned his bottom as best I could. As soon as I'd finished, more diarrhea came. He frowned, an expression I hadn't seen since our car ride right after I'd picked him up. His little eyes crinkled; he was cramping up.

I thought about the river, those bodies, the water washing over them and then downriver to my Otto, and wished I'd been quick-thinking enough to stop him from drinking. "Otto, honey," I said, rubbing his clammy hand. "It's just a little longer, okay? We'll probably be there by tomorrow."

I cleaned him up again and lifted him. He sighed. Usually he clamped on with his hands and went in for a kiss, but this time he kept his arms at his side, holding on to me with only his legs. So I carried him like a human baby, his body heavy in my arms, singing the same lullabies I'd sung to him back when we'd first started knowing each other. Only now he let himself sleep, gurgling away as I tromped along.

I concentrated on moving forward as quickly as I could. The amount of fluid that had come out of his little body . . . I needed one little pill of Cipro, or a couple of tabs of Imodium. A pharmacy. But there was nothing like that for thousands of miles. All I had was Otto, and all Otto had was me.

I stopped often to check on him, but every time I gently brushed the hair back from his forehead I found him sleeping. I couldn't tell if it was just the rain forest humidity, but his brow felt hot and moist.

I was getting very thirsty, and couldn't really tell anymore if my own hot forehead was from a rash or dehydration. I had returning visions, annoying in their insistence, of the tall tumbler of club soda I used to enjoy on Friday nights with my parents. Clinking ice.

I had a jangling headache, and each footstep was sending bolts up my skull. When we came across a broad flat stone in the muddy earth, remarkably free of termites and ants, I decided to stop us early for the day. I sat with Otto, laying him flat on the warm stone. He didn't sit up, but lifted his arms in the *come and hug* move. I embraced him hard, and when I let go he slumped back to the stone, murping at me.

We both needed hydration, but I couldn't stomach taking in river water, not after what the last gulpful had done to Otto. Most of the fruits the bonobos ate, though, contained water. If I could find some of those and get him to eat . . .

Promising Otto that I wouldn't leave his sight, I explored the wooded area to see what I could find. There were none of the usual shoots, nor could I find any figgy fruits. I went back to check on Otto and found his face in a grimace, body sweaty and twitching.

I gave him a kiss and started exploring in the other direction. There wasn't anything much to eat there, either, but on the way back to Otto I came across a short tree with glossy leaves. Guava. I combed through the branches, hoping to find something to nourish us, but my heart sank; it was the wrong season and the tree wasn't in fruit. But the leaves . . . I remembered Mama Marie-France chewing on her guava leaves for diarrhea. They might help Otto, and might even give us some sustenance in the process. If nothing else, we'd get some tiny amount of water out of them. I ripped down a few branches, feeling very bonobo as I did, and headed back to Otto.

I pulled him into my lap and tried to get him to eat. Nothing doing; he kept dozing off. Running the leaf under his nose, flying it in like an airplane — nothing worked. He kept making his kissy face, which I knew by now meant he might want me to spit water into his mouth. I would have, gladly, but I had none to give.

Otto watched disinterestedly as I selected three particularly luscious leaves from a branch, delicately placed them into my mouth, and started chewing. It was hard going, as the saliva refused to come; it felt like my molars were crushing paint chips. Finally, though, I got the leaves into a semimoist mush. I leaned forward, blew on his lips so he'd part them, and let the wad drop into Otto's mouth. His eyes widened, like I'd committed some minor betrayal, and he pushed the bundle out of his mouth with his tongue. I shook my head, put the wad back in my mouth, chewed it a little more, and let it drop in again.

By now Otto seemed to have come around to the idea. He absently chewed and swallowed while he looked at me. Once the wad was gone, I put a fresh leaf in his mouth and he casually chomped it, looking here, there, and everywhere, as if I couldn't have asked him to do anything more boring. But he swallowed it. I put in another.

That was how sunset found us: huddled together with our bottoms on the sun-soaked stone for warmth, eating guava leaves one by one, otherwise motionless, Otto's frail little shoulders pressed into my belly.

Before we tried to sleep, I took off my T-shirt and tented it on four sticks in the hopes that I'd be able to collect dew come morning. At one point during the long night, Otto rolled away from me and returned a minute later. I wondered what he'd gone off to do, but come morning I found no remnants of anything alarming;

he must have peed. I unhitched my T-shirt and wrung the dew that had soaked it into Otto's mouth. I saved one of the sleeves for myself; the few drops of water disappeared onto my parched tongue like they'd never been.

After a reluctant breakfast of a few guava leaves, we continued our journey. As we walked, my body started to rebel against me. My stomach cramped despite the guava, and I wondered whether it was a matter of time before Otto's fate would be my own. The sun beat down, and I could feel my skin heating and cracking. Otto grew heavy and quiet on my back. I had to force myself to go on.

Step by step. There was no other way to do it.

Even so, I wasn't sure I could. It was a small relief that I eventually stopped feeling my skin and stomach and head, could sense nothing more than the distant pressure of the ground against my feet. I couldn't walk anymore; I could only lumber.

It was amazing how close we'd been to Ikwa that terrible night. Just an hour after we started out I came across the first village houses. I collapsed out of view at the tree line while a mother walked by. She had a bundle of logs on her head and was holding the hand of a crying child, another baby strapped to her back. Three young boys in ratty shirts walked by. One had been stricken by polio, keeping up with his friends by agilely dragging forward with his hands while his ruined legs trailed behind. An old woman followed them, hauling a jug.

We needed that water.

These people were poor, with barely any clothes on their backs, but they were living everyday lives. I had hopes that Ikwa was safe.

I wanted to close my eyes and let myself sleep. But instead I mustered up the courage to leave my hiding spot. As I stepped out of my crouch, my stomach lurched and sensation ripped back through my body, the sudden pain doubling me over. Only by digging my fingernails into my arms could I make the other agonies relent. I trusted to sisterhood first and approached the mother with her crying child. By then she was washing clothes by a stream bank, and she stiffened as I softly called. She stood up, but didn't raise any alarm. I tried to speak to her in French, Lingala, and then English, but she knew none of them. She stared at my agonized smile, and her little daughter stopped crying when she saw Otto, her eyes widening in fascination. The woman left her washing and got up from the bank, gesturing for me to follow.

She brought me to one of the three young boys I'd seen earlier, the one who'd had polio. Struggling to form words, I asked him if he spoke Lingala, and he responded "no" in French. So, in French, I asked him if he could tell me where a great ape release site was nearby. Propped up on his arms and staring up at me, his hands heeled in plastic shoes, he shook his head. But I didn't think he'd understood what I meant. Maybe it was my fault; maybe I was too delirious to make real sentences. I tried again more slowly, and still no luck.

The woman touched my arm and made a spade with her fingers, tapping them on her lips. I nodded. Yes, I was hungry.

We were given cold water to drink that the boy explained in pidgin French was fresh and safe. Squatting beside a blackened tin pot outside the woman's hut, I ate burned rice, crispy and gooey. And bananas. I was blissful and queasy at the same time — I could only just force the food down, even though I was desperately hungry. Otto didn't eat more than a piece of banana, but he did gulp down a ton of water. After we ate, he even allowed the little girl to take him into her lap. Through my haze of discomfort, I pantomimed some of the games he liked to play, and even though Otto was sluggish, they were soon having a companionable time.

A crowd had gathered around us by then, and I asked again in multiple languages if anyone had heard of a release site. They shook their heads in incomprehension, even the boy who spoke French. I pointed at Otto, who was dangling in the little girl's arms, and asked if they knew where any more bonobos were.

Their only response was still the shaking of heads, but an old man said something in their local language, and the boy with polio nodded and gestured for me to follow him.

I pulled Otto from the protesting little girl and wrapped my arms around his sweaty skinny body — *Sorry, but the bonobo comes with me.* Once I stood the world went back to being hot and unsteady, and it was all I could do to stagger after the smiling boy. We finally approached a hut on the far side of the village. He pulled back a dangling grass curtain and ushered me in.

It was cramped inside, the air a stale haze, the char of many fires scarring the dirt center. Otto struggled down from my arms and crawled to the pile of old straw on the far side. There was a body turned away from us on top of the makeshift bed, and without a moment's pause he reached up his little arms and pulled himself right on top of it. "Otto!" I scolded. But then the body turned toward me, and it became a person, more than a person, and all words that were going to follow stopped.

The fever. The pain. I had to have lost my senses. I had to be imagining this. I had to be wrong.

She shook her head and sat up, wrapping her arms around Otto and giving him a big kiss on the top of his head.

Then she looked up at me. Saw me.

It couldn't be happening.

It couldn't be her.

It couldn't be.

She cried out my name.

TWENTY-FOUR

For long moments I lay in the bed, Otto wrapped around me and me wrapped around my mom, her heart beating its familiar rhythm against my ear. I thought I could pick up traces of her usual rosewater scent deep in the fabric of her shirt. With the smell came memories of what we'd once had, of cool mornings sitting in the garden of our Kinshasa house. Her hair, once an even curve from part to shoulder, was now unkempt and frizzled at the roots and tips, smooth only in the middle. She was thinner; Florence Biyoya would never be a skinny woman, mind you, but I did feel the suggestion of a collarbone under my chin.

I must have looked worse for wear, too. She cried when she saw me in the light. Shocked by her shock, I tried to see myself through her eyes: shoes that were little more than oozy soles rattily laced to the bottoms of my feet; gray and wilted socks; pants stained with blood and mud; T-shirt a fungal petri dish; hair a frazzled mess. The smell coming off my flesh had gone from simple stinkiness to something weird and almost appetizing, close to sour-cream-and-onion potato chips.

But none of that changed that we were back to mom and daughter. Well, mom and daughter and ape.

"Mom," I said, "why are you here?"

We sat up and faced each other. Her arms never left me. "Let me look at you again. Oh, my Sophie. I can't say a thing." Her voice cracked, and tears rolled down her red and peeling cheeks. Finally, she got words out. "Why are you here?"

Since she clearly wasn't ready to tell me her story, I told her mine, from the first weeks with Otto to the evacuation van to the attack. I paused there, seeing my mom's face fall, and we hugged for a while. Then I barreled forward and answered her unspoken question by telling her that at least some, and maybe all, of the workers at the sanctuary were dead. She went into a scary, turned-inside place, asking me gray-lipped questions: Who had I witnessed killed? Whose bodies had I seen? Any sign that anyone escaped? I didn't have much information to give, and what I did have wasn't promising.

"I should have been there," she said, blood rushing back into her face. "I'm so sorry I wasn't there to protect you."

It wasn't to me that she was apologizing, I knew; it was to everyone who worked at the sanctuary. But since I was the only one there to accept her regret, it was up to me to bear its weight. "It's okay, Mom. How could you have known?"

"I left you there, *chérie*. I thought you were the safe one, that I was the one in danger, while all this time . . . What did you do, Sophie? How did you survive?"

So I continued. I told her about entering the enclosure, rescuing Songololo from the nursery, meeting the bonobos for the first time. Mom was awestruck. "Eventually you need to tell me everything," she said. "Every last detail. It's lucky that you're a girl. They trust women."

I told her about the weeks I spent in the enclosure, what Otto and I ate and drank, and then about the electricity going off. She cried when I told her about Banalia, then her mouth dropped open again when I told her about Pweto saving us from the hunter and being chased off by Anastasia, about the short time we spent in the countryside as a group, about drugging the bonobos and getting away. I told her about the school for boys, my time at the UN camp, receiving her letter, the two little dead bonobos, the slog to the river, catching a boat up, our capture in Mbandaka, and finally our arrival here.

Long moments went by in the hut, her hands hot against mine. Finally she spoke. "It's a miracle the two of you are alive. I haven't stopped praying for you. When news trickled in here of what was happening in the south, and then Mbandaka was taken, I realized how dangerous everything had gotten. I'd been foolish to assume you were okay because you were near Kinshasa. But by then the rebels were swarming on the river and it got too dangerous to police the island with my bonobos, much less travel downriver. On top of it all I got malaria —"

"Mom!"

She held up a hand. "I'm better now — you've caught me on the mend. I got my men to bring me to this village before they went off to find their families. I had money with me, and someone here is hooked into the black market and was able to get me Malarone. I'm a lot luckier than the villagers themselves."

"I'm so glad you're alive."

"The village chief was willing to take me on as a pensioner," she continued. "I've been stuck in this hut for weeks. For two dollars a day, they've fed me and kept me alive."

"And the bonobos at the release site?"

"As far as I know, fine. There's been no one there to examine them for over a month, but one of the village fishermen passed by a few days ago and heard them calling in the forest."

"When do you think you'll be well enough to move?"

"It's not really a question of how well I am, *chérie*. It's more about when it will be safe enough to head out. The chief of Ikwa has made a truce with one of the warlords, giving him a portion of their crops in return for protection from attack or having to work the mine. We'll be stuck here until help comes, I'm afraid, until the situation gets better enough that your father can work his magic and get us out."

"I'm fine staying here as long as it takes. So long as the three of us are safe and okay," I said.

"And how's our little bonobo?" Mom said, lifting Otto into a standing position. He picked up a handful of straw and threw it at her head, hoping to start a game.

"He was wonderful, Mom. I couldn't have made it here without him, that's for sure."

"Otto!" she said. "Do you hear that? You're my daughter's savior!"

We spent a month recuperating in Ikwa. Even if it had been safe enough to travel, we wouldn't have been able to, since I had pretty bad stomach problems. It was like I'd been staving it all off for survival's sake, and now that things looked better, I allowed myself to be sick.

My mother kept all of us on a diet of rice and guava leaves in the form of hourly cups of steamy tea, with sugarcane swizzle sticks. Otto was particularly fond of those.

Even once I was well enough to walk around, I didn't go far. Like Otto weeks ago, I'd feel an almost constant need to check on my mother and confirm that she was still there. She always was.

It was hardly a chore, our quiet village life, but I was still relieved when a break came. One afternoon a local farmer raced into town providing breathless word that almost all the rebels had left Mbandaka. The rumors were even more promising: International forces had supposedly come through and taken back Kinshasa. The army general was serving as interim president until the UN could organize elections. In ordinary circumstances, having the military in control would hardly be good news, but it felt like the best thing I'd ever heard. Around that same time my mom's hand-cranked field telephone found a signal.

Even better than a recognized government: phone reception.

The first call that reached us through the jammed circuits was from Dad, just minutes after the phone came to life. He must have been dialing my mom's number nonstop since August. I'd been off foraging in the forest with Otto and heard a whooping cry of joy from the distant hut. I ran back, and the sight of my mom's tears and the way she stared straight at me was enough to tell me who had called.

I kneeled beside her, both of our ears against the phone, me pinning Otto down so he didn't try to chew on the receiver. It was astonishing to hear Dad's voice. Even better, he told us he was in Kinshasa; he'd flown in as soon as aid flights had opened up and was calling from Mom's living room. Our home was in bad shape, but the basic structure was still there. He'd already contracted some day laborers to get to work repairing it.

"And the sanctuary?" Mom asked.

TWENTY-FIVE

We took a bumpy prop-plane flight from Mbandaka to Kinshasa, Otto buckled onto my lap by special permission — he thought that was really cool and spent the whole time pressed against the window. When we arrived, I fell into Dad's arms on the freshly paved tarmac. He and my mom shared a quick, complicated hug, parted, and looked away. We didn't go home, but went straight to the sanctuary, lurching up the road in a borrowed Jeep. It was a stunningly sunny day; Congo had entered its rainy season, with its dramatic showers followed by clean and invigorating sunshine.

We rolled down the windows and waved at the local villagers. Familiar women were back to their stalls selling fruits and vegetables; I even recognized the families of goats crossing our path. We could have been entering our prewar lives. When we rounded the final bend, the old wooden sign announcing the sanctuary's visitation policies was still standing there, untouched.

Behind it we could see the sanctuary buildings, soaked in sunlight.

Silent.

For a while after the Jeep rumbled to a stop, none of us got out. I sat in the back, grappling with Otto as he tried to get the door handle open so he could explore. My parents remained in their seats, steeling themselves.

Clément came down the walk. My dad rolled out of the Jeep, followed by my mom. I lay in the backseat with Otto, toying with his ears. We'd have to get out soon, but I couldn't face it yet. There would be bonobo corpses. Many bonobo corpses.

When Otto and I finally got out, I was surprised to see not only Clément, Mom, and Dad, but ancient Mama Marie-France — apparently she'd been away negotiating for extra milk when the rebels had attacked. We stood there for a while, Dad speaking to Clément in a hushed voice and Mom hugging Mama Marie-France. I stood there with Otto, staring at the enclosure fence. It had been violently bent back, and the combatants had been in and out so many times, they'd beaten a muddy trail.

Marie-France confirmed to Mom and me what Dad had already warned us to be true: Many of the sanctuary workers were dead. Mama Brunelle. Emile. Patrice. Others had escaped but hadn't surfaced after the war's end, including Mama Evangeline. After long hugs and sad greetings, Clément took Dad for an appraisal of the buildings, while Marie-France led us to the enclosure.

The first place we passed was the nursery. It was eerie and distancing, like we'd fished an old movie of the nursery out of a vault and played it back without volume. The bright-colored mural was still streaked in blackened mashed banana, but the painted figures stared at us in reproachful stillness. I spotted where Mama Brunelle had died, the mussed dirt and clawed tracks grown over with weeds, but didn't point it out to my mother. When we stopped at various points to discuss the state of the sanctuary, Otto would quickly lose interest, pressing his face against me and play-biting my shirt.

We approached the enclosure fence. Beyond the trampled chain-link we could hear bird songs and the hum of crickets, but no bonobo calls. It was quiet and awful.

My mom put her head in her hands. "It's true. They're all gone."

Marie-France's wizened old eyes crinkled in sympathy as she

explained in Lingala that no one had thoroughly searched the enclosure yet, that maybe some were deep in hiding. But Mom shook her head.

"I'd know it if they were there. I can feel it. It's over."

We trudged on. "We'll put it back together," I said. "Now that the war's done, orphans will start streaming in. I can help you. It'll be hard at first, but with a little —"

My mom gasped and stopped in her tracks.

We'd arrived at Pweto's tiny enclosure. There he was, lying by the water in the classic bonobo relaxation pose, an ankle against the opposite knee. Somewhere during the ruckus of the last few months, he'd found a muddy pair of women's pants and spread them out to lie on, like a beach blanket. He was staring at the sky, broke off for a moment to look at us, and then went back to his meditation.

"Okay, there is one," Marie-France said, beaming. "I wanted it to be a surprise."

"Pweto!" my mom said, grinning. "You devil."

Of all the bonobos . . . I thought, amazed. But I guess it made sense. Being antisocial and aggressive was a flaw in peace and an advantage in war. And because he'd tried to follow us, he hadn't been stuck in his enclosure when the soldiers went in.

"We'll keep everyone else away until we can get his enclosure re-electrified," Marie-France said.

My mom had a little more spring in her step after seeing one of her bonobos alive, and even within my sadness I bubbled on with her about how amazing it was that Pweto would return to his tiny enclosure even though it wasn't electrified anymore. Our voices soon trailed off, though — our tour had come full circle, back to the nursery and its accusatory silence.

After setting a time to reunite with Clément and Marie-France, we slumped back to our car and to our hollowed-out home in Kinshasa. Every belonging that could be carried or unscrewed had been stolen long ago, so for the first few nights we camped on the floor. Over the following days, the living room became our base for dealing with the aftermath, Mom and Dad constantly on their cell phones, recharging them at the American embassy's generator while we waited for the capital's power grid to light back up. It would be an ordeal, putting our home back together, but we were far better off than most: We had international connections and the wad of hundred-dollar bills my father had brought with him.

Mom spent the first few days tracking down the families of her dead employees — though Dad and I kept telling her that their deaths weren't her fault, she vowed to pay for the upkeep of parentless children and partnerless spouses. It made the cost of getting the sanctuary back and running higher and higher, but if she debated whether it was all worth it, she didn't let on. "Our sanctuary was the most functional part of the Kinshasa economy," she kept saying. "Investors know that. I'll find enough funders to get us going again."

My mother chose a picture of Pweto sunbathing as her cell phone wallpaper. For the first time in years, the sanctuary's problem bonobo was an asset. If it hadn't been for him and Otto, I don't know if she would have tried to rebuild. But there were still bonobos to take care of, even if only two, and so the decision was made: Florence Biyoya was officially back at work.

I, too, had things I needed to do. We tripled the payment I had promised Wello. I sealed the money into a pouch with a note and my e-mail address, not that it was likely he'd ever have access to the Internet, and sent it off with the first of my mom's friends to venture north along the river. He wouldn't be back for a few months, so I'd have to wait a while to hear about Wello. Chances were we wouldn't be able to track him down; at least he had the silver necklace.

But that wasn't the most important thing.

The most important thing would require me to go back to the difficult days of August and September.

I had to see for myself if the other bonobos were alive.

TWENTY-SIX

Early one morning, I took Otto and my mother and Clément and retraced the path I'd taken after leaving. I didn't have much optimism that Anastasia and the rest were still alive, but I hoped to find a clue as to what might have happened to them.

Getting to the manioc fields was a lot easier this time, since it was safe to take the road. I was unfamiliar with this way, though, and overshot, realizing I'd gone too far only when we unexpectedly came across a peeling plywood sign that read *SIDA*.

I could sense the old house was empty long before it came into view. Heavily so; some stillnesses are full. Deep greenery had grown over the entrance and ant columns crisscrossed the walk. The front door groaned and tilted free in my hands. Inside, everything was gone. Not only the teacher and the boys; also missing were the furniture and fixtures, and there were long winding gashes puckering the walls where someone had ripped out the wiring. Upstairs was much the same. The room I'd stayed in was stripped clean. In the boys' room, all that remained were the bolts that had attached the bunk beds to the wall; I guess that wood had built someone a cooking fire.

I pondered what had happened. The possibilities were wonderful and terrible. Maybe the teacher had gotten the boys together and escaped. Maybe soldiers had come and recruited the whole bunch. Maybe tearful families had come with open arms to collect their children. Maybe the water had gotten contaminated and cholera had done everyone in, wild animals dragging away the bodies. I would never find out.

It was with heavy footsteps that I continued on my way, my mother and Clément allowing me a respectful silence. The abandoned village wasn't too far off, and already showed signs of rebuilding. Two old women were at work on one of the burned-away roofs, beating thatch against the earth to clear it of bugs before twining it to the roof timbers. We greeted them as we passed, and they briefly acknowledged us before returning to their task. One of them gave Otto a long puzzled look that was hard for me to interpret. I asked her if she had seen any apes like Otto nearby, and she shook her head.

Once on the far side, we patrolled along the jungle line, peering into the vegetation. Excited by this new game, Otto took to the trees, following me from up above.

There was no sign of Mushie, Anastasia, Ikwa, or Songololo.

We continued our investigating, delving deeper into the growth. It was late afternoon, around the time the bonobos would have been eating their fruit lunch back in the sanctuary, when I first heard a high-pitched call. Otto cried back exuberantly, bounding down from a tree and climbing up me to straddle my head, a foot on each of my shoulders as he waved his arms in excitement, slapping a hand over my eyes whenever he lost balance.

Calls answered Otto's, followed by frantic shrieks and crashing sounds from deep in the trees. Clément fled, taking shelter behind the wall of a wrecked hut, but Otto and Mom and I stood ready.

First to bound out of the tree line was Mushie, menacingly brandishing a tiny branch. When he saw who it was, he dropped it and rushed me, in his excitement climbing a nearby sapling and falling off, then picking himself up and racing near, only to skid in the dirt and present his back to me to groom. I did so happily.

Next out of the trees was Songololo, approaching more timidly. She was excited to see Otto, grinning broadly, but still she didn't approach near. I found out why when, a few seconds later, a tiny bonobo clumsily pushed through the leaves to join her. When she saw me and Otto, she froze, chirping, and threw her skinny arms around Songololo's leg.

Mushie threw up his arms, and the little baby toddled over, climbing up his belly so she rested up near his neck. The baby stared at Otto and me with wide eyes. She was frail and wrinkly, probably no more than a few weeks old.

A baby! I couldn't figure it out. Someone in the group had given birth. But Songololo was far too young to get pregnant. That left Anastasia, and maybe Mushie as the father.

She must have been pregnant when we fled the enclosure. They'd been surviving out here in the forest and fields around the abandoned village, and Anastasia had given birth in the wild.

But where was she? And where was old Ikwa?

While I stood there thinking, Songololo and Otto were already working on bringing their friendship back into full swing, shrieking and humping and wrestling.

With the loud calls that Mushie and Otto had made, with the clamor they were making now, Queen Anastasia should have come running from wherever she was to take charge of the situation. Especially with her infant right here. Mushie and Songololo were paying no attention to the jungle behind them, which made me think they weren't anticipating any more bonobos.

Which meant Anastasia and Ikwa were gone. Probably dead. And not too long ago, at least in Anastasia's case, if that infant was alive without a nursing mother around.

To make sure, I tromped through the jungle where Mushie and

Songololo had emerged, the others following curiously a few paces behind.

There was no sign of them.

Finally seeing my mother — whom he'd known since he was a baby, when she'd nursed him on formula in our backyard — Mushie rushed over. As my mom embraced him, the baby transitioned to her, gamely placing frail arms around my mom's neck. Her instant appeal for bonobos appeared not to have diminished one bit. She buried her face into the baby's hair, her expression indecipherable.

We led the ape parade back to the sanctuary, reversing the course I had taken weeks ago. We passed through the sanctuary gate shortly before dark. I was there to witness Mama Marie-France cry for joy for the first time.

Mushie and Songololo were installed back in their old home, only now with a new baby to take care of. My mom entered the enclosure multiple times a day to feed milk to the infant. We discussed names, but nothing stuck. Mom wanted Mbandaka, I guess in honor of what the city had gone through, but I refused; I couldn't think about that horrible place every time I saw this sweet little bonobo.

Otto and I took on the massive administrative tasks involved in reestablishing the sanctuary, maintaining constant phone contact with the new government's rapidly changing Ministry of Environment and keeping track of which officials to curry favor with and which to hold to the fire. Well, that was actually all me. As I made my calls, Otto would munch bananas and stare out the window, or go outside to teach the new arrivals jungle-gym techniques. He wasn't allowed near the youngest orphans, since his lingering cough had returned full force. All human drugs work on bonobos, so whenever his wheezing kept him awake at night I gave him precious cough syrup I bought from the US embassy commissary.

One afternoon, as I sat at my mother's desk, filling out and stamping paperwork, my cell phone rang. Recognizing a government number, I picked up quickly. "Hello?"

"Yes, I'm calling for Florence Biyoya, please."

"This is her daughter, Sophie. May I ask who is calling?"

"Yes," said a female voice. "This is the assistant to Monsieur Ngambe, Social Minister."

I sat up straight. "The social minister? Of all of Congo?"

"Yes. Mademoiselle Biyoya, how can I phrase this? First I could ask this: Do you have a truck to transport bonobos?"

"We have a small vehicle, yes. Do you have a confiscated orphan? Let us know where you are keeping it, and we can —"

"Mademoiselle Biyoya, that is not quite it."

"Tell me what I can do to help you."

"Ah. Well . . . we have eighteen."

It took me a moment to find words. "You have eighteen orphans?"

"Not exactly. You see . . . the new president has finally gotten around to cleaning out the former president's winter palace. But when we went to recover and renovate it, we . . . were not able to enter. There are bonobos inside. And they do not want us to disturb them."

I smiled so widely it hurt. "I see. Where is this palace located?" She told me. It was no more than ten miles along the road. "Is someone there now?" I asked.

"I'm actually outside the gate right now," the assistant said. "We're at a loss here, and the minister is getting angry. Please come as soon as you can."

Clément drove me and my mom there right away. Otto was particularly under the weather that day, so I left him in the care of

Mama Marie-France, knocked out by cough syrup, snoring under a tree.

We found the assistant midway down the drive, pacing next to her black SUV and wringing her hands. She led us to the palace gates.

What a sight. On the other side of the elegant wrought-iron entrance lay what looked like a bonobo theme park: bonobos draped over cupid planters; bonobos pooping in a birdbath; bonobos chasing one another up and down Grecian statues, leaping from the head of Aphrodite and swinging around Poseidon's trident to land in the arms of Zeus. They'd stolen clothes and furniture from the palace and strewn it on the lawn. Most were ruined, but one of the bonobos ran past wearing a dripping-wet military beret over her face.

There had to be half the nursery here, and a handful of the adults. They'd escaped the soldiers.

And they were having the time of their lives.

I put my arms around my mother. "It seems a shame to make them leave."

PART SEVEN: CONGO

TWENTY-SEVEN

I still have it, all these years later, there on my bookshelf.

The sneaker.

The knot Otto made in the laces when I was trying to escape from Bouain was a convoluted mess, made worse by repeated bathings in river muck. In the end, I had to cut the shoe off to remove it. But that wonderful chaotic sphere of shoelace that Otto had created, and in so doing saved my life, still crowns it on top.

I didn't wind up going back to Miami after the war, instead staying with my mother and attending the American School of Kinshasa. After a month or two, my dad returned to the States, and my mom and I settled into life in Congo. I'd harbored a fleeting hope they'd get back together, but it never happened. I guess the divorce had been for more reasons than I'd been old enough to realize. Once high school was finished, my parents insisted that I go to the States for college — and given the state of the universities in Congo, I agreed. So I moved to Atlanta and went to Emory.

The only souvenir I've kept of that war year is the sneaker. Visitors who come over — friends, boyfriends — often ask me about it. At first I'd put on a pot of coffee and go into the whole story, not starting with the attack on the sanctuary but going way back, to the nineteenth century when the Belgians invaded Congo up through the wars in the nineties. But the memories were so raw and so painful that my friends' inability to find words to say after

I'd finished only pushed me deeper into the sadness of what had happened. They'd want to see photos of Otto, and I couldn't stand to bring them out, not now that he was gone. It's like I'm back to when I was eight starting school in Florida, and people would ask me what Congo was like; I'd say, "Poor," and move on. Except now it's "That was the shoe I wore during the war," and we move on. No mention of the bonobo no longer by my side.

But I didn't move on from Congo, not in the most important parts of me. I wound up concentrating my course work on international politics and development, and now I've graduated and am on an AirFrance plane beginning its descent into familiar old Kinshasa. The business plan for a community development nonprofit is nestled in my carry-on briefcase, alongside a photo of that sneaker and its jumble of shoelace.

They say Congo is improving, but you can't tell from the airport. It's still a mess of barely paid employees searching for any excuse to exact a bribe. A big goal I have for my new organization is to make Congo accessible to tourists; I'm trying to network with European and American travel sites to arrange group visits to my mom's sanctuary and to the gorilla hot spots in the east, and in so doing infuse money into the economy, not the bureaucrats' pockets where so much foreign aid ends up. First step is reining in the bribe-happy airport employees. It's going to take a long time, so today I've got a ten-dollar bill in each pocket of my pants, one for each person who extorts money from me just to get out of the terminal.

Mom's waiting outside, and gives me one of those long warm hugs that I crave so much. We get into the backseat of the sanctuary vehicle, and before we're halfway home she's going on and on about all the eligible Congolese boys she knows, friends of friends of her friends, every one of them extraordinarily handsome and well-educated. This has been a recent development, my mom getting boy crazy on my behalf. It all triggered when I told her I'd gotten engaged to a Senegalese guy I met at Emory; I guess she was hoping that I'd settle down with someone from Congo.

My fiancé is thrilled that we're moving to Kinshasa, and once he's here I'm sure my mom will come around. He's a teacher, and wonderful with children, so my hope is maybe he'll lead up the education arm of the sanctuary, introducing Congolese schoolchildren to their national heritage, doing something to make animals in Lingala more than the plural of *meat*.

To stave off the impending marriage argument, I ask my mom about the sanctuary. It's got multiple enclosures now, and is bigger than it ever was before the war. And her release project, after a rough start, has turned out to be a great success. She has more bonobos living in the wilds of the release site than she has in captivity, an achievement she brings up often. The sanctuary is still the best-functioning part of the Kinshasa economy and an important model for how the country can lift its people out of poverty; her staff roster has reached one hundred, not including the many farmers who produce the tons of fruit the sanctuary goes through each month.

I don't mention Otto, and I'm relieved that she doesn't bring him up.

I've timed my arrival to coincide with the latest phase of her release project, partially because it means I'll get to go back to Mbandaka with her. Now that a few years have gone by, I want to see the city again for myself and come to terms with the site of my personal horror.

When we arrive, I see that the city is doing pretty well — it's even got an outdoor café with real espresso drinks! And a botanical garden! Many people say it's made more progress than Kinshasa, and I can see why. The rotting post office is now a little movie theater, for example. After fifty years' absence, movie theaters are back in Congo.

The people of Ikwa are still scrawny and smiley, and they host a big feast of fish and groundnuts and safou fruit for our crew. In return, we present them with burlap bags of salt and a few kilos of precious soap. I also give them a stack of clothing from America, and they're most excited by the price tags and labels, which get posted as artwork throughout the village. We spend the night there on the way to the release site, leaving the bonobos tranquilized and snoozing in their transports. Despite our efforts to shoo them away, the local children spend hours staring at the bonobos and trying to get them to wake up. The next day we're into motorized pirogues and heading to the site.

There are four bonobos in this release group. When Mom told me who was included, I knew I had to be here. Mushie is among them, as is Songololo, now an adult. The pair has been pretty much inseparable since their return to the sanctuary. The smallest of the release bonobos is only seven years old. She's Anastasia's war orphan, whom I named Congo. I was still in my wound-up postwar state when I named her, and I think the name's a little silly now. Sometimes I call her Democratic Republic to tease myself, but I don't think little Congo likes that very much.

It's late afternoon by the time our pirogues reach the island. It takes four men to lift each crate, with its groggy bonobo contents, onto the beach. There's a lot of shouting, and the pirogues nearly capsize multiple times in the process. But the crates are eventually all onshore. To make the bonobos feel secure, we decide to keep them in the crates until morning, sleeping in tents alongside them while we wait for the tranquilizers to wear off. Tonight we'll position the crates on the other side of the electrified gateway, then tomorrow we'll release these bonobos to join the wild ones.

But that's all for later. Right now I have a different mission. I ask my mom if I can take a pirogue and do a circuit of the island. She nods, with a half smile that tells me she knows exactly what I have in mind.

One of the porters offers to take me, but I tell him I want to do this alone. And so, in the pink-blue light of the approaching sunset, I motor off to the far side of the island.

To Otto.

I kept him by my side all that first year, only gradually introducing him to the nursery. I weaned him off me by spending half an hour at a time out of his presence, then an afternoon, and finally days away once he was comfortable with his new friends. Whenever I returned, though, he would leap to me with his arms over his head, desperate for a hug, like he'd only been biding time until I came back. I'd cry, he'd giggle, and I would immediately start dreading the next moment we'd have to part.

By the time I left for college, Otto was a full-on adult bonobo, slender and elegant, with a part right along the center of his head, wiry hair flopping on either side. Dashing, I thought, in a scrawny poet kind of way. He had huge, expressive eyes like a manga character, and (I'm proud to say) was catnip to the ladies. And to the gentlemen, for that matter — such is the way of bonobos.

A couple of years ago, my mom called to tell me that Otto had a goiter, and even though it was the middle of exam week, I almost got on the next plane to come save him. But it turned out that goiters are fairly common in bonobos, and harmless. It went away on its own after a few months, but until then he never left my mind. He's always on my mind, to tell the truth. My thoughts don't wander anymore; he's where they go as soon as they're idle.

Except for the hum of the motor, being in this pirogue feels familiar from my time with Wello. The lapping sounds are both soothing and anxiety producing. As I circle the island, searching for signs of bonobos, my heart races with a sense of all that's past and all that's happening now.

As I near the top of the island, the trees give way to low marsh. Mom told me the bonobos don't spend much time here, preferring the coverage of trees during the rainy season. So I speed along, slowing only after I've gone around the tip and am on the island's other side and back to a forested zone. But I still can't find any bonobos.

Though I have only a half hour more of sunlight, I cut off the motor and idle; I fear that the noise is chasing the bonobos away. I hear occasional crashes from the tree line, but each time it's a lizard plopping into the water or a bird taking flight.

But then a black shape appears at a treetop. It disappears almost immediately, and I question what I saw: It was definitely a bonobo, but was it Otto?

The bonobo reappears on the shallow beach, and I know it's him. The part in his hair, the searching eyes, the delicate limbs. My Otto! I stand in the pirogue and wave. He sways uncertainly on his two legs and peers at me. I cry out his name.

Immediately he shrieks, grinning and jumping and slapping the ground. He runs back and forth, keeping his eyes on me. He lifts his arms: *Come give me a hug.*

Teary, I lift my arms back. It's an essential principle of the project that humans not come in direct contact with the released bonobos. To keep them safe from people who might come to the island to do them harm, the bonobos mustn't stay too used to us.

He lifts his arms again, more energetically. *Come give me a hug! Come give me a hug!*

Oh, Otto, I wish I could.

I stand in the pirogue, calling his name over and over, talking nonsense to keep him near. But I don't need to work to keep his attention; he seems like he would never leave. He paces back and forth on the shore, makes a couple of steps into the water as if to swim out. But bonobos can't swim, so he heads back to land, arms fussily over his head to keep them dry. He paces the bank and murps at me. Eventually he gives up and slumps on the beach, head in his hands, sun glinting gold in his eyes. He stares at me.

"Otto," I say finally as the sun pulls back its last rays. "I love you so much."

He stares back and lifts his arms one last time. *Come give me a hug.*

But I can't.

Before it gets too dark, I motor up the pirogue and head back to camp.

My mom helps me off when I get there. She asks me if I saw Otto, and knows the answer when I'm unable to respond. She leads me to our tent, where I stare up at the fabric walls until sleep finally takes over.

The next morning, I wake up to the sound of my mom unzipping and then zipping up our tent. I roll over and try to go back to sleep, listening to the hissing gas as she cranks up the camping stove to make tea. Then the tent unzips again, and she's shaking me awake. "Sophie! Get out here!"

I slip my feet into my shoes, slapping at the mosquitoes that have already whizzed into the tent. "Mom," I say, "you have to be careful about letting the —"

I stop midsentence.

There, not more than a few feet away on the other side of the enclosure fence, is Otto. He's curled up on his side, fast asleep, facing us, arms reaching out and hands curled in the soil.

And not just Otto. Next to him is a young female bonobo with an infant, also asleep. His little legs are flung over his mother, slowly rising and falling on her belly.

Bonobos aren't monogamous, so it's impossible to know who is whose father, but these feel like Otto's close companions. He followed my pirogue in the dark, found out where the camp was, went back into the forest, and brought these two out to meet me.

"Mom," I whisper, "I know we aren't supposed to get close to them, but I . . . could I . . . ?"

She looks around guiltily. "Only for a minute, before anyone else comes out of their tents. They can't know I'm soft on this rule."

Mom flips a switch on the line from the solar panels to the enclosure, and the electricity flicks off. I creak open the door and step inside. Back into an enclosure: It's in such a different circumstance this time, but memories return of my flight from the UN peacekeepers so many years ago. Then I draw near Otto and his family and all of that history vanishes. This is now.

I kneel by sleeping Otto and watch him. Those are the same feet I blew raspberries into. This is the same wrist Patrice held tight to force in an IV. Those are the hips, now so sturdy and muscled, that once were covered in blisters. Those are the hands that had looped so easily around my neck.

Otto stirs from sleep and opens his eyes. When he sees me, they widen further and he sits up. He murps quietly and lifts his arms, lean muscles flexing. This time I can hug him, and the clasp he returns is powerful, many times stronger than any human embrace I will ever experience.

He sighs quietly into my ear, and in return I stroke the thick hair of his back. The activity has woken up the baby, and the little guy groggily lifts his head and stares at me, calm and curious. I try to extract myself from Otto's fierce grip, but he won't let go. So I talk to him. "He's very cute, your boy," I say. "Looks a lot like you once did."

It's only by digging my fingers into his ribs that I'm able to make Otto let go. He gives great big raspy laughs, rolls onto his back, and smiles, exposing strong creamy teeth. His baby clambers over his sleeping mother to join in, crawling right over Otto's face to get closer to me. I don't tickle him, though — this little bonobo has never had direct contact with humans, and I'd like to keep it that way.

I take advantage of the distraction to stand up. Otto's immediately on his feet, placing the infant on his back and stepping toward me. When I reach the fence he shrieks to warn me about the electricity. But I know something he doesn't, of course, and step through the doorway and shut it quickly. My mom flicks the power back on.

Otto stands as close as he can to the fence and purses his lips, making his kissy-kissy face. I lean as close as I can and blow air over his mouth. He smiles and purses his lips again, bobbing his head.

On the other side of the fence lie the release bonobos. Within her crate, Songololo is now awake and down from her nylon hammock, standing at the bars and watching Otto curiously. There's nothing apprehensive about her expression; she remembers Otto and seems excited to get out and greet her old friend and his new companions.

Mom wakes up the porters and the vet and gets them ready for the release. Ropes have been tied to the crate gates, threaded through the fence to our side of the enclosure. All we have to do is pull. While the rest of the group sips tea and discusses potential complications, I stand at the fence, blowing on Otto's face and saying my good-byes.

Once they've heard the commotion, the rest of the semiwild bonobos will soon be here, so my mom decides now is the time. Three of the porters take up the other ropes, and I ask for the fourth. Otto watches me, intrigued. I see his eyes follow the rope to the crate, and he goes over to it, sitting in front and waiting for the door to open. My smart boy.

He lies down on all fours, peering between the bars. With a creaking slide, the door pulls open. Otto lays his arms down, palms open, in the bonobo sign of trust, as little Congo takes a wide-eyed look around and ventures out.

AUTHOR'S NOTE

Though the specific conflict I've written about in *Endangered* is fictional, the lengthy history of violence in the Democratic Republic of Congo is not. Though as of publication there is still widespread fighting in the east, Congo is not officially at war today. That's a semantic technicality rather than a reality: Numerous rebel groups are active near the Rwandan border, plundering resources and recruiting child soldiers and raping women — by UN estimates, a thousand a day. Attempts to rein in the violence are often ineffective and, even worse, can lead to retaliatory massacres.

The Congolese began the twentieth century toiling under colonialism and ended it in the midst of armed conflict. There is more reason for optimism today, however, than there has been for years. Violence may still be endemic, but the existence of the nation itself isn't in question, as it was in the 1990s. Though the last twenty years have seen assassinations and regime changes, in the current moment few are anticipating the capital could fall as it does in *Endangered*. But the United Nations still sees a need to maintain its largest peacekeeping operation in the world in Congo, keeping forty thousand units on the ground. Whenever there is an election, as in 2006 and 2011, the world holds its breath to see whether the first stirrings of Congolese democracy will hold.

The conflict and the reasons for it are diffuse. This book is a work of fiction, and is neither a recounting of real events nor an attempt to get to the bottom of the reasons for the fighting. The Democratic Republic of Congo is an enormous country, rivaling Western Europe in landmass, and, with almost seventy-two million people, is the world's largest francophone country. The scale of what has happened there — the five million and counting dead, the grotesque brutality of much of the slaying — is hard to comprehend. Unlike the cases of the most infamous villains of recent history (Hitler, Stalin, Pol Pot, Milosevic), the killing in Congo is less the product of an ironfisted regime than of the lack of one, the consequence of a government so impoverished by corruption that it doesn't have the resources to combat the lawless factions terrorizing a huge territory.

In the midst of all this live the bonobos. The Democratic Republic of Congo is the only place in the world where they exist in the wild. Though monkeys have always been eaten in Congo, almost all of the tribes in the country have had taboos against eating great apes, the tailless intelligent primates known in most local languages as "mock men." But with the rampant starvation that comes along with such a long war, those taboos have eroded. The story of each orphan that arrives at the bonobo sanctuary in Kinshasa is virtually the same:

Hunters enter the forest. They wait for nightfall, when the bonobos call loudly to one another while bedding down in their tree nests. They hide out beneath them and, come morning, shoot or machete as many as they can. The adults they eat immediately or smoke to sell as bushmeat. Infants can fetch upwards of $50 on the black market, or $1,500 if they're smuggled out and sold internationally. (One of Lola Ya Bonobo's orphans was rescued after being imaged in a Paris airport security scanner, crammed into a carry-on.) When the average DRC income is $12 a month, either amount is a windfall, so the infants are caged and transported to marketplaces in the larger cities. Most don't survive the trip. Each bonobo who grows up in the sanctuary serves as an effigy for the many more that have died in the process of getting him there.

In *Endangered* I've strived to remain true to what scientists know of bonobo behavior. I'm sure there are inaccuracies and errors, for which I of course take sole responsibility. Similarly, the conflict I've fictionalized is, I'm sure, untrue in a hundred ways to how a full-on civil war might transpire. I have a lot of hope that the Congolese people are heading into better times. But, all the same, writing about war didn't require that much speculation.

NEW YORK, DECEMBER 2011

A Q&A WITH
ELIOT SCHREFER

Q: How did you wind up writing about bonobos and Congo?
A: Congo, formerly known as Zaire, is the same land Joseph
Conrad wrote about in *Heart of Darkness*. The state department sug-
gests no nonessential travel there. I'm not quite what you'd call a
tough guy, so how did I end up going? The answer's more *GQ* than
National Geographic: a pair of pants.

I couldn't figure out where my new Bonobo brand khakis had
gotten their name, so I hit the Internet. A few months later I was
sitting on a porch in Congo, talking with the founder of the world's
only bonobo sanctuary about how odd it is to find yourself
reflected back in a creature that isn't even human.

I knew Congo was the home of the world's deadliest conflict
since World War II, but not much more than that — I'd always
skipped the page if I found an article on the violence, figuring it
was depressing and there was nothing I could do. But the bonobos
were a new way in. Their evolutionary history and their current
plight are closely linked to what it means to be a human living in
a world divided between development and deprivation. In my first
days reading about them, I found my apathy punctured and was
gulping down more and more material about both primates and
politics.

The moment I knew the bonobos would become a novel,
though, was when I read about Kinsuke, an orphan who had
arrived at the bonobo sanctuary too frail to survive. In her final
moments, she had held tightly to the rope that her captors had
used to restrain her, refusing to let it go. It was her only possession

left after everything else had been taken from her, and she died clutching it to her cheek. Sometimes your greatest torment can also be your greatest treasure. Writing *Endangered* was a way of trying to get my head around that.

Q: You traveled to Kinshasa in June 2011 to stay at the bonobo sanctuary run by Claudine André. Were you intimidated by the trip?
A: The first sign that I was leaving my comfort zone was that Expedia and Travelocity didn't permit Kinshasa, a city of ten million people, as a destination. Luckily for me, Orbitz had no such qualms. When I sent my passport to the DRC embassy, it came back with a fuzzy rubber-stamped visa, hand-numbered.

When I went to the doctor and asked him to give me whatever inoculations I would need for DRC, he started chatting about malaria and cholera while he lined up a drawer's worth of syringes on his desktop. Eight needles later, I walked out of there with massively punctured biceps and a bad case of nerves.

Months of research and one highly anxious mother later, I was on my way, flying from New York to Washington to Ethiopia to Brazzaville and finally to Kinshasa. I was scared, sure, but mostly I was excited. I was about to meet my first bonobos.

I flew into the western part of Congo, almost a thousand miles away from Goma and the Rwandan border, where the worst fighting is. The Lola Ya Bonobo sanctuary is very well run, and they took great care of me. There was even air-conditioning! It was the easiest way imaginable to visit Congo.

That said, being in Congo also meant losing the safety net I'd had living in America. I felt it most as I was leaving Kinshasa and got hassled for bribes at the airport. A lot of bribes: A good half-dozen people, from airline representatives to security agents, pressed for handouts. I had read about the airport kleptocracy and came supplied with granola bars, which I gave out instead. For some reason passing people food instead of dollars made me feel like less of a dupe. I realized, though, as I made my slow and almost amusingly harassing passage through the airport (one security agent even told me she wouldn't let me through unless I married her and got her a US passport) that in the back of my head was running a ticker-tape thought that *if this gets bad I'll ask for a supervisor.* But the supervisor had already asked me for a bribe. And the police can't always be trusted, so outside of the US embassy, there was nowhere to escalate the problem, if it came to that. It all made me realize how much faith we have in our Western institutions, and how important that faith is to our going about our daily lives in relative calm. Michela Wrong writes that it's a discomfort common to first-time visitors to Congo, realizing "their well-being depends on the condescension of strangers."

Q: Obviously, in a book about an endangered animal in Congo, suffering is going to be a theme. Did you discover anything about it that surprised you?
A: How people get through suffering was on my mind as I started, but in spending time learning about the bonobos and the recent history of Congo, that question got a little more tailored.

My own personal journey was realizing that you don't have to ignore a lesser suffering because there's a greater one out there — that's a sure route to paralysis. This one Sophie is able to come to terms with fine; she wonders how people can devote their lives to improving the lot of animals when there is so much human anguish, but the presence of Otto in her life is enough to settle the debate. He needs her, and she loves him; it's that simple. I had a much harder time getting my mind around it. Though I've always been more of an environmentalist than a humanitarian, writing a book about Congo that focused on bonobos first and humans second, when there is such a humanitarian crisis going on, gave me pause. I asked myself: Is it moral to concern ourselves with nonhuman suffering? But that artificial classroom question of human vs. animal disappeared when I actually visited, because it became clear that the two issues can't be separated. How we treat the environment is inextricably linked to how we treat one another. The same systems of social power — in Congo's case, a corrupt government and rapacious corporate forces — treat underprivileged humans and animals in much the same way.

Q: Since gaining independence from Belgium in 1960, the Democratic Republic of Congo has suffered from a succession of dictators and widespread violence, while other neighboring countries, such as Congo-Brazzaville or Central African Republic, have had a somewhat easier time. What's kept Congo back?
A: Everyone's got a different theory for why Congo has had such a hard time. A lot of the seeds were planted back when King Leopold II of Belgium was in control — he was merciless in using slave labor on his rubber plantations, including cutting off the hands of slaves who tried to run away, and that devaluation of human life stayed on after the Belgians fled. There was an attitude among the colonists that empowerment of native Congolese would subvert the country: *"Pas d'élites, pas d'ennemis."* ("No elites, no enemies.") After the Belgians left, there were only seventeen Congolese with college educations. Untrained men were rushed into government posts with the American CIA playing a major part, and the country was born with a cramp in its side.

Obviously there's more to it than that, though. It seems DRC's main curse is the very richness of its land. Elsewhere politicians, even the most selfish, need a tax base to get money. In Congo, all a politician needs is to pull minerals out of the earth and sell them. People — and bonobos — are less important than efficient mining. It's an irony about Africa that its most resource-rich countries are often its most unstable.

Q: Bonobos are closely related to chimpanzees, and for a long time weren't thought of as a separate species. Even once they were, they were called pygmy chimpanzees until the classification was changed to bonobo in 1954. Now that they're standing on their own two feet, so to speak, what other differences between the two species have come out?

A: What I love most about the peaceful, matriarchal bonobos is that they prove war and conflict aren't inevitable.

When anthropologists first looked to find our evolutionary origins, they settled on *Australopithecus*, which is seen as a now-vanished midway point between us and chimpanzees. *Australopithecus* wasn't thought to be a friendly guy. It behaved a lot like a chimp. It killed infants so its own offspring could prosper. Its sexual life was pretty close to continual rape.

Bonobos didn't enter into anthropologists' picture of our origins because their natural shyness meant no one knew much about them until recently. They're as genetically close to us as chimps, if not more so, and yet they aren't nearly as violent. The big difference: the Congo River. It split the two groups, with bonobos getting the south of the river, where they didn't have to compete with gorillas for food. Given their relatively plentiful resources, they didn't have to evolve the same systems of intense competition and squabbling. Social interaction and support became more important than fighting for resources, and so they turned to sex as their means of structuring society instead of violence, and the resulting profound sense of intimacy and companionship led to a far better lot for females and children. With bonobos, mothers are in charge, and everyone benefits.

Q: What do you make of the irony that a symbol for humankind's potential to avoid war and aggression lives only in one of the most war-torn countries in the world?

A: I don't think it's reductive to say that the bonobos have a lot to say about how Congo can get out of its plight. Studying how bonobos diverge from chimps (and why) reminds us that the difference between widespread conflict and widespread harmony lies in access to resources. The Congolese in the east have scant support from the government — little education, roads, hospitals, police — and so are vulnerable to militia groups who rove, raping women and recruiting boys. But would the militias persist if there weren't such a struggle for resources? When there's enough to eat, you don't have to use violence to get your dinner. Just ask the bonobos. They're right there in Congo's backyard.

Q: What do Congo and its bonobos need now?

A: I'm no Congo scholar. But a strong legal system would be a start, with a court of justice that could hold the country's highest executives responsible for misdeeds and stolen money. With that faith in authority at the center, the rest of Congolese society could follow suit. Beyond that, as Congo's economy continues to grow it will be able to employ more people and give them a baseline of subsistence that will prevent them from needing to trek into the jungle to trap food. Tourism will be essential for this, and in that way Lola Ya Bonobo serves a dual function: providing a home for orphans and serving as what many say is the best-functioning element of the Congolese economy.

Q: What can someone sitting in relative luxury do to help?

A: Conservation takes money, and holding fund-raisers to help those working to maintain environmental integrity throughout the world is a great way to help them do their work and simultane-ously get the word out about the plight of the bonobo. There are only a few thousand bonobos left, and the numbers continue to diminish. But the fledgling national parks in Congo can reverse the downward trend, for the bonobos and the other animals — like the forest elephants and okapi — that will also benefit. Congo's lack of economic development has a silver lining, since a lot of its land is still pristine and untouched by roads or logging. Now is the time to act and preserve it.

Among the best groups working in conservation today, with projects that directly impact the well-being of bonobos, are:

African Wildlife Foundation (www.awf.org)
World Wildlife Fund (www.wwf.org)
Conservation International (www.conservation.org)
Arcus Foundation (www.arcusfoundation.org)

And, focusing more specifically on bonobos, are:

Bonobo Conservation Initiative (www.bonobo.org)
Terese and John Hart (www.bonoboincongo.com)
Friends of Bonobos, the nonprofit behind Lola Ya Bonobo (www.friendsofbonobos.org)

While I was in Kinshasa, I spoke to Terese Hart, a conser-vationist who has been fighting for bonobos for years. I asked her what someone who is getting started could do to help. Her answer surprised me: Learn how to do field observations. She meant taking college courses that involved fieldwork, but I was reminded of Jane Goodall's description of her youth in her remark-able memoir for children, *My Life with the Chimpanzees*. She would lie for hours in the garden of her English house, staring at dogs, cats, and birds, and take notes. For her, that's how it all started. Observation. Dr. Hart was talking about how to make a good research scientist, but I think her advice can apply to us all: Look. Notice.

ACKNOWLEDGMENTS

The book that cemented my desire to write about bonobos was the terrific and heartfelt *Bonobo Handshake* by Vanessa Woods, detailing her time spent learning about and living with bonobos in Congo. I took frequent inspiration from her accounts of her real-life experiences. Vanessa was so patient with my questions and queries, and it was through our conversations and her book that I discovered Claudine André, founder of Lola Ya Bonobo. Learning about Madame André's years of work creating a great ape sanctuary in one of the most corrupt countries on earth, I felt my affection for bonobos become fascination and eventually determination. For those of you who read French, her memoir, *Une Tendresse Sauvage*, is fascinating. The character of Anastasia in *Endangered* is an homage to Mimia, one of André's most precious bonobos who came to the sanctuary after living a life among humans in Kinshasa and unfortunately died in childbirth in 2010. I've borrowed Madame André's method of naming bonobos after places in Congo.

The gorillas had Dian Fossey, the chimpanzees have Jane Goodall, and the bonobos have Claudine André. She's perhaps the most charismatic person I've met, and the bonobos couldn't ask for a better figurehead. Evelyne Pitault and Jeanne d'Arc, two long-term volunteers, made me feel very welcome at Lola. The surrogate mothers Yvonne Vela, Henriette Lubondo, Espérance Tsona, and Micheline Nzonzi walk softly and carry big sticks. Thanks, Nurse Anne-Marie Ngalula, for the many strolls around the sanctuary. Terese and John Hart, I'm so glad you were able to take time out to have lunch right before setting off for Kindu.

Hairy little Oshwe, thanks for spending your banana-and-peanut breakfasts on my lap.

Of all the books about Congo, I keep coming back to Bryan Mealer's *All Things Must Fight to Live*. Bracing, distilled, and unfiltered. Bryan was also kind enough to take time out from lawn mowing to talk to me on the phone. For learning more about life in Congo during a time of conflict, Human Rights Watch's reports "Trail of Death" and "The Christmas Massacres" were difficult reading, but very informative. Michela Wrong's *In the Footsteps of Mr. Kurtz*, Jason Stearns's *Dancing in the Glory of Monsters*, Adam Hochschild's *King Leopold's Ghost*, Charles London's *One Day the Soldiers Came*, Jeffrey Tayler's *Facing the Congo*, Tim Butcher's *Blood River*, and Philip Gourevitch's *We Wish to Inform You That Tomorrow We Will Be Killed with Our Families* were also useful.

Those wanting to learn more about bonobos would do well by starting with Vanessa Woods's book. Also very useful were Frans de Waal's *Bonobo: The Forgotten Ape* and *Our Inner Ape*, Desmond Morris's *Planet Ape*, Paul Raffaele's *Among the Great Apes*, and Boesch, Hohmann, Marchant, et. al's *Behavioral Diversity in Chimpanzees and Bonobos*. *NOVA* also released an episode, titled "The Last Great Ape," all about bonobos. Radiolab's episode 702, reporting on a chimpanzee named Lucy, who was raised by humans and later released in Gambia, was also inspirational.

Marie Rutkoski helped me edit this book over pasta, Daphne Grab over scones, and Donna Freitas over olive oil cake. The rest of my writing group, Marianna Baer, Elizabeth Bird, Kekla Magoon, and Jill Santopolo, did most of their work over chicken sandwiches. All were invaluable. My mother remains my best line editor. My partner, Eric Zahler, has listened to more facts about bonobos than anyone ever should have had to, and I'm so grateful that his passion for them rivals my own. Next time I go to see the bonobos, he's coming with me.

Team Bonobo wouldn't be complete without the tireless and inspired help of my agent, Richard Pine, who has been one of this book's fiercest advocates. And David Levithan: If it weren't one hundred percent morally reprehensible I'd smuggle you a baby bonobo to look after. If you took care of her even slightly as well as you took care of this book, she'd be one lucky little ape.

ELIOT SCHREFER

is the author of *Threatened, The Deadly Sister, The School for Dangerous Girls, Glamorous Disasters,* and *The New Kid.* He lives in New York City when he is not visiting bonobos in Congo. Visit him online at www.eliotschrefer.com.

TURN THE PAGE
FOR A SNEAK PEEK
OF ELIOT SCHREFER'S
THREATENED.

While Prof drank his tea the next morning, I examined the snare. Making it must have taken a lot of effort; it had an elegantly carved disc of wood at its center, with fasteners of the perfect thickness for the vine to slip through. But that work had paid off — I remembered how easily I'd been hoisted into the air, the amount of force the simple device had been able to muster. The snares spent their existences like I'd spent mine, announcing themselves only in the quietest moments.

The moment Prof had finished his mint tea, I eagerly led him toward the spot on the faint trail where I'd heard the chimpanzee scream and crash away. He pulled us short well before we got to the site. "Look," he said, grabbing my arm and whirling.

It was a dead body.

The skeleton dangled from a wrist, still striped with sinew and scraps of skin and straight black hair. At first I thought someone had hung a human skeleton from a tree to warn us. But then I realized it wasn't a human and that it hadn't been hung; it had been trapped. The liana vine was older and brown this time, but I recognized the snare's knots.

"Is that a mock man?" I whispered.

Prof nodded sadly. "Yes. It was a chimpanzee. Do you still have the knife on you?"

I nodded, then climbed the tree and cut the skeleton loose. It clattered to the ground, flies and maggots and scraps of skin falling from it. Some rotted tissue opened up at the center of the corpse, letting out a terrible smell. I tugged at Prof's sleeve. "We'll be sick! There's nothing you can do with the body."

Prof dry heaved for a moment, then approached the corpse. Clutching the vine, he dragged the skeleton to the river and hurled it in. We watched it disintegrate in the current. When Prof returned he had tears in his eyes. "It is illegal to hunt chimpanzees! They are endangered! And this hunter set a snare that he didn't return to. This chimpanzee probably took over a week to die from infection on its wrist. An exquisitely sensitive creature, with family and hopes, died a very painful, lonely death."

I imagined hanging by my wrist from a tree, crying alone. The pain spreading from my wrist to my arm, watching my body rot until I died of thirst. That was often how I'd seen snared animal corpses for sale in Franceville: One limb had rotted too much to eat and had been chopped off. Even if these mock men were monsters, no creature deserved to die that way.

"It is awful," I said.

"The irresponsibility of it," Prof said. "We will find this hunter!"

"Okay, Prof. Of course we will," I said quietly.

I thought Prof might want to return to camp after that, but he wordlessly pressed on.

Once we'd reached the clearing where I'd heard the chimpanzee, we stood still for a long time. Omar had followed us at a distance, emerging from the green and clutching my shirttail like Pierre once had; but he soon got bored, climbed a nearby tree, and nodded off. Prof was patient and still, staring into the foliage with intense focus. At points he rolled out his rug, kneeled, and prayed to his god. But even with the power of his prayers, no chimpanzees came.

"We must be very patient," he said in a hushed voice once he was back up, shaking soil from the rug. "The chimps are smart creatures, and clearly they are already being hunted by humans. Why should they trust *us*, who are also humans?"

Asking Prof to stay where he was, I returned to the mango tree. There I gathered up more of the wormy fruit. Inspecting the mangoes, pink grubs waving from between the plates of their cracked skins, I realized they might be too far gone to attract any mock men. I let them fall with a wet thud, wiped my hands on my pants, and shinnied up the trunk until I reached a couple of choice ripe mangoes still on the branches. I got bitten by some insects as I scaled the tree, and already had a raised rash from a vine that had broken my skin as I rolled across it, but I thought these delicious fruits would be worth it.

When I returned to Prof, he realized my intention right away and nodded toward the far side of the clearing. Once I'd laid the fruit there in a small pile and returned, we stood behind a tree and watched.

All was quiet. Omar woke and chirped down at us, as if asking what was supposed to happen.

"Mangoes are not native to Africa," Prof whispered. "Maybe the chimpanzees know this and do not like them."

"I bet the chimpanzees don't care where mangoes originally came from," I said. "They care that they taste very good."

But still — the fruit didn't seem to be working very well so far. All that happened was a red-brown snake wandered across them, flicked its tongue into the air, and then disappeared into the brush.

"What if the mock men decide *we* are tastier than the mangoes?" I asked. "What if something is watching, waiting for *us* to be eaten?"

Prof considered my words. "All the literature I have read indicates that chimpanzees will not eat us."

I gave him a long look, then returned my gaze to the mangoes. "Does *Jane Goodall* write books about —" I cut off.

The drumming was loud and purposeful, like a chief preparing his people for war. And it was getting louder.

I crouched as the noise approached, heart thudding. For many seconds in a row there would be no drumming, then it would start again, each time much closer than before. I pointed high when I realized nearby treetops had started trembling along with the thuds.

The shaking branches were no more than a dozen yards away. Alarmed, Prof clutched my forearm. Then all was still.

Until a mock man came into view.

He was low and muscular, stiff black hair messy over a tan face and pouting pink lips. Easing forward on all fours, he sniffed curiously at the pile of mangoes. When the chimp grunted, Omar bounded to the top of the highest tree. He was a smart monkey, choosing a thin branch where it would be impossible for the heavier animal to follow. The chimpanzee's attention snapped to the vervet. He stared at Omar for a few seconds, then brought his attention back to the fruit. Before taking any of the mangoes, he approached a nearby kapok, which he drummed by going into a half handstand and flailing his feet against it. It was a loud, impressive sound, and the chimpanzee paused to look at Omar, as if to see whether the monkey had been as awestruck as he ought to be. Making soft hooting sounds, the chimp drew nearer to the mangoes.

The chimpanzee was shorter than me, but his hands made deep indentations in the ground, so I knew he was heavy and strong. Though he mostly walked on all fours like a beast, occasionally he would stand on his two feet to look around. Then he'd go back to walking along the narrow forest path. The chimp seemed to have forgotten about the mangoes, and didn't appear to have anything else to do with himself. He sniffed a branch and grasped along it to pluck a single berry. His hairy black fingers drew the red treat close to his lips. There were more berries on the branch, but he didn't bother with them, instead plopping down in the grass, head resting on his joined palms. He looked like a boy kicked out of his home for the day, walking the streets and looking for trouble so he'd feel part of something.

I thought Prof might take his notebook out to make notes, but he was quietly watching the chimpanzee, face full of joy. He'd gone so long without blinking that tears were falling down his chin and dripping to the ground.

As he sat, the chimp held one of his feet to his nose and sniffed it; I saw that the bottom of his foot had no hair on it and was as brown-orange-pink as a person's.

He lay still for a minute or two, then unexpectedly took off at a run. When he tripped over the pile of mangoes, he skidded to a stop and peered at them. After scanning the scene like a burglar, he placed one in his mouth, easily biting through the tough skin. The others he piled into his arms. Then he hurried away.

"Come on," Prof said once the chimp was out of sight. "We're following." He took off down the path, moving surprisingly fast considering his limp. I trailed a safe distance behind, Omar bounding down from the tree and holding tight to my shoulder. We must have looked like nervous children trailing after Father.

Prof led us fast enough to keep the chimp in view, tracking the black figure against tangled flashes of green and brown. One time the chimpanzee halted and looked back at us, his black eyes meeting ours, but he didn't seem alarmed; he clutched his mangoes tighter and continued on. Eventually the chimp stopped in a clearing and began hooting. Prof and I froze at the opposite end, hiding ourselves in the greenery as best we could.

The chimp held still, his hoots softening. While we waited I idly kicked at one of the large flat tree wings — and it made no sound at all. The chimpanzee must have been incredibly strong to make that drumming noise.

I decided to call him Drummer.

There was an answering chimp cry nearby, and then Drummer shot out of the clearing. We rushed to follow, and when we peeked around the bend we saw him with more chimps: a female with an infant playing at her feet. I figured she was older, since her skin hung loose, with hairless patches. The infant seemed healthy, rolling around on the ground and insistently climbing up her mother to suckle, even though the old female kept casting her off.

For a while Drummer stood near the old mother, swaying, the stack of mangoes tight in his hands. Then he turned away from her, squatted, and began to chew through the mangoes. The female crossed in front of him. For a while she kneeled there, infant wrapped around her belly, and stared longingly at the mangoes. Drummer pivoted again so she was out of his view and continued to eat. Then the female lay on her back, arm flat out on the ground. While Drummer ignored her, she flicked her fingers against his back, trying to attract his attention.

I named her Beggar.

Once Drummer had finished his second mango, he placed his free hand, downturned, on top of Beggar's. She panted softly and cautiously reached for one of the remaining fruits. Drummer continued eating calmly as she pulled it and then the other mango away from him. She bit into the thick skin and peeled, rapidly eating one and then the other. As the peels dropped, the infant played with them, tossing them between her hands. When her lack of coordination made them fall, she got down from her mother's lap to retrieve them — kicking them farther away in the process. Then she returned and began to suckle.

I decided to name the infant Mango.

Drummer's attitude toward the old female was so dismissive yet respectful that I guessed he was no longer a child but not yet an adult; I suspected that he was even her son. Prof and I didn't dare speak and risk drawing attention, but I made mental notes of what I wanted to tell him so he could record them in his notebook. I wondered if this was a little family alone in the jungle, or if there were other chimpanzees nearby.

Prof refused to leave the trio all day, but at one point I got hungry, so Omar and I returned to the campsite. Some small, fat brown monkeys, like yams with arms and legs, were poking around our stuff. I chased them off. Omar scolded the intruders even louder than I, though never leaving the security of my shoulder. Once we were alone I cooked some more rice, indulging in salt this time to make the meal taste at least a little different from breakfast. Omar seemed to feel at home at the campsite; he climbed into the plastic basin and stayed there when I headed back to check on Prof.

Along the way I foraged more mangoes. We ate them in our hiding spot, watching Beggar and Drummer and Mango. The chimps were conscious of us, but didn't seem wary. Maybe they had already been around humans. I made a mental note to tell Prof that later: The hunter might have been someone the chimps already knew.

Prof's head bobbed as he ate his salted rice. We'd been in that clearing for hours, and squatting so long had worn on the old man — like all foreigners, he crouched on the balls of his feet, instead of on his heels as he should have done. I leaned in and risked whispering, "Do you want to head back to the campsite? I can stay here a while longer and remember everything I see."

Prof shook his head, then reconsidered and nodded. He must have seen I was upset to be alone, though, because he leaned down to look right in my eyes, hands squarely on my shoulders. "I know it's frightening out here. But if we lose track of the chimps we might not find any again for weeks. I need your help; do you think you can give it?"

I nodded solemnly. I didn't want to separate, but I owed Prof everything. If he wanted me to do this, I would. I pressed the knife into his hands. "You should have this. If that hunter or Monsieur Tatagani comes to me, I can run. You can't run from the campsite."

"Monsieur Tatagani? He doesn't know where we are, Luc," Prof said. But he did take the knife, and limped back toward the campsite. When he was gone I felt very much alone, even with the chimps so near. Once it was dark there would be no tracing my steps back to the campsite; whatever happened out here, I'd have to deal with it myself. I wedged myself between two baobab trees to feel safer.

As the afternoon wore dim, the chimps focused less on eating and more on relaxing. Beggar reclined at the base of a tree, arms behind her head and legs crossed. As soon as she was laid flat her eyes closed, as if she'd been waiting all day for this moment. Mango scrambled over her mother's torso, slapping her head. Throughout it all, Beggar resolutely scrunched her eyes shut. Even though I was only a few yards away, neither of them paid me any attention.

Drummer, though, was a different story. At one point a stream of army ants shifted routes so that they passed near my shoe, and when I'd finished shaking my foot clear, I looked up to see the young male a few feet away, hunched over his knuckles, the hairs on the back of his neck raised. He'd stalked over soundlessly and now stared at me, the glow of the fading afternoon sun rimming his hard shiny eyes with rust. He took a step forward, his eyes locked on mine. Then he took another.

I'd confronted aggressive dogs before. I knew that you weren't supposed to run from a violent animal. As this muscular creature crept toward me, teeth bared, all I could think was *hold still*, and all I could feel was *get away*.

I backed up, heedlessly stepping through the crust of a termite mound. I was sure the insects, plump with venom, were biting my ankles, but I couldn't feel them. I could only stare at the beast before me. I sensed our locked gazes were only making things worse, but I couldn't look away. Like I'd once done for Monsieur Tatagani, I had to learn as much as I could about his anger and how I might survive it.

Suddenly Drummer sprinted toward me, dragging his hands along the ground. Rocks and branches scattered before him, making a terrible noise. I sensed Beggar sitting up and heard Mango shrieking in fright even as all my thoughts turned to escape. As I leaped over a stream and into a thick stand of ferns, there was a rush of sound and a beating black wave. For a moment I thought another chimp was in front of me, that I'd been hunted and surrounded. But then it turned out to be a cluster of startled black birds, their underwings blurred arcs of white within black as they rose to the sky.

When I stumbled into the campsite I surprised Prof at his prayers; he leaped to his feet and blinked wildly while I doubled over and wheezed.

"What happened? What is it?!" he cried.

I tried to tell him, but the words wouldn't come out right. "One . . . of those chimps . . . charged me."

Prof nodded, suddenly calm. "I see. Is that him?"

I whirled and looked where Prof was pointing. There was Drummer, standing at the base of our hill. He steadily turned his gaze to me, then to Prof. Now that I'd run from him, his fury seemed to have drained. He was holding a hefty rock, which he hurled vaguely in our direction; it went far astray, but he still hooted triumphantly.

"Yes," I said. "That's him."

"We appear," Prof said, "to have met our neighbors."